CRITICAL ACCLAIM FOR

'Brilliant and chilling, Leigh Rus... ... of a read!' – **Marti...**

'A million readers can't be wrong! Loyal fans of Geraldine Steel will be thrilled with this latest compelling story from Leigh Russell. New readers will discover a terrific crime series to get their teeth into. Clear some time in your day, sit back and enjoy a bloody good read'
– **Howard Linskey**

'Taut and compelling' – **Peter James**

'Leigh Russell is one to watch' – **Lee Child**

'Leigh Russell has become one of the most impressively dependable purveyors of the English police procedural'
– **Marcel Berlins**, *Times*

'A brilliant talent in the thriller field' – **Jeffery Deaver**

'*Death Rope* is another cracking addition to the series which has just left me wanting to read more'
– *Jen Med's Book Reviews*

'The story keeps you guessing until the end. I would highly recommend this series'
– *A Crime Reader's Blog*

'A great plot that keeps you guessing right until the very end, some subtle subplots, brilliant characters both old and new

Also by Leigh Russell

Geraldine Steel Mysteries
Cut Short
Road Closed
Dead End
Death Bed
Stop Dead
Fatal Act
Killer Plan
Murder Ring
Deadly Alibi
Class Murder
Death Rope
Rogue Killer

Ian Peterson Murder Investigations
Cold Sacrifice
Race to Death
Blood Axe

Lucy Hall Mysteries
Journey to Death
Girl in Danger
The Wrong Suspect

The Adulterer's Wife
Suspicion

LEIGH RUSSELL

DEATHLY AFFAIR

A GERALDINE STEEL MYSTERY

NO EXIT PRESS

First published in 2019 by No Exit Press,
an imprint of Oldcastle Books Ltd,
Harpenden, UK
noexit.co.uk

ISBN
978-0-85730-301-1 (print)
978-0-85730-302-8 (epub)

2 4 6 8 10 9 7 5 3 1

Typeset in 11pt Times New Roman
by Avocet Typeset, Bideford, Devon, EX39 2BP
Printed and bound in Great Britain by Clays Ltd, Elcograf S.p.A.

For more information about Crime Fiction go to @crimetimeuk

To Michael, Jo, Phillipa, Phil, Rian, and Kezia
With my love

'And thus the native hue of resolution
Is sicklied o'er with the pale cast of thought,
And enterprises of great pith and moment
With this regard their currents turn awry,
And lose the name of action'

William Shakespeare

Glossary of acronyms

DCI   – Detective Chief Inspector (senior officer on case)
DI   – Detective Inspector
DS   – Detective Sergeant
SOCO – scene of crime officer (collects forensic evidence at scene)
PM   – Post mortem or Autopsy (examination of dead body to establish cause of death)
CCTV – Closed Circuit Television (security cameras)
VIIDO – Visual Images, Identification and Detections Office

Prologue

Strictly speaking he was not a killer. Not yet.

Tonight, for the first time, conditions were perfect. He passed several people scurrying along the pavement, hoods and umbrellas up against a light drizzle that had begun to fall. No one would pay any attention to the hood which concealed his own face. He looked unremarkable in every way. The street was deserted, but another pedestrian could appear around the corner at any moment. If he failed to seize the opportunity, right now, he might never have another chance.

If intention were the same as action this would be easy, but he had underestimated the gulf between thought and deed. Shakespeare, who understood human nature perhaps better than anyone, had warned that overthinking could 'make cowards of us all'.

Best not to think about it at all then, now the time had come. He had already given more than enough thought to this, weighing up the risks and playing it out in his mind while he lay in bed at night.

It was not as though a likely victim had fallen into his lap. Far from it. It had taken him months to find someone who used a covered step as a bed, where he was likely to sleep when it rained. Having identified a suitable target, he had prepared for this moment with care, following his shuffling victim for several evenings along Coney Street to the doorway of an empty shop where he spent the night.

Winter would soon be on its way, signalling the end of his

opportunities until the spring because, when the weather turned cold, the homeless would seek out bricks and mortar shelter from the elements, safe from predators roaming the streets – and killers. But York in early September was warm, with only a slight chill in the air at night, and homeless people could still be found sleeping rough, even in wet weather.

The tramp settled himself down in his doorway, exactly as he had done for the past few evenings, unaware that this was the last time he would pull his grubby coat around his bare ankles and pat his bundle into shape before using it as a pillow. Oblivious of his watcher, he reached into his coat pocket and drew out a small bottle. Laboriously, he heaved himself into a semi-recumbent position, leaning on one elbow, so that he could fumble with the lid before taking a swig. A trickle of pale amber liquid dribbled down his chin and disappeared into his straggly beard.

Pressed motionless against the opposite wall, the watcher waited.

At last the tramp settled down on his rough bed, curled himself into a foetal position, and lay still. Perhaps he heard a cautious footstep or a nearly silent breath because, just as the hooded figure reached him, the tramp stirred and his eyes flickered open. He half sat up, the expression in his watery grey eyes shifting from surprise to fear as he struggled to clamber to his feet, but his hoarse croak of protest came too late. The noose was already tightening around his throat.

The tramp's arms flailed helplessly for a moment before he grew limp, very suddenly, like a puppet whose strings had been cut, and his filthy fingers stopped scrabbling at the sleeves of his assailant's jacket. Had the sagging body not been held upright by the stick relentlessly turning at the nape of his neck, the victim would have collapsed. And still the noose tautened, carving a dark runnel around the unwashed neck.

Finally, satisfied that his victim was dead, the assailant

released the tension and stepped back. His hood was still pulled forward, masking his face. The only unforeseen complication was that fibres from his own jacket might be found lodged beneath the dead man's fingernails. It was the kind of detail that could lead to a conviction. He would have to get rid of his jacket. That was a nuisance because his wife was bound to notice, but he could not risk keeping it. He would have to find an identical replacement for the jacket, or invent an excuse for its disappearance. Annoyed with himself for the oversight, he turned and slipped away along the glistening pavement.

It had taken him less than a minute to become a killer.

1

EVEN THOUGH HER MARRIAGE was a mistake, Ann had never intended to break her vows. It was not as if David was a bad husband. After all, he had done the right thing in offering to marry her as soon as he had learned she was pregnant. She was the one who had blundered by saying yes, but she had been seventeen at the time, and scared. Even then she had known she did not love David, certainly not enough to want to spend the rest of her life with him. The thought of years stretching ahead of her, spending every night in bed with the same man in married monotony, had made her cry when she was alone in her single bed in her parents' house. Only she had not been alone, not really, because there was a baby growing inside her. Besides, her parents had given her little choice, and at seventeen she had not developed the strength of character to withstand their hectoring.

'Of course I love him,' she had lied to her mother, choosing to waive any possibility of future happiness rather than admit the humiliating truth, that her affair with David had been thoughtless and meaningless.

'In that case, we won't stand in your way. You must marry him,' her mother had promptly replied, as though she wished to support her daughter's decision and was not merely concerned about what other people might think.

The truth was that Ann's parents had been keen for her to marry David from the moment they learned about the pregnancy. He was a qualified lawyer, and they thought she was lucky to have found a man with a steady profession who would stand by her and take care of her and her child. If anyone had asked Ann what she really wanted, the outcome might have been very different. But everyone had been happy to go along with the marriage because, of course, there was the baby.

David was not a bad man, but he was hardly the partner Ann would have chosen to spend the rest of her life with. To a naive seventeen-year-old, the attentions of a tall and well-spoken man in his late thirties had been exciting at first. Compared to the boys of her own age she hung around with, his maturity had been part of the attraction, and she had been flattered by his interest in her. Before long she had realised the problem. It was not just that he was twenty years older than her, but he was boring. Right from the start he had barely said a word when they were together. He seemed to want to speak to her. Sometimes she caught him looking at her with unnerving intensity, but when she challenged him he would stammer and look away. What she had at first tolerated as shyness became tedious.

Looking back over the years, it was hardly surprising that one of them would end up being unfaithful, but she had not expected it would be her. Her only justification for having embarked on an affair at all was that since the age of eighteen her life had been filled with nappies and teething rings, trips to the doctor, leaking washing machines, cooking, cleaning, packing for holidays, and homework. Not that she regretted having her daughter. Aimee kept her busy and relentlessly cheerful. And her life could have been a lot worse. Perhaps nothing would have changed had she not met another man during the interval at her daughter's school concert.

'Can I get you a drink?'

She turned and saw a young man. He had neatly cropped fair hair and green-blue eyes that almost disappeared when he smiled, giving an impression that he did not take life seriously. She liked that about him instantly. Returning his smile, she was dismayed when he turned and vanished into the crowd.

'Was it something I said?' she muttered.

Considering she had not said a word to the man who had just approached her, she felt unreasonably disappointed as she began to make her way back to the auditorium.

'Hey, you can't leave yet, not now I've paid for this.'

The young man was back, with a pint in one hand and a glass of wine in the other, which he held out to her. He told her that his name was Mark and he was a music teacher.

'Music teacher?' she repeated. 'I like music. Not sure about teachers though.'

'We should get along famously then,' he replied. 'Most teachers I know are insufferable.'

His flirting became more blatant but she did not object and, by the time he bought her another drink, she felt as though she had known him for years. She must have had too much to drink because she agreed to visit him at his home the following week. He lived in a flat above a shop in Gillygate. All that week she thought of little else but the man with green-blue eyes. Even when she made up her mind to forget all about him she knew, deep down, that she was going to accept his invitation. As soon as she arrived, he offered her a glass of wine. One drink turned into three then four until Ann was tipsy and, unusually for her, she found she was having fun, thrilled by a rare sense of freedom.

'I feel like a teenager again,' she giggled.

'You're pissed.'

'Isn't it wonderful?'

She was on the point of thanking him for the drinks and telling him she had to go home. He had no right to expect anything else. Yet when she felt his leg touching hers she did not move away but let things unfold, not unlike when she had fallen pregnant at seventeen.

She could hear her mother's voice inside her head, warning

her as she followed Mark into his bedroom: 'Have you learned nothing?' But she did not want to listen, nor did she want to learn. Her mother could teach her nothing. She had been sensible for long enough. So although she had never intended to cheat on her husband, that was exactly what she did. The trouble was, it did not end with that one night. Because despite the difference in their ages, or maybe because of it, Mark and Ann hit it off. That was a pity. If he had turned out to be a good-looking but callow dullard, she would have walked away from her secret fling and gone back to her normal life with hardly a backward ' glance. She could have forgiven herself one fleeting encounter in fifteen years of loyal duty to a man she had never really loved. But Mark listened to her, and he made her laugh. He insisted on playing music and dancing with her when they went back to his flat, and he flatly refused to let her help him clear up when they ordered a takeaway.

'Next time, I'll cook for you,' he promised her, when they were lying in each other's arms, naked.

'Next time?'

'That's what I said.'

Gazing into his smiling eyes, she realised he was right in supposing she would see him again.

'What makes you think there'll be a next time?' she asked. 'You do know I'm married.'

Mark shrugged. 'Yet here you are and, as long as you are here, nothing else exists, does it?'

Cocooned in the warmth of his embrace she realised he was right. Never before had she felt so overwhelming a rush of love for another adult. Intense infatuation, passion, she did not understand what she was feeling; she only knew that it was wonderful. It was not about sex, although his prowess was undeniable. It was like a drug, as though she had only seen in black and white before and now everything appeared to her in glorious colour. She wondered if this was love. As long as her husband remained ignorant of her affair it could not hurt him, and she would make sure he never found out. Whatever happened, she had to carry on seeing Mark.

2

THE EVENINGS WERE DRAWING in and there were a few other hints of approaching winter with the leaves beginning to fall and a noticeable drop in temperature, especially at night. First thing in the morning there was a chill in the air and Geraldine had begun wearing a jacket on her short journey to the police station. She preferred to get to work early to avoid the traffic and often had breakfast at her desk. The office seemed dull without her fellow detective sergeant, Ariadne, who was away on a week's holiday. Geraldine had become accustomed to her colleague's smiling greeting each morning. They had a lot in common, being around the same age and single, and it had not taken them long to slip into the habit of spending their lunch hour together. Without Ariadne sitting opposite her, punctuating the hours with her occasional quips, Geraldine's day dragged. She was on good terms with her other colleagues but, after living in York for seven months, Ariadne was the only one with whom she could let her guard down. Generally focused on her work in the serious crime unit, it was not in Geraldine's nature to be frivolous, and her new friend's lighthearted approach to problems often lifted her spirits.

There had been a time when Geraldine had regarded another of their colleagues as her closest friend. She and Detective Inspector Ian Peterson had known one another when he had been her sergeant in her days working as a detective inspector. But their roles were now reversed and since he had become her superior officer he had become aloof, only rarely showing flashes of his former warmth towards her. Having missed Ariadne, Geraldine was pleased to hear from her on her return, and they arranged to meet for a drink.

'So, what's been going on while I've been away?' Ariadne asked as she put a couple of pints on the table between them and pulled up a chair.

'Honestly? Absolutely nothing.'

'Oh well, no news is good news I suppose.'

They exchanged a shamefaced look. Much as they both abhorred the crimes they investigated, for detective sergeants working in serious crime, their jobs could be monotonous when they were not working on a case.

'A mugging, a ring of shoplifters, a stolen car,' Geraldine said, reeling off a list of relatively minor infringements, 'and mounds of reports to write. So, how was your week off?'

Looking unusually despondent, Ariadne described her trip to visit her cousins in Athens. 'I mean, it's great seeing my family – I get on really well with my cousins – but it's depressing to see how the city has changed since I was last there. A lot of the buildings look derelict and it's more like a slum every time I visit. There's graffiti and litter everywhere. Honestly, people think things are bad here, but they've no idea how well off they are...' she broke off and rolled her eyes. 'I can't tell you how dreadful conditions are there. And the frightening thing is, it's all degenerated so quickly. I know it's unfashionable to complain about Europe,' she went on, lowering her voice, 'but really, the joint economy hasn't served everyone's interest. Greece was better off before it joined up with Germany and France. They've decimated the Greek economy.'

'Would Greece have been any better off on its own?'

Ariadne shrugged. 'Probably not. But what's really worrying is not so much the poverty, although that's distressing enough to witness, but the numbers of people unemployed, so many youngsters who've never had a job. It's frightening.'

Despite her Yorkshire accent, with her striking long black curls and eyes as dark as Geraldine's, it was easy to believe Ariadne's mother was Greek. They chatted for a while. Geraldine suggested going out for something to eat, but Ariadne said she was worn out and wanted to get home to unpack.

'Sure,' Geraldine smiled. 'To be honest, I'm pretty tired myself.'

'From doing nothing?'

'Exactly. It's hardly been a stimulating week while you've been away.'

'Well, now I'm here, I'm sure your life is about to get a whole lot more exciting.'

She laughed and Geraldine joined in. It was good to have her friend back. They parted and Geraldine returned to her flat. It had taken her a few months to settle down in York but she felt at home now in her new apartment overlooking the river. She made herself a plate of spaghetti with tomato sauce, a recipe she had been experimenting with for a few weeks. It was not quite right yet, but it was her best effort so far. Leaving her blinds open, she ate staring out into the darkness of the night, wondering what crimes were being committed while she sat safely indoors, eating and drinking wine.

The next morning she was woken by her phone ringing before her alarm went off.

'Oh, bloody hell,' she grumbled. 'Hello? Hello?'

Still listening to the message, she switched on the light and grabbed her clothes with her free hand.

'OK,' she replied, scrambling into her jeans, 'I'm on my way now.'

Her colleague, Detective Inspector Ian Peterson, arrived at the location in the centre of the city at the same time as Geraldine. Together they approached the cordon. Without exchanging a word they pulled on protective clothing and followed the common approach path to the crime scene. A dead body had been discovered by a postman on an early morning round in the doorway of an empty shop in Coney Street which ran alongside the river, not far from York Minster.

Shivering, Geraldine gazed down at the hump of ragged clothing that concealed a corpse. The lower part of the dead man's face was covered by a grizzled beard and his lips were concealed beneath a straggly moustache. Above a large nose, dark eyes glared blindly up at them.

'He looks like a tramp,' Ian grunted, turning away.

Geraldine suppressed a sigh. Having worked as Ian's mentor when he was still a young sergeant, she was possibly his only colleague who was aware of the queasiness he experienced when viewing corpses. Without mentioning the subject, she did her best to protect him from the need to attend post mortems. But she could not shelter him from the brutal ugliness of crime scenes.

'He hasn't got any form of identification, only a few pounds in coins in one pocket, and an empty beer bottle in the other,' a scene of crime officer said. 'But you're right. He looks as though he might be homeless.'

Geraldine nodded. The stench of death masked any other smell from the body, but he was certainly filthy, his fingernails black with grime, his face speckled with dirt.

'What did he die of?' Ian asked.

He refrained from wondering aloud why the major crime unit would be summoned to investigate an old hobo who had no doubt drunk himself to death, but Geraldine thought his voice seemed to imply the question. She hoped she had misinterpreted his tone.

'He was strangled,' a scene of crime officer replied quietly.

'I suppose it's too much to hope the killer used his bare hands?' Geraldine asked.

Craning her neck to peer under the rough sleeper's collar, she saw a short section of a red band around his throat. Ian must have noticed it too because he muttered something inaudible under his breath.

'Who the hell would bother to do that – to him?' the scene of crime officer asked.

Something in the dismissive tone of his voice prompted another officer to add, 'And why are we spending so much time and effort on him?'

Geraldine glared at her colleagues, too angry to trust herself to respond. Unwashed and homeless, the dead man had been a human being. Any one of the officers there might have become homeless had their lives panned out differently. Drugs, legal or controlled, could render anyone dysfunctional, and the decline into penury was often swift and unforgiving. If her work had taught her anything, she had come to understand that the boundary between coping with life and falling apart was flimsier than most people realised. This tramp's murder deserved the full attention of the authorities, no less than any other victim. Justice had to be indiscriminate, like death.

She kept her indignation to herself, determined to channel her anger into finding the killer. A cordon had been set up and the forensic tent was expected imminently. Although the weather was fine, being outside they needed to protect any evidence at the scene from the threat of deterioration and contamination. In the few moments that would elapse before the forensic tent arrived, Geraldine focused on the scene, doing her best to ignore the white-coated forensic officers and uniformed police who were guarding the cordon. She had stood in such a position many times before, but the visceral thrill she experienced never lessened. Her colleagues' offhand reaction to the body made her uneasy, and she wondered whether the rest of the team could be relied on to devote their usual level of attention to detail at this particular crime scene.

'Do you think they'll be thorough –' she began, and paused.

'What? Who are you talking about?' Ian replied.

His terse response reminded her of his discomfort when viewing the dead, a handicap for a detective that he had worked hard to overcome.

'Nothing,' she muttered. 'Don't worry about it. I'm sure everything will be fine.'

Ian gave her a curious glance. 'Not for him, it won't.'

Their awkward conversation was interrupted by the arrival of the forensic tent, and they headed back to the police station to attend a briefing.

'It looks as though he was sleeping in the doorway when he was attacked,' Ian said. 'The body hadn't been moved, as far as the SOCOs could tell.'

The detective chief inspector was a solidly built woman. Her authoritative manner proved effective when she challenged suspects, but made her seem heavy-handed in her dealings with colleagues. Initially put off by Eileen's didactic manner, Geraldine had come to respect the kind and generous nature that lay concealed behind her ferocity.

'Were there any defence wounds?' Eileen asked, squinting at an image of the dead man.

'We're not sure yet,' Ian replied.

The post mortem would be able to tell them more about the nature of the attack.

'He was strangled, so he was probably attacked from behind,' Eileen said.

Ian nodded. 'And he might not have had any warning.'

'He was probably too drunk to know what was going on,' a constable added.

'He might have been partly responsible for what happened,' another constable said.

'What does that even mean? You're not suggesting he strangled himself?' Geraldine asked.

'No, but he probably got into a fight while he was pissed, so it's hardly surprising that –'

'Just because he was homeless doesn't mean he was either drunk or belligerent,' Geraldine snapped, unable to control her irritation at the constables' inane comments.

'Let's have no more of this idle speculation before we have gathered enough information to make a case,' Eileen said firmly. 'Ian, you're in charge of the investigating team on this one, and Geraldine you can assist him in running the enquiry.'

Pleased to be conducting the investigation with Ian, Geraldine barely listened as Eileen proceeded to reel off a list of officers who would be working with them.

'It's obvious what happened –' the disgruntled constable insisted, but Eileen interrupted him.

'That's enough,' she snapped. 'We need evidence, not supposition. This is a murder enquiry, and the status of the victim when he was alive is not the point. Homeless or not, he was murdered, and we need to find out who killed him. Now, we all have work to do, so let's crack on, shall we?'

3

WHILE A TEAM WAS endeavouring to identify the victim, Geraldine was sent to question James Harrison, the postman who had discovered the body. After stumbling on the corpse, he had been in no fit state to continue his delivery round and his boss had sent him home. He lived on the outskirts of Heslington, a few miles from Lendal Post Office where he was based. Geraldine drove out to his house to speak to him, and a middle-aged woman came to the door. When Geraldine introduced herself and asked for James Harrison, the woman nodded.

'They sent him home,' she said. 'He was pretty upset, although from what he told me it was just some rough sleeper who got himself killed. So, can you tell us what happened? No one seems to be telling James anything.'

'I'm afraid I can't discuss our investigation. And now, I'd like to speak to James, please.'

'Of course.'

James Harrison was young, tall, dark-haired and long limbed. Geraldine suspected his pallor might be a consequence of the shock he had experienced, and his shaky voice confirmed her impression.

'I was just doing my rounds, you know,' he told her.

He spoke very fast, and so softly that she struggled to catch the words, while his eyes flickered nervously to meet hers and away again.

'It was... well, it's not what you expect to see, is it? I've never seen a dead body before. Never. I suppose you see them all the time, don't you?'

Geraldine wondered fleetingly what it would feel like, to be so distressed by the sight of a corpse. She had seen so many, but she had never felt anything other than fierce curiosity to discover who had been responsible for the victim's death. Perhaps it made a difference that she did not usually come across corpses unexpectedly. Being mentally prepared made a difference, besides which she had become accustomed to the sight of the dead. She sometimes wondered if her work had made her become detached from all normal human feelings.

'I was delivering the letters. Most of it was junk mail anyway. And he was just lying there, across the step. I assumed he was drunk, or asleep. So I –' he paused and heaved a sigh. 'I gave him a kick. Well, I didn't know, did I? I mean, how was I to know he was dead? It wasn't a real kick, more of a gentle nudge with my foot, but I didn't know he was dead, did I? Anyway, he didn't wake up.' He paused, lost in his memory.

'What happened then?' Geraldine prompted him.

'I leaned down and yelled in his ear, didn't I? And he still didn't stir. Well, of course he didn't, because he was dead, wasn't he? But I didn't realise straight away. So I – I kicked him again, a bit harder. I figured if he was unconscious it wouldn't hurt him. He half rolled over and that's when I saw.'

'Did you see the mark on his neck?' Geraldine asked.

'What? No. I saw his eyes, staring. That's when I knew he was dead. So I called 999. I didn't know what else to do.'

Geraldine nodded.

'It's my first week at work,' he said miserably. 'My third morning. What a way to start a new job.'

'You did the right thing calling us,' she reassured him. 'And you did nothing wrong.'

Only kicked a dead body, shifted it from its position, and contaminated the evidence left behind by the killer, she thought, but she said nothing about his carelessness, instead explaining that the police would need to take a sample of his DNA.

'And we'd also like to examine the shoes you were wearing this morning. We need to eliminate you from our list of suspects.'

'Oh, Jesus. All this is enough to put you off your job,' the postman said.

It *is* my job, Geraldine thought.

From everything the postman was able to tell her, the only significant pieces of information were the time he had discovered the body and his physical contact with the victim.

'Where exactly did you kick him?' she asked, aware that the pathologist might even now be studying injuries sustained by the victim post mortem.

The postman became cagey. 'I didn't kick him, really. Not deliberately. I just pushed him with my toe, to wake him up.'

'You kicked him hard enough to make him roll over.'

'Not exactly,' he muttered. 'He just – he just rolled over...'

Geraldine leaned forward. 'What you did was perfectly understandable. No one is going to criticise you for trying to wake him up. You have a job to do, an important job, and he was obstructing you. But you must tell me exactly what you did, or the injuries you inflicted could mislead our investigation.'

'I didn't injure him –'

'No, probably not. In any case, he was already dead, so you couldn't have done him any harm.' She smiled, trying to encourage the man to talk. 'But you must tell me where your foot made contact with the body, or the pathologist might be misled into thinking the killer kicked the body after garroting him.'

'What difference would it make if he did?'

'It makes a difference,' she replied. 'We're going to need to build a picture of the killer and this could affect it.'

'Why do you want my shoes?'

Painstakingly, Geraldine repeated her explanation and

eventually the postman seemed to understand and left the room to fetch a pair of large black trainers.

'When will I get them back?' he asked as he handed them over.

'As soon as we've finished examining them and identifying any footprints you left at the scene.'

'I didn't leave any footprints,' he said. 'I'm going to need them back for tomorrow morning, very early.'

'You'll get them back when we finish with them,' Geraldine said, beginning to lose patience with the witness. 'James,' she added, quickly regaining control of her temper, 'this is important. What you're doing is helping us to find a dangerous killer.'

'It was just a tramp,' he muttered crossly. 'Those people get in fights all the time.'

'But this man wasn't killed in a fight,' she said. 'We think he may have been murdered deliberately.'

James shrugged. 'It comes to the same thing, doesn't it? He's still dead.'

Geraldine did not bother to point out that an accidental fatality in the course of a fight was very different from a planned murder.

4

DAVID OBSERVED ANN THROUGH narrowed eyelids. He did not want her to catch him looking at her, because he knew how much she hated it.

'What are you staring at?' she would ask, whenever she noticed him watching her.

'Nothing.'

'You're looking at me.'

'So? What's wrong with that? A man can look at his wife, can't he? I like looking at you,' he would reply.

'Why?'

'Because you're beautiful.'

It was a glib response, but it happened to be true. Even after fifteen years of marriage, he still felt his breath catch in the back of his throat whenever he saw his young wife. With blue eyes, wispy, fair hair and very pale skin, she looked ethereal, like an angel. The first time he had set eyes on her, he had been smitten. He had been having a quick pint on his way home to his empty flat. Drinking alone in the pub had felt less lonely than sitting at home on his own and besides, one of the barmaids in his local always gave him a friendly smile. God knows he had received few enough of those when he was younger. There was nothing wrong with him but he was not exactly outgoing, always the first to be overlooked in a group of people. He spent every day studying legal documents in a quiet room, where no one ever spoke to him.

That evening, Ann had walked into the pub with a group of

teenagers, but the barmaid had refused to serve her.

'No ID, no drink,' she had said.

Ann's crestfallen expression touched David. On a sudden impulse, he stood up and offered to buy her a drink. He knew he could be in trouble for infringing the law, but he did not think it would matter this once. No one would ever know. And the girl was beautiful. Giggling, she accepted and asked for a glass of white wine. The barmaid must have known who it was for, but she handed over the drink without demur. With a frisson of pleasure, David handed the glass to Ann. He saw a flash of gratitude in her lovely eyes and felt his hand tremble. Expecting her to take the drink and hurry back to her friends, he was surprised when she followed him to his table and sat down beside him. The silence between them grew awkward, so he took a chance and introduced himself. He was sure she was merely leading him on for the sake of another drink, but he was happy to sit there exchanging desultory remarks and could hardly believe his luck when she responded to his advances. Her cheeks reddened slightly as she asked whether he had a car. That appeared to be the deciding factor in her agreeing to go home with him; he was glad he had recently had his car cleaned.

To begin with they had kept their affair a secret. With about twenty years between them he had never expected the relationship to last, but as soon as she had fallen pregnant he had seized his chance. When her parents had supported his proposal, he knew he had won. Now, at fifty-two, he was old enough to know better than to remain obsessed with his young wife, but he could not help his adoration. He had always known she would never love him as he loved her, with an all-consuming passion that made everything else seem pale and dull. Meeting her had given purpose to his dreary life, and their marriage ceremony had been the best moment of his life. Right up to the very last minute he had expected her to do a runner. Relief, not happiness, had nearly reduced him to tears on seeing her arrive at the registry office flanked by her parents, one on either side of her, holding her by her arms. She had been visibly shaking and her parents had looked grim, as though they were attending a funeral.

He had let her think he was happy about the baby for its own sake. In reality he was pleased because he thought the baby would tie her to him, making her need him as he needed her. Their relationship could never be equal though, because she could walk away from him at any time and move on with her life. As far as he was concerned, she *was* his life. Before the baby arrived he had lived in fear of her leaving him. Once Aimee was born, he felt he had been granted a reprieve. But Ann had been unable to conceive again after problems with her first delivery and, now their daughter was fifteen, he worried about what was going to happen when she grew up and left home.

He provided a home for Ann, but he was afraid that would not be enough to keep her. She was only thirty-two, with nearly all of her adult life ahead of her. If she ever tried to leave him, he would do everything in his power to stop her going. He knew what it was to be lonely and the thought of living in the house without her terrified him, as did the prospect of facing old age without her. Ann said she loved him, but he knew that was not true. If love had not been kind to him, he knew that solitude was worse. So he was grateful to his wife for her feigned affection. He understood she was fond of him, and he had to be satisfied with that, even though he wanted her to love him with a fierce passion he suspected she was capable of feeling, but not for him.

He gave up speculating what his life might have been like if he had never met Ann, and whether he might have been happier with a woman who was able to love him as he loved her. He could not help his feelings, and he would never give Ann up. After a while he stopped telling her how he felt; it was too painful watching her pretend to reciprocate his feelings, and they found a way to live together in spite of the difference in their attachment. He wondered if every marriage was like his, with one partner loving, while the other was loved. It comforted him to think he was not alone in his desperation.

When Ann suggested she look for a job, David was horrified and insisted she stay at home.

'We could put the money aside for Aimee,' she said. 'She's going to want to go to university.'

'Whatever she wants to do, I've taken care of everything,' he told her. 'We're perfectly comfortable as we are. There's no need for you to worry. And there's certainly no call for you to go looking for a job.'

He was immensely relieved when she backed down without further protest. He told her he was happy to take care of the bills but the truth was he hated the idea of her finding a job and working with other men, some of whom would no doubt be closer to her in age. He could not imagine other men would be able to resist falling in love with her, as he had done. He had never had any close friends, and he dropped his few desultory social acquaintances once he was married, and refused to socialise with Ann's friends. They were all much younger than him, and likely to find him a bore, and he could not risk allowing them to influence her. He worried sometimes that Ann would find her life with him dull, but she assured him that running their home and looking after Aimee kept her fully occupied.

'I don't know how other women have time to go out to work,' she told him. 'How do they ever find time to wash the curtains and clean out their cupboards regularly?'

As long as Aimee was living at home he felt relatively secure, but that would not continue forever. Already Aimee was considering her options for the sixth form, and talking about higher education. She grunted dismissively at him when he pointed out that the university in York was one of the best in the country, and there was really no need to look anywhere else.

'I'm not staying in York,' she said. 'No way. The whole point of going to university is –'

'Is to study so you can get a better job,' he interrupted her.

Aimee rolled her eyes. 'The whole point of going to university is that you can get away from your parents.'

'We're not that bad, are we?' he asked with a smile.

Aimee heaved an exaggerated sigh. 'Oh Dad, that's so like you, missing the point again.'

To his surprise he had found he got on well with his teenage daughter, who seemed to seek out his company whenever she could. Ann called her a 'daddy's girl' and he detected more than a hint of envy in her voice. Unused to being liked, he regarded this show of affection from his daughter as an unexpected bonus life had thrown him, but he knew it would not last forever. Aimee would leave home and then it would be just him and Ann. He looked forward to that time with trepidation, terrified he would not be able to keep her.

'You won't leave me when Aimee goes off, will you?' he asked her once.

'Goes off? What do you mean goes off?'

'I mean when she leaves home.'

'Oh, well why didn't you say so?'

'Well? Will you?'

'Will I what?'

'Will you leave?'

'What? Aren't we talking about Aimee leaving home?'

He was convinced she was being deliberately obtuse, avoiding giving him a straight answer, but somehow his question was lost in the apparent misunderstanding. He never dared ask her again.

5

GERALDINE ASSURED IAN SHE was happy to attend the post
mortem by herself and he smiled in relief, claiming that he
had to study a stack of documents connected to the case. Her
readiness to visit the mortuary alone was unforced, since she
understood the real reason for Ian's reluctance to accompany
her. It gave her a sense of deep satisfaction to know she was
helping Ian in some way.

Jonah Hetherington greeted Geraldine with a cheery wave of
a bloody hand. An ugly little man with a face like a pug dog,
he was surprisingly attractive, thanks to his cheeky grin. He
had carried out post mortems on the victims in quite a few of
Geraldine's cases so far, and they had built up a strong mutual
trust through their professional encounters. He joked that
he might not recognise her were they ever to meet without a
cadaver for a chaperone.

'This one's a bit of a puzzle, isn't he?' he asked, nodding at the
body lying on a table in front of them. 'Oh well, I don't suppose
you'll be wanting to spend too long on him?'

Jonah could have been referring to a crossword clue he had
not yet solved. Once again Geraldine was dismayed at the
offhand way her colleagues referred to the victim but, before
she could challenge him, the pathologist carried on speaking in
his characteristically good-humoured tone.

'His clothes and poor personal hygiene seem to confirm the
suspicion that he was a vagrant, living on the streets. He had
an empty beer bottle in one of his coat pockets and quite a lot

of alcohol swilling around in his guts, and he hadn't eaten for a while. His trousers were several sizes too large for him so either he'd lost weight since he bought them, or else they were second-hand. If I had to hazard a guess at his age I'd say he was in his forties, although he looks a lot older than that. It's hard to be sure. And I suppose there's not much hope of identifying him?'

'What about dental records?' Geraldine asked half-heartedly.

They both knew it was unlikely the dead man had paid regular visits to a dentist.

'So, he'd been drinking,' Geraldine said when it was evident Jonah was not going to respond to her question. 'What else can you tell us?'

'He'd not eaten much recently. In fact I'd say he hadn't been eating very much for quite a while. He was badly malnourished.'

'Does that mean he'd probably been living rough for a while?'

The pathologist gave a helpless shrug as though to say, 'Your guess is as good as mine.' After a pause he answered her with a question, 'You know there are centres in York that provide breakfast to rough sleepers?'

'Yes, we're asking around. How did he die?'

'He was strangled. You can see the imprint of the noose here.'

'Was he strangled with a rope?'

Jonah frowned. 'No, it wasn't a rope, it was a length of fabric of some kind. The width of the injury and the neatness of the edges suggest it could have been a tie.'

Once again Geraldine had the impression that he was not being as attentive to detail as he would normally be in a murder case. She hoped the fact that no one appeared to have cared about the victim was not going to make her colleagues slapdash in their approach. As far as she was concerned, the fact that no one was likely to call them to account was irrelevant. She tried to ignore her concerns and focus on the victim.

'What can you tell us about the murder weapon?'

Jonah shook his head. Instead of answering her question, he

raised one of his own. 'Who would bother to do such a thing to *him*?'

With growing irritation, Geraldine repeated her question.

'Murder weapon?' Jonah chuckled with his usual good humour. 'Doesn't it ever strike you when you see a man in a tie, that we're surrounded by men wearing lethal weapons around their necks every day?'

'I'll never go near a man in a tie again,' she promised, returning his smile. 'Unless it's a bow tie. Now, what can you tell me about the tie that was used on this poor guy?'

'Yes, poor in every sense of the word, I fear. Well, first off, we can't say for sure that the killer used a tie to strangle him. It could have been any narrow strip of material, but there were no rough edges so it hadn't been torn off from a larger piece. Under magnification you can see the threads, so yes, it was fabric of some kind, but I'm only speculating about what it might have been. But,' he paused and glanced at her as though to check she was listening, 'a few minute strands of fabric we found adhering to his skin have gone off for analysis. We'll know more when the report comes back. We might have a colour and be able to tell you exactly what kind of fabric it was.'

'Excellent,' Geraldine said. 'Let's hope the lab don't take too long to get back to us.'

Once they had some idea of what had been used to strangle the victim, they would be able to search CCTV footage of the area with a clearer idea of what they were looking for. With luck they might spot someone arriving or leaving the crime scene at around the time they thought the tramp had been killed, wearing a tie that appeared to match the strands of fabric found on the body. That way they would at least have a visual image of the killer which might enable them to narrow the field of suspects down to a man or woman, with dark or fair hair, with a certain build and an individual gait. While that would not necessarily lead them to the killer, any such information would certainly assist them in getting a conviction once the killer had been traced. But that was still a long way off.

At this point in an investigation, Geraldine's attention usually turned to the family of the victim, and how to communicate the news of their loss. That, generally, was the most harrowing part of her job. But on this occasion there was as yet no one to tell, because they did not know who the victim was. It was possible they would never find out. She found that prospect almost unbearably sad.

Jonah's cheery voice broke into her reverie. 'All we need now is CCTV footage of an easily recognisable individual, wearing a tie of the appropriate colour, leaving the scene, preferably looking around with a furtive expression. And if we can trace that individual to a car with a visible registration number, the case will be solved.'

Geraldine smiled. 'That would be nice.'

Aware that reality was likely to prove far more challenging than Jonah's suggested scenario, Geraldine returned to the police station to write up her report.

'Are you all right?' Ariadne asked her, looking up from her own work.

'Yes, I'm fine. Why do you ask?'

Ariadne shrugged. 'You just looked very solemn.'

'I'm thinking about the man who was killed. How do you want me to look?'

Her friend hesitated and lowered her voice. 'Did you know him?'

'No, I didn't, and as far as we know so far, nor did anyone else. He's dead and...' On the verge of becoming emotional, Geraldine broke off with a slightly embarrassed laugh. 'Anyway, I dare say we'll get to the bottom of it eventually.'

'You're right, it's going to be tricky, not knowing who he was,' Ariadne agreed, misunderstanding what Geraldine was saying. 'But we'll track him down eventually.'

Geraldine was not sure whether Ariadne was referring to the identity of the victim or his killer, but she felt too despondent to care. She was not sure why she felt so depressed about the death of an unknown man.

When Ariadne suggested going for a coffee, she agreed gladly. 'Only if we don't talk about the case,' she said. 'I don't know why, but this one is getting to me,' she added. 'It just seems so sad that no one knew him when he was alive and no one cares now he's dead,' but Ariadne had already walked away and did not appear to have heard her.

6

AT TIMES MARK ALMOST wished he had never agreed to Ann's regular weekly visits. Like so much that happened in his life, it had seemed like a good idea at the time but, although it was still fun, the glamour of having an affair with an older woman had palled and he was growing tired of her demands. She was so needy. The sex was still great, and he enjoyed her appreciation of his skills in bed almost as much as the excitement of the act itself, but the novelty was wearing off. Ann was not the only woman in the world, and he was beginning to find her attention suffocating.

They had met at a school concert he had attended with his own sixth form choir. Ann's daughter had been singing in a choir from another school. He had noticed Ann in the audience straight away, and had sought her out during the interval. With only a short time to introduce himself to her, he had worked quickly to arrange a meeting, and their affair had developed rapidly after that. Within a couple of months, he felt he had lost all control of the relationship.

He was not used to having a woman reorganise his flat, and he did not appreciate her meddling with his possessions. To be fair, he was not exactly tidy, but he knew where to find things. Even searching for something as small as his phone when it was silenced never took long in the flat, but once Ann started moving everything around, he struggled to find anything. Eventually he accepted her interference as the price he paid for having a clean flat. In many ways, he would miss her if she stopped coming to see him. Without them exchanging a single word on the subject, she had worked her way through the dirty laundry piled up on his bathroom floor and now did his washing every week. And that was not all. She also wiped around the kitchen and bathroom, and hoovered the carpets. Basically, it was like having a cleaner with benefits. So he let it ride.

'You're as good as a wife,' he had once quipped, immediately regretting the joke when he saw the hungry expression in her eyes.

The relationship was never going to develop into anything more than a weekly visit, and even that was too frequent for his liking, but he was loath to lose her because that would mean having to do his own cleaning again. These days he just left his washing-up to accumulate in the kitchen and by the time Ann left, it was all done. On the face of it, there really was no downside to the arrangement, other than the risk that her husband might find out about their affair. If that ever happened, which seemed unlikely, it would hardly be Mark's problem to deal with. He had no wish to cause Ann any trouble, but she had entered into the affair with her eyes open and, of the two of them, she was the one who insisted on keeping their relationship going. If she had told him she wanted to end it, he would not have objected. She was not that important to him, yet from the way she behaved and spoke she made it sound as though he was the centre of her existence. He was both flattered and irritated by her infatuation.

'You may not always feel the same way about me, you know,' he said when she complained, wistfully, that he never told her he loved her.

'I'll always feel the same way about you,' she replied.

'How can you be so sure?'

She shrugged. 'I just know that I will. You can't stop loving someone.'

'What about your husband?'

Frowning, she asked what he meant.

'You say I'm the only man you've ever loved –'

'Because you are.'

'Are you saying you don't love your husband?'

'Yes, that's exactly what I'm saying.'

'You must still love him, even if only a little?'

'No, not at all. I love you, you know I do, but I never loved him, not really.'

'But you must have loved him once,' he persisted, 'or why on earth would you have married him in the first place?'

She shook her head. 'I was just swept away by circumstances. Marrying David was the biggest mistake of my life.'

Mark felt a tremor of anxiety in case she went on to say she wanted to leave her husband. As long as she stayed married to someone else, he felt safe.

'I only married David because of the baby. I told you, I was pregnant when we got married. I wasn't given any choice.'

He frowned. 'There's always a choice.'

'I was only seventeen.' She hesitated. 'I can't help how I feel. They're my feelings. They just happen. We can't control our feelings.'

'So are you saying you wouldn't have married him if you hadn't been pregnant?'

'Not in a million years.'

She was so emphatic he could not help feeling sorry for her, trapped in a loveless marriage, but it was not his problem if she had been rash enough to tie herself to a man she did not love. Although he was fond of her, in a way, he was not going to let his feelings for one woman dominate his life. They had only ever agreed to spend time together for fun. The idea that they might one day commit to one another in any serious way had never entered his mind. Her married status not only suited him, it was necessary for the survival of their relationship.

'Now you've got your daughter, I don't suppose you'll ever be able to leave her father,' he said cautiously.

'Aimee will be leaving home in a couple of years,' she replied.

Mark nodded, but he could not trust himself to speak. Certainly he was not thinking what Ann clearly hoped he had in mind, that with her daughter gone, the way would be clear for her to move in with Mark. He sighed. In many ways he would be sorry to see their affair come to an end, but the writing was on the wall.

'Things are going to change once she's left,' Ann added with a coy smile.

Mark nodded. 'I guess they are,' he agreed, turning away.

He could just imagine the scene she was going to make when he told her their affair was over. He would have to make sure she understood his position before she ended her marriage, or it might be difficult to chuck her. Certainly it would be cavalier of him to abandon her right after she had given up her marriage to be with him. Still, he hoped it was just talk, and she would not act on her threat to leave her husband. There was a good chance that she would decide to stick it out for the sake of her daughter. In the meantime, he would continue to see her, but he would watch out for any signs that she was about to make the break from David. As soon as she told him she was ready to end her marriage, he would drop his bombshell. It would be briefly painful, but after that he would never need to see her again. He almost felt sorry in anticipation of the break-up, but he banished such depressing thoughts from his mind. He had always believed in living for the moment. After all, death could strike anyone at any time, and in the most unexpected ways. There was no point in spoiling the time they had left together. He turned to her with a smile and pulled her, unresisting, into his embrace. He might as well enjoy the affair while he could.

7

MARK HAD PLANNED TO leave as soon as the concert finished. He could have found a plausible pretext for declining to attend in the first place but, although he was not pleased about having to spend a Saturday evening at school, he knew the visiting violinist would be worth hearing. It had been something of a coup for the head of music to engage her to perform at the school and, besides, it would have been churlish of him not to support an event organised within his department. Few of the pupils appreciated the brilliance of the performance but his applause at least was heartfelt. Afterwards, elated by the music he had just heard, he hung around for a glass of wine, instead of setting off home immediately the performance finished. Chatting with a few parents and sixth formers on this occasion was far more relaxed than the parents' evenings he was obliged to attend where he always felt it was he, rather than his pupils, who was being judged.

The violinist's performance proved a perfect prompt for inconsequential small talk.

'Wasn't she wonderful,' they told one another.

They commented variously on the programme which comprised a well-thought-out combination of traditional favourites and more obscure pieces, some of which Mark had never heard before. After a couple of glasses of wine, he would have been happy to stay longer, but all too soon the head of music wound the evening up with a short speech of thanks to the performer, and after a final round of applause, the audience trickled out of the building.

As Mark reached the centre of the city, he had to weave his way along streets packed with Saturday-night revellers, most of them drunk. A raucous gang of women dressed in pink and silver costumes went by, shrieking and waving bottles of Babycham. They were followed by another gang of women accompanying a woman dressed in white with a veil fluttering on her head. After listening to uplifting music, the women's shrill screeching laughter grated horribly.

Several other people were hanging around at his stop, waiting for buses. His eyes slid past a tall figure in a grey hoodie and lingered on a young woman with striking red hair. Beside her a boy was smoking the end of a cigarette, a trail of smoke spiralling upwards in a breeze blowing through the shelter. As the bus drew up, the boy dropped his cigarette butt. It continued to send a thin thread of smoke into the night air as Mark followed the woman on to the bus. Focused on his rear view of the woman as he climbed aboard after her, he paid scant attention to other passengers. Sitting across the aisle from her, he stared at her, willing her to glance in his direction so he could catch her eye and smile, but she never looked up. When she stood up and left the bus he was almost tempted to follow her, but he stayed in his seat. Even after a few drinks, he knew it would be weird to follow a complete stranger. Besides, his love life was well catered for and he had no need to meet anyone else. With a sigh, he watched the woman walking along the pavement as the bus drove off and she disappeared from view.

As the red-haired woman moved out of his line of vision, reflected in the window he saw the face of a man who appeared to be staring straight at him. In the instant their eyes met, Mark caught a brief glimpse of sharp features, high cheek bones, a pointed nose, and eyes that looked back at him in the reflection from the window. It was only a fleeting impression of a face half hidden below a hood pulled down over his forehead. As soon as Mark's eyes fell on his reflection the other man looked away, as though he was reluctant to be observed watching.

Reaching his stop, Mark jumped down and set off towards the side street where he lived. He was only vaguely aware of another passenger leaving the bus behind him. As he turned the corner into the side street where he lived, at the periphery of his vision he saw a hooded figure walking along the main road a few feet away. For no reason, Mark began to walk faster. The side street was well lit, but deserted apart from him and the man in the hood. Glancing over his shoulder, he saw that the other man had also turned into his street and seemed to be gaining on him. Mark increased his pace until he was almost trotting. It could have been a coincidence, but he was almost sure the man hurrying along the street behind him was the one who had been watching him on the bus. It was uncomfortable to think that he was being followed. He began to run and heard footsteps tapping rapidly along the pavement behind him.

Panting, he came to an abrupt halt. If the other man really *was* pursuing him, he wanted to know why, a question fuelled by anger rather than curiosity. He spun round so the other man could not catch hold of him from behind. The pavement was empty. His pursuer had vanished, perhaps slipping along the side of one of the properties in the street as soon as Mark stopped running. There was no point in searching for him. Mark turned and hurried home, baffled and uneasy. Once he was back in the safety of his flat, he realised he must have been mistaken, unnerved by the darkness and unsettled by having drunk too quickly on an empty stomach. Clearly the other man had not been following him. Shrugging off his unease, he put the kettle on, and then thought better of it and opened a beer. It was Saturday night, and he wanted to enjoy the rest of his evening alone.

The following morning, walking home from the local supermarket, he spotted a hooded figure on the opposite pavement apparently waiting for someone. With a slight shock, as he drew near Mark recognised the sharp features of the man he had seen on the bus. He hurried up the path to his front door but before opening it he looked round. The man was standing motionless on the opposite side of the street, watching him from the shadow of his overhanging hood. Dumping his shopping bags in the kitchen, Mark ran back outside to confront the hooded man, but he had vanished. Going back indoors, he cast a glance at the sink where his washing-up was accumulating for Tuesday's visit from Ann. This time it was not easy to convince himself that he was mistaken because he knew what he had seen, and he was scared.

His hand shook slightly as he poured himself a drink. He was aware that alcohol probably wouldn't steady his nerves, but he gulped down a shot of whisky, followed by another one straight away. The drink did not help. Now he felt just as scared as before, and slightly groggy as well. He poured a third whisky and took it through into the living room. Sprawling on an armchair, he examined his options. He could hardly go to the police to complain he had been followed home by a hooded man. The whole idea sounded silly and paranoid and, in any case, he had no idea who his stalker might be. Even if the police took his claim seriously, they were hardly going to offer him protection from some nebulous stranger who might or might not exist. The likelihood was that he was being targeted by an ex-pupil playing a stupid prank, but it was also possible that his stalker was the aggrieved husband or boyfriend of a woman Mark had enjoyed a fling with. If that was true, the stalker could turn violent. Mark resolved to be vigilant and confront his stalker as soon as he had an opportunity to do so. Possibly the whole episode was a mistake that would be easily resolved if they could only talk to one another. But he determined to carry a knife from now on, in case things turned ugly.

8

THIS WASN'T THE FIRST time Eileen had let her frustration show in the course of an investigation. Although it was less than a week since the rough sleeper had been found in a shop doorway, no one was satisfied with how the investigation was going, least of all the detective chief inspector. The victim's identity remained a mystery, and very little was known about his death, other than that he had been strangled with some sort of noose made of fabric. For the past week a higher profile murder case had taken priority over the investigation into the homeless victim, and the man hours available for this case had been curtailed. Now that the other case had been wrapped up, Eileen was focusing her attention on the dead tramp.

'We need to work harder and faster on this,' she said, as though the members of the team were each personally responsible for the lack of progress they had made. 'This case has been hanging over us for days and we're no further ahead with it than we were when the body was first spotted. We have to step up our efforts, starting right now.'

Listening to the detective chief inspector's rhetoric, Geraldine wondered how she would have behaved if she had found herself in Eileen's position. Until recently, she had been a detective inspector herself, heading for promotion to an even higher post. Now, having followed an impulse to protect her twin sister, she had been demoted to detective sergeant. She did not regret the actions that had led to her disgrace; by sacrificing her own career prospects, Geraldine had been able to save her sister's life. As a direct result of Geraldine's selfless action, her sister had finally agreed to attend a rehabilitation clinic in an attempt to kick her addiction to heroin. As long as Helena remained clean, Geraldine's sacrifice had been worthwhile.

'I screwed up your career for you, didn't I?' Helena had asked her one day.

Hoping Helena would not realise the extent of the sacrifice she had made, Geraldine's response had been cagey. 'What do you mean?'

'If it wasn't for me you would've been an important cop by now, wouldn't you? You'd have been really high up,' Helena had gone on, staring intently at her. 'You'd probably have been chief of the whole country, instead of being shunted off to York in disgrace.'

Geraldine had managed to force a credible laugh. 'Listen, Helena, I've not been "shunted off" anywhere. I like York –'

'Sure. And you really like being a sergeant instead of an inspector, don't you? That's just what an ambitious woman like you wants, isn't it? To move down the ranks instead of up. Don't give me that bullshit. How do you think it makes me feel, knowing you made this oh-so-noble sacrifice to save me from my evil ways. At least you could be honest with me about it.'

Geraldine had hesitated only briefly to work out a plausible excuse to help assuage her sister's guilt and anger.

'Actually,' she had replied, 'I wanted to go to York because there's a guy there I've worked with before, and I wanted to see more of him. So you don't need to feel in any way responsible for what happened to me. Your impact on my career wasn't that important.'

Helena's eyes had narrowed. 'Do you mean you fancy him?'

'I... yes, I like him,' Geraldine had admitted.

'You could have followed him there anyway, without all the drama.'

'It's not always that easy to get a transfer.'

Helena had shrugged. 'Whatever you say.'

50

Geraldine was not sure whether Helena had believed her or not. She was not even sure herself about her feelings for Ian Peterson. At one time she had believed their relationship might become closer than platonic friendship, but he seemed to have lost interest in her. She could not have said why, but she understood that following him to York had been a mistake. She cast a fleeting glance over at him before switching her attention back to the detective chief inspector. Ian was gazing at Eileen with a blank expression on his face. Geraldine thought he looked tired and somehow disconnected from his colleagues. She wondered what he was thinking about.

'It's time to ramp up our efforts,' Eileen was saying. 'We need to question everyone who lives and works on Coney Street. Someone there might have noticed something, and if that doesn't come up with anything we're going to have to spread the net wider.'

'What about the other rough sleepers?' Ian asked, clearly more engaged than he appeared. 'Shouldn't we be talking to them?'

'If you can get them to co-operate,' someone else muttered.

'Of course they'll co-operate,' Geraldine said. 'One of their community has just been brutally murdered. They must all be wondering if they'll be the next victim.'

A few other officers murmured in agreement.

'We'll talk to everyone we can find,' Eileen said.

Ariadne frowned. 'That's going to be a massive operation.'

'We're drafting in more officers to help,' Eileen replied. 'It's time to sort this one out before any more vulnerable people are targeted. At the moment we're dealing with one random death, but who knows what's behind it? We can't afford to let the situation get out of control.'

'Do you think this could be the start of a concerted attack on homeless people?' Ariadne asked Geraldine when the briefing was over.

Geraldine looked up from her desk. 'What makes you say that?'

'It's what Eileen was implying. She said this might not be the only attack on people sleeping rough. What do you think?'

Geraldine hesitated. 'That's certainly the kind of line the press would love to pick up on,' she said at last.

'I know, I know, we keep this to ourselves, of course. Although I dare say reporters have already made the leap from one murder to a blood bath. They hardly need us to feed their sensational bollocks.'

'Who's got sensational bollocks?' a young constable asked, overhearing Ariadne's closing comment. 'Really, what you women talk about when you're supposed to be working never ceases to amaze me!'

Ariadne laughed at his affectation of surprise, but Geraldine did not feel like joining in with the lighthearted exchange. The implications of the murder were worrying. Eileen had been right to demand more resources for this particular investigation. If it turned out to be one attack on a rough sleeper, that would be serious enough, but the murder appeared to have been carefully planned by a killer who had covered his tracks. That raised a number of possibilities, one of which was that the victim had been deliberately selected precisely because he was homeless. And homelessness was on the increase in York, despite the work of the council resettlement centres. For a killer targeting rough sleepers, victims could be relatively easy pickings.

'What if someone really is targeting rough sleepers?' she muttered. 'And if that's what's happening, is the killer going to be satisfied with one victim?'

Ariadne looked round. 'What did you say?'

Geraldine sighed. 'We have to get this case sorted as soon as we can.'

With a nod, Ariadne returned to her banter with the constable who had interrupted them.

9

ANN REFUSED TO GIVE Mark the number of her landline, and told him she was careful to leave no trace of their assignations at her home. In addition to those precautions, she had bought a pay-as-you-go phone which she kept hidden from her husband, topping it up with cash. Mark was happy for her to keep their affair a secret from her husband. When he assured her that breaking up her marriage was the last thing he wanted to do, she thanked him for his sympathetic grasp of her situation. The truth was that he was as keen as she was that her husband should not find out about their affair.

Several times she had hinted that if Mark begged her to move in with him, she would willingly abandon her marriage, and she repeatedly told him that she would do anything for him. But he never encouraged her to leave her husband, even though he knew she was miserable with him. Instead, he did his best to convince her he was only doing what he thought was best for her, and so they slipped into a comfortable routine, seeing one another most Tuesday evenings.

'I'm so happy here,' she told him as she lay in his arms one evening. 'I still can't believe it. I go to sleep every evening thinking about you, and wake up every morning thinking about you. Sometimes I dream about you. I don't believe in fate and all that, but it really seems as though we were destined to be together. Loving you is the only thing that gives my life meaning.'

'You know I care about you,' he replied. 'But you have to

stay with your husband. I'm only thinking of you, and your daughter,' he added, seeing her crestfallen expression. 'You know I'm right. It would be cruel to your daughter if we allowed our affair to break up your family.'

'You're right,' she agreed. 'Not many men would be as thoughtful as you. When Aimee's older we'll talk about what we're going to do. Once she's left home, things'll be different.'

One evening she yanked the duvet off the bed and found a pair of lacy scarlet knickers that did not belong to her. Furious, she picked them up by the label and brandished them in his face.

'What the hell is this?'

He forced a smile, inwardly cursing the careless girl he had brought home the previous night.

'It looks like a pair of knickers,' he replied.

Her voice grew shrill with anger. 'They're not mine!'

'No? Really? Are you sure? They must be my sister's then,' he replied, with what he hoped was a disarming smile.

'Your sister's?'

'Yes, she was here on a flying visit. She only stayed for a night. I slept on the sofa and let her have the bed.'

Ann scowled at him.

'What's wrong now?' he asked.

'You never told me you had a sister.'

He laughed at her indignation. 'So?'

He turned away, but she was not ready to let it go. 'What was your sister doing sleeping in your bed?'

'Where else was she supposed to sleep?'

'How do I know the woman who slept in your bed was really your sister?'

Mark raised his eyebrows, then burst out laughing. 'I can't believe you'd think for one moment that I'd lie to you,' he said, when he was able to catch his breath. 'You must know by now that I'm crazy about you. Come on. Come here, you silly thing. Why won't you trust me?'

When she refused to be placated, he pretended to lose his patience with her.

'All right,' he snapped. 'If you refuse to trust me, why don't you just go home?'

She immediately capitulated, as he had known she would, and she kissed him passionately.

'Of course, I trust you,' she murmured as his lips moved down her neck.

Mark wondered if it was his conscience that prompted him to suspect he was being watched, when really it was the married women he was seeing who ought to be feeling guilty. He was single, and free to sleep with anyone he fancied. He thought Ann would sympathise with his fears, so he confided in her. To his annoyance, she mocked his suspicions.

'This is no laughing matter,' he insisted, struggling to control his irritation. 'I'm telling you, I'm being stalked.'

'Stalked? As in, you have a stalker?'

'Yes.'

'What on earth makes you think that?'

'I don't just *think* I'm being stalked, I *know*. I'm telling you, someone's following me wherever I go.'

'Who is she? Is it someone from the school where you work? Perhaps there's an obsessive psycho there who fancies you?'

'I don't know who it is,' he replied, 'but I don't think it's a woman.'

She frowned. 'You think a man is stalking you? Really? What makes you think that?'

'I don't know, exactly, but it's true. I'm not an idiot. I wouldn't tell you about it if I wasn't sure.'

Ann looked baffled. 'And you're telling me this isn't a woman?'

'No, I just told you, it's a man.'

'Can you prove it?'

'Prove it? I've got the evidence of my own eyes.'

'I mean actual proof, like photos or something, because if it's true, you're going to need to tell someone and you need to be able to prove you're being stalked.'

'I told you, I've seen someone following me. I don't know who it is.'

'Well, what did you see, exactly?'

'A figure.'

'What sort of a figure?'

He shrugged, making no attempt to hide his irritation. 'I don't know. I don't know who it is. Whoever it is keeps to the shadows and follows me around whenever I go out. I'm telling you, someone's stalking me. He's out there in the street, watching me. Every time I go out, he's there, waiting for me. I can't go to my car, or walk down the road, or to the station, without being followed.'

'Why don't you go to the police? Let them sort it out.'

'The police? Why would they listen to me?

'That's their job.'

'They're not going to listen, are they? Even you don't believe me, and you know I'd never lie to you.'

He paused, struck by the irony of his words.

Ann hesitated, gazing at him with a worried expression. 'Have you ever experienced anything like this before?'

Realising she suspected he was mentally unstable, he felt a surge of rage, because her conjecture stirred up his worst fear.

He glared at her. 'I'm not schizophrenic, and I don't suffer from paranoid delusions.'

'That's not what I meant,' she lied.

But obviously it was. Outraged by her scepticism, he stood up and stalked over to the window. Reaching to close the curtains, he recoiled suddenly, as if he had been slapped. A figure was standing on the opposite pavement, staring directly at his window.

He summoned her rapidly, in a low undertone. 'Come here, quickly, and you can see for yourself.'

Heaving a sigh, she climbed off the bed and went over to join him.

'Look down there,' he said.

She leaned forward and peered out of the window. 'What am I supposed to be looking at?'

He turned his head to look at the empty street below.

'There's no one there now,' he said. 'But there was a moment ago.'

Ann reached out and put her hand on his arm. 'If that's true, you need to report it to the police.'

'If it's true? I'm telling you I just saw him. He was there.'

Struggling to control his panic, he flung himself down on the bed and buried his face in the pillow.

'Mark, you have to go to the police,' she said. 'What does the man look like?'

'I don't know,' he replied, sitting up. 'It's just a shadowy figure in a hoodie.'

She nodded, frowning. 'You need to get close to him and get a photo of him. That way we can see if we recognise him.'

He realised what she meant. 'You think it's your husband, don't you?'

She nodded uncertainly. 'More likely a private detective he's hired to follow me around.'

'But I'm the one who's being followed, not you.' He was nearly shouting at her. 'This isn't about you. Don't you understand, someone is threatening me, and I can't do a damn thing about it.'

She left soon after, for once eager to get away. Although he was scared to be alone, he was pleased to shut the door behind her. Her bland disbelief had upset him more than he had let on. Passing the window, he glanced down and saw that the hooded man had returned. Standing motionless between the street lamps, the stranger stared up at him from the shadows. Mark swore helplessly, then realised that he was turning himself into a victim. He did not have to allow the anonymous stranger to terrorise him. Determined to take control of the situation, he armed himself with a sharp knife from the kitchen, and set off to confront his antagonist. Flinging the front door open, he burst out into the street. In the time it had taken him to race downstairs, the man had vanished. But the unspoken threat remained.

10

BY THE TIME GERALDINE had gone to bed on Monday, the forensic report on threads found on the victim's neck had been received. The traces of fabric came from a cotton material that had been dyed dark red. It had been difficult to establish the exact colour at first sight as the red dye had been stained with blood where the victim's skin had broken with the friction of the noose, but with close analysis the colour was now confirmed. They now knew for certain that the tramp had been strangled with a strip of red cotton material. It could have been a tie. The details of his noose made no difference to the dead man, but Geraldine felt cautiously encouraged by the new information, as though the police were closing in on the unknown killer. She went to bed feeling more positive than she had been for a few days, and woke up early on Tuesday morning. Since there was nothing more she could do until she reached the police station and was given her duties for the day, and the sun was shining, she decided to have breakfast on her narrow balcony overlooking the river.

Sitting with coffee and cereal, she did her best to focus her attention on the boats sporadically passing by, and the pedestrians out on the far side of the river, having a morning stroll. But at the back of her mind she kept picturing the victim, probably pissed, staggering along the street. He might have been singing drunkenly to himself as he walked. Perhaps he had paused as he reached the doorway in Coney Street where he slept. Swaying, he might have been fumbling in his coat pocket for a drink when a shadowy figure stole up behind him, flung a tie around his neck, and twisted the ends swiftly and strongly, round and round, while he scrabbled at the noose with fingers frantic, then limp, and finally lifeless. The assault had probably lasted less than five minutes, enough time to kill a man no one cared about.

'So, we have no idea who this man was,' Eileen said. 'We're still waiting for a DNA report. We're hoping someone will come forward to report him missing, but we can't rely on that, given that he appeared to be sleeping rough.' She paused. 'It's possible no one will ever realise he's missing. In the meantime, we'll be checking with the local homeless shelters to see if anyone there can recognise him.'

That morning Geraldine went to the Fishergate Resettlement Centre, where homeless people were prepared for independent living. She found herself in a newly refurbished building, which she learned housed two dozen single rooms and half a dozen double ones. The man who let her in explained that he was a volunteer who had been working there for nearly ten years. He was a sprightly grey-haired man in his seventies and Geraldine guessed he had been helping at the centre since he had retired. He asked if she would prefer to talk to one of the key workers, but she decided that someone who had been there for around a decade was likely to know more than an employee who might not have worked there for long.

'The residents all want rooms to themselves,' the volunteer explained, 'but we have a waiting list. Sometimes there's only a bed in a double room available, but we move them into a single room as soon as a single becomes available. It never usually takes long because we try to move them on as soon as they're ready. What we offer here is a stepping stone to independent living. Not all of our residents are down and outs. Some of them have been thrown out by their families, or they've lost their jobs and their homes. You know what they say: we're all of us only two pay days away from being homeless. And not all of the rough sleepers who come here stay for long. Some of them don't settle. We look after them, but they have to follow the rules. We have to be strict – no alcohol or drugs on the premises, and they're responsible for keeping their own rooms tidy – it's all part of preparing them to move on to independent living. We offer workshops in raising self-esteem, literacy, cooking, all the skills they're going to need when they leave. We do everything we can to support them but even so, not everyone likes it here.'

Geraldine wondered whether her own sister had ever stayed in a similar shelter. If she had, she would have been thrown out for failing to kick her drug habit. The thought made Geraldine shiver. Dismissing the memory of her sister, Geraldine turned to the reason for her visit and showed the volunteer a photograph of the dead man.

'Oh yes, that's Bingo,' he said straight away.

'Bingo?'

'Yes. That's the name he goes by. He's not been a resident here, but he's used the crash pad a few times.'

'Crash pad?'

The volunteer nodded. 'Yes, in severe weather we try to pack in as many of the rough sleepers as we can, so it's a case of laying out mattresses in the communal lounge. There are quite a few of them who come in when they have to find shelter from the weather. Bingo stayed with us from time to time, but he was never here for long. He would drift in here in the bad weather, and then leave. He's been coming here, on and off, for years now. And,' he leaned closer and lowered his voice, 'every time we saw him he looked worse. He didn't look after himself at all. I think he was pretty sick towards the end. We tried to get him to see a doctor, but he flatly refused, don't ask me why. People can be stubborn like that.'

Geraldine wondered how a sick man living on the streets was supposed to look after himself but she did not comment.

'He was a gentle soul, poor old Bingo,' the volunteer went on.

'I can't imagine why anyone would want to do away with him. I mean, he wasn't the sort to get into fights or anything, not like some of our clientele who are involved with drugs. I guess some vicious bastard must have set on him. He would have been easy prey for a violent attack. He wasn't the sort to fight back, even if he had the strength.'

'Do you know his full name?'

The man shook his head. 'He told us his name was Bingo, but we never knew if that was his real name.' He gave a sad smile. 'You will catch whoever did this, won't you? They shouldn't be allowed to get away with it.'

'I assure you we're doing all we can.'

He hesitated. 'The papers are saying you're not interested, on account of no one caring about the homeless, but –'

Geraldine interrupted him briskly. 'This man was unlawfully killed and we are investigating his death in exactly the same way as we would any other murder on the streets of York. Murder is murder, regardless of the victim's identity.'

The man nodded uncertainly. 'That's good to hear,' he replied.

Geraldine had the impression he did not believe her.

'Do you think any of your other residents might be able to tell me more about him?'

'What is it you want to know?'

'Discovering his identity might help us to find out who killed him.'

But no one knew the victim, and those who remembered him did not know his full name, or even whether Bingo had been his real name.

'It sounds like a name he adopted for himself,' Eileen said when Geraldine told her what she had discovered. 'Perhaps he thought it would bring him luck,' she added with a sour smile.

'He might have been an educated man,' Geraldine said. 'There's a character called Bingo in PG Wodehouse.'

'Is that his surname?'

'No, he was called Bingo Little. But I'm not sure if it was supposed to be a real name, or a nickname.'

'Well, let's look into the name Bingo and see what we can come up with,' Eileen replied.

11

MARK DID NOT ANSWER the door the first time the bell rang. He could not imagine why Ann would want to return at such a late hour, and he was not sure he wanted to see her again so soon. He lived in fear of hearing that she had decided to leave her husband. If that happened, he would have to face her wrath when she learned that he had no intention of letting her move in with him. When the bell rang again, he almost did not open the door and, when he did, he nearly shut it again without listening to what the man on his doorstep had to say. It was growing dark outside and he was surprised that anyone would be cold calling so late.

'Whatever you're selling I'm not interested –' he began.

The other man cut him short, speaking in a strangely flat voice. 'I'm not selling anything. You don't know who I am, do you?'

Mark squinted at the stranger as he introduced himself as a neighbour, adding that he had 'seen Mark around', and was surprised Mark did not recognise him. Mark studied the man on his doorstep. With a pale face beneath hair cropped very short, a straight nose, full lips and dark eyes that were curiously intent, there was nothing memorable about him apart from his piercing gaze. So although it was slightly surprising that Mark had never noticed him, he could quite plausibly have passed the other man in the hallway a few times without registering his appearance.

'How can I help you?' Mark asked.

'It's about your car.'

'My car? What about it?'

The other man gave a helpless shrug. 'I guess you'd better come and take a look. Assuming it is your car I'm talking about.' He reeled off the registration number of Mark's car.

Mark nodded. With a sinking feeling he grabbed his keys and followed his neighbour down the stairs to the underground car park, grumbling that the CCTV cameras were not working again. When they reached the bottom of the stairs, the neighbour stood back to allow Mark to go in front of him. Approaching his car, Mark frowned because there did not appear to be anything wrong with it. He leaned forward, and did not know what hit him next.

When he regained consciousness his head was pounding. What he was suffering felt like a bad hangover, only far more painful. Gradually he realised he was lying on a hard floor in a poorly lit room. Without moving his head he swivelled his eyes slowly and saw that he was in a cellar of some kind, with a very low ceiling and no windows. A free-standing lamp cast long shadows across the dusty floor. Other than that, the room was bare. Not until he tried to call out did he recover consciousness sufficiently to realise that he had been gagged, and his hands had been tied together. Whoever had brought him here had not given any thought to keeping him comfortable. He had no idea how long he lay there feeling his joints stiffen, before he finally heard a door open and footsteps approaching. With an effort he turned his head and saw the lower half of a pair of legs wearing jeans and trainers. Looking at the shoes, he guessed he had been joined by a man. Unable to talk, Mark groaned as loudly as he could and blinked as tears slid from his eyes.

He became aware of a figure crouching down beside him and shifting his gaze upwards saw the angular profile, dark eyes and fleshy lips of his neighbour. He could have cried with relief when fumbling fingers removed his gag. For a moment he was too overcome to thank his rescuer. While he struggled to control his emotions and express his gratitude, a voice murmured close to his ear.

'Good. He's still alive.'

'Help me,' Mark blurted out. 'My hands are tied.'

'We don't want him dying on us yet,' the voice continued, paying no attention to Mark's words.

'What are you talking about?' Mark asked, confused. 'I'm tied up here. Can you release my hands please?'

'He wants us to let him go. Does he think we are stupid?'

Mark swivelled his eyes around but could see no one else in the room with them, and the man did not appear to be talking into a phone.

'Who's there? What do you want with me?' he cried out.

'He knows why he's here. He's played fast and loose for long enough. Now it's his turn to suffer.'

'Let me go at once!' Mark shouted, his eyes wide with terror.

Ignoring Mark's outburst, the other man asked a question of his own. He spoke so calmly, it took a few seconds for Mark to take in what he was saying.

'How long can a man last without food or water, do you suppose?'

'What the hell's going on?' Mark said, his own voice rising in fear with the growing realisation that the man might not have come to rescue him after all. 'Do you want money? Is that it?'

For a moment the other man did not answer, then the silence was broken by a guttural laugh.

'He's offering us money,' the man said in his odd singsong voice. 'He thinks he can buy his way out of his predicament.'

'Tell me what you want,' Mark said, trying to keep his voice steady, as though this was a normal conversation. 'If it's not about money, what are you after?'

'How long can a man last without food or water?' the man repeated. He sat back on his heels. 'I guess we're about to find out, aren't we? Assuming we can all be patient, that is.'

'What do you want?' Mark asked, even though he had already realised the other man was insane. Not only was he apparently talking to himself, but he seemed to be threatening to kill Mark. 'You're making a mistake. You can't want to do this to me. I don't even know you.'

'But you know my wife, don't you?'

'What? What wife?'

Mark felt sick. It was true, he had been sleeping with another man's wife, but he had never seen her husband. Not having met him face to face before, there was a chance he might be able to persuade his captor that he had the wrong man. Although his voice was shaking with fear, he tried to sound indignant.

'What are you talking about? I've never slept with another man's wife. You've got the wrong guy. I'm not like that. I – I'm gay.'

'He's pretending he's gay,' the man sniggered. 'Of course, he's used to lying, isn't he? His whole life is built on deceit. Well, he has to learn that he can't get away with it. Not this time. Not with me.'

'What do you want? Listen, you're making a mistake. Tell you what. You let me go right now and we'll say no more about it. I won't say a word to anyone about this. We'll put it down to a practical joke, just a bit of fun. How about that? I don't even know who you are. You don't live in my block of flats really, do you? I don't know who you are or where you're from and by tomorrow I won't even remember what you look like. I'm hopeless with faces. I just don't remember them.'

It was terrifying, trying to persuade this lunatic to let him go, while his hands were tied together and his head was aching horribly. He thought he might throw up. But he kept babbling, until the other man snapped at him to stop talking.

'What are you going to do with me?' Mark asked. 'You can't really be going to kill me? You can't do this.'

'He's not happy about it but he's going to get what's coming to him. No, not yet. He's not ready yet.'

'What do you mean, not ready? I don't understand. What are you talking about? What's going on?'

'He's too well fed for us.'

Although the words did not make sense, they had a horrible ring of premeditation. What was more, Mark could not fail to notice that his captor was wearing black gloves and was making no attempt to conceal his face. It seemed that Mark's incarceration had been planned in advance, and was going to end in his death. In a panic, he began to yell, but the other man slapped him, hard, across the face. Before Mark recovered enough to resume shouting for help the gag was pulled across his mouth again.

'Now we wait,' the man said. 'Shall we come back tomorrow? Will he be ready to do what we want by then?'

Mark nodded his head, as far as he could, to intimate he would do whatever his captor wanted. He was ready to comply right now. But his protestations of surrender came out as unintelligible moaning. He heard footsteps moving away, the floor vibrated with the movement, and then the door closed softly and he was on his own again.

12

IT WAS A WEEK since the body had been discovered. The police had got nowhere with finding the killer or even establishing the victim's identity. He was known only as Bingo. In the absence of family or friends on their backs to complain about police inaction, the investigation was proceeding without any sense of urgency. In theory, it was desperately sad that a man had been murdered and no one cared, but without any outpouring of grief, the complexion of the case was altered. In some ways it felt more like an impersonal puzzle to be solved than a restoration of human justice. Subtle changes in her colleagues' behaviour alerted Geraldine to their attitude towards the murdered man.

'Bingo,' Ariadne said. 'It sounds like an old time music hall artist, or the name you might give to a dog. I mean, it's an odd sort of name, isn't it? I've never met anyone called Bingo. It could be a surname, I suppose.'

'It's probably a nickname,' Geraldine replied. 'We haven't been able to find anyone called Bingo, first name or surname, who's been reported missing. He's like an inconvenient loose end,' she added glumly.

'Who is?' Ariadne asked.

Geraldine shrugged.

'I thought we were getting somewhere,' Ariadne said when Geraldine explained herself.

It was true, they were making progress. Only that morning the forensic laboratory had confirmed that the threads found on Bingo's neck matched a fabric used in the manufacture of garments made with a particular cotton. They were able to pinpoint the area of the globe where the material originated, and the factory where the dye was produced. They had even said where that particular batch of cotton had been dyed. The disappointing news was that it was a common colour used in the mass production of millions of garments, including a brand of tie that could have been purchased from any number of stores, or online. Thousands of such items were sold every week, and in any case the one used to strangle the victim might have been bought years ago so there was little point in trying to trace where it had been purchased. Even though the specific fabric and dye had been identified, discovering the likely nature of the murder weapon had not moved the investigation forward.

'At least we now know the killer was male,' a constable said.

His comment provoked a barrage of dissent.

'Women can get hold of ties,' a female constable said.

'Women wear ties,' another officer added.

The constable who had made the thoughtless comment looked at the floor.

'Don't make assumptions and don't take anything for granted,' Ian said.

Geraldine wondered if Ian remembered how she had drummed those instructions into him when she had been his superior officer. The days when she had been a detective inspector and he had been her sergeant seemed a lifetime away. She smiled sadly at him but he either did not notice or else chose to ignore her glance of complicity. She understood. As an inspector, he had moved away from his former reliance on her guidance. Stifling her regret at the distance that had grown between them, she went to speak to the team who had been studying CCTV footage of the area around Coney Street.

The constables were excited that they had spotted a hooded figure near the crime scene. They had done their best to follow it, but had lost their possible suspect in the streets leading away from the site. With a light drizzle falling on the evening the tramp had been killed, there were several hooded figures hurrying along the pavements and waiting at bus stops. It was impossible to be sure which of them had walked hurriedly along the street away from the crime scene at around the time the tramp had been strangled. Geraldine shivered as she watched one of the figures who was probably a perfectly innocent pedestrian, but who might have just killed someone.

Armed with photographs of the dead man before and after he had been cleaned up, that evening Geraldine and Ariadne went to talk to anyone they could find sleeping rough in the warm weather.

'You'd hardly think it was the same man, would you?' Ariadne asked, gazing at the two images.

With his face washed, and his hair combed neatly, the man known as Bingo looked very different to the grubby corpse that had been discovered lying on the pavement. It made the circumstances of his death somehow more poignant, a pointless death at the end of a wasted life.

'He doesn't look that old, does he, now he's been cleaned up?'

'Younger than us,' Ariadne agreed. 'What was he? Late thirties?'

'Jonah said it was difficult to assess his age because he was so unhealthy before he died, but he thinks he was in his forties. He'd barely eaten for days and had been drinking a lot of cheap spirits.' She sighed. 'It's so sad, isn't it?'

'What? That he was homeless or that he was killed?' Ariadne asked.

'Both. I wonder what reduced him to poverty.'

'Oh well, there's nothing we can do about that and thank

goodness it's not our job to try and sort out the homeless. What a depressing task that must be. Hopeless.'

Geraldine was not sure whether Ariadne was feeling pessimistic about the task or the homeless people, but she did not pursue the matter. Leaving Ariadne talking to any rough sleepers she could find, Geraldine went along to the other resettlement shelter in York. The manager of the shelter came to meet her in person. After signing her in, he led her upstairs to his office which was small but well maintained like the rest of the building she had seen so far.

'How can we help you?' he asked. 'I take it this is about the rough sleeper who was murdered?'

'Yes. We're trying to establish his identity. So far we only know him as Bingo.'

'That's right. We heard about it from the shelter at Fishergate.'

'Did he have another name?'

The responses were almost identical to those she had been given at the first shelter she had visited.

The manager gave a helpless shrug. 'He must have had other names, of course, but he didn't tell us. We only knew him as Bingo.' He gave a twisted smile. 'It happens. Some of them never tell us their full names and when they do they often just make the names up. They don't always give the same name because they forget what they've already told us. We don't judge here. If they're referred to come and stay then we need their details, but many of the rough sleepers are too accustomed to their lifestyle to want to change and only come here to use the crash pad in severe weather. We're under no obligation to try and force them to stay, even if we had the resources to accommodate them all. We can only try to help those who genuinely want to learn to live independently. We offer all sorts of support, and workshops and training, but there's not much we can do for those who are happy to stay on the streets. They can use the facilities here, like the showers, but that's all some of them want. We can't work miracles.'

'Of course not. But the point is we're trying to trace his identity. This man has been murdered and there may be someone somewhere who would like to know what's happened to him, or who can maybe even help us to find out who did this.'

The manager nodded. 'I want to introduce you to some of our volunteer helpers here, as well as our paid staff, as they may have heard something.'

Several of the people working there mentioned a resident called Tommy.

'He's in his room,' the manager said. 'I'll pop up and fetch him. It sounds as though he knows Bingo.'

He knew him, Geraldine thought.

At first sight Tommy looked nothing like a stereotypical tramp, apart perhaps from his shuffling gait as he entered the office. His hair was neat, his face clean shaven and his shirt crisply ironed. Well spoken and articulate, he launched unbidden into an apologetic account of how he had been laid off by a bank in the latest crash. Paid off in shares that became worthless overnight, he went from a high-earning banker to a rough sleeper, abandoned by his wife, alone and homeless. Quitting the city, he had walked and hitched his way north to Scotland, and had ended up returning to York where he had been referred to the resettlement shelter. Geraldine did not enquire whether it was drink or drugs that made him jittery but he told her anyway, extending a trembling hand.

'It's the drink that makes me shake. I'm doing what I can to control it. They'll throw me out if I don't.'

When Geraldine asked him about Bingo he nodded. 'Yes, I know Bingo. We used to look out for each other, before I came here.'

'I'm afraid Bingo's dead.'

Tommy did not show any emotion on hearing the news of his friend's death. He merely raised one inquisitive eyebrow.

'Bingo's dead?' He frowned, gazing at Geraldine speculatively. 'I heard a rumour to that effect, but there are always rumours flying around.'

'I'm afraid it was more than a rumour. Bingo is dead. I'm sorry to bring you the sad news.'

Tommy shrugged and a flake of dandruff floated off his shoulder. Geraldine watched it for a second as it drifted aimlessly to the floor.

'You're sorry? Why? I wouldn't waste your sympathy on guys like us. If you ask me, he's well out of it.'

'He was murdered.'

'Shit.' Tommy stood up and went and opened the office door. 'Hey, you guys,' he called out in a commanding voice to a couple of men walking past. 'Did you know Bingo was murdered?'

'I told you it's not safe out there,' one of the other residents replied.

'Who's going to protect *us*?' an old man whined. 'Any one of us could be next.'

When it came to talking about the dead man, all Tommy admitted to knowing about him was his name, and he freely conceded that even that was probably no more than an untraceable nickname. Geraldine had expected it to be easier to deal with a murder when there was no one living suffering as a consequence, but in some ways Bingo's death was turning out to be even more distressing to investigate than the victims she was used to dealing with: a man had died and no one actually cared. Even Tommy, who claimed to have looked out for Bingo, was unmoved at the news of his violent death.

'It's a shame about Tommy,' the manager said as Geraldine was leaving. 'We've tried to encourage him to stop drinking but he just says, what for?'

'Are you all right?' Ariadne asked as Geraldine arrived back at her desk. 'You're looking a bit down.'

Geraldine did not reply that she was wondering who would care if anything happened to her.

Instead, she smiled. 'Sure. I'm fine.'

'Those places are depressing, aren't they?'

Geraldine nodded, content to let Ariadne misinterpret her long face.

13

THE PLAN WAS WORKING out perfectly so far. Mark's cries would probably have been inaudible regardless of where he was kept, since he was gagged and tied up. But to make absolutely sure, he had not been trapped in a shed at the end of a garden, or in a garage at the side of a house, where he might somehow have managed to attract attention by banging loudly on the door. Instead, he was imprisoned in the locked cellar of a locked house where no one could possibly hear him or come across him by accident.

Even though he could not help gloating, he was not acting out of petty resentment. This was far more important than his own personal revenge. What he was doing was carrying out a just and reasonable execution. It was exactly what Mark deserved. In principle, he would agree, it was never a good idea to take the law into your own hands, but in this instance the law was impotent, leaving him with no other choice. With Mark gone, the world would be rid of a toxic presence; an evil rooted out and destroyed could only make the world a better place for everyone. He smiled, savouring Mark's terror as the finishing touch to his triumph.

'I wonder how long it will take him to die, down here, alone in the dark?' he asked after a few minutes of silent contemplation.

He stared into his captive's stricken eyes, as though awaiting a response. It was tranquil down in the cellar, and silent. Shielded from the world above their heads, they could have been on a different planet. Watching the terror in Mark's eyes, a sense of

76

wellbeing flooded through him at the knowledge that he was righting the wrong. This was a good place to find tranquillity. He almost hoped Mark felt the same way about his death, although that was a kindness he did not deserve.

'A man can be at peace in here,' he said, still smiling and looking around the bare room. 'It's quiet, and he knows he won't be disturbed. No one ever comes down here. No one but me has a key to this place, so he's quite safe from interruption. He can use the time to think about what he's done, and why he deserves to be here.'

His captive responded with a series of muffled cries, while the expression in his eyes grew increasingly wild.

'Oh, shut up,' he snapped, losing patience. 'There's no point in fussing like that because no one can hear anything from down here. No one but me, that is.'

He smiled, his good humour restored. For reply, Mark resumed his moaning. He really was annoying. He had been told, quite clearly, that no one would be able to hear him down here, however much noise he made, yet he persisted in bleating. It was such a waste of energy. Not that Mark had any reason to conserve his energy. In some ways, the sooner he exhausted himself, the sooner all this would be over. But he did not want his captive to die too quickly. That, too, would be an undeserved mercy.

'He's going to have to suffer for a little while longer,' he said. 'It's only fair. This is his punishment, after all. He's not been here nearly long enough. And once he's dead, his punishment will be over.'

After that, it would just be a question of somehow disposing of the body before it began to smell. He wrinkled his nose, disgusted at the thought. But that was merely an unfortunate consequence of what he had to do. He would deal with it when the time came. For now, he simply wanted to enjoy the sight of Mark, tied up and helpless. It was intensely gratifying. The way

Mark was looking, this was going to take a while. With a sigh, he stood up and Mark's eyes flickered. Much as they expressed loathing, he was evidently panicking at the prospect of being left on his own. In a way that was frustrating, because he could not be present to witness Mark's worst terrors. He could try to set up a camera, but it was too dark in there to catch the subtleties of changing facial expressions. He moved towards the door, staring into his prisoner's eyes, which were wild with a mute plea for clemency.

He shook his head in answer. 'No,' he said softly, 'we can't let him go. That would ruin everything.' His voice grew hard. 'He'll never leave this place alive. That's the whole point. God, he's slow. I mean, let's be reasonable, shall we? Would we really bring him all the way down here, and tie him up, only to let him go? And what then? What's to stop him going to the police and telling them everything that's happened?'

Mark shook his head furiously.

'Besides, if he's still too stupid to work out who I am, he can describe me to the police, can't he? Because he's seen my face, hasn't he? Oh, he can shake his head until his eyes pop out, but he knows what would happen, doesn't he? No, we all know there's only one way this can end. But not yet.'

Listening to the muffled sobs of his prisoner, he walked over to the door and glanced over his shoulder for one last look at Mark, grovelling in the dirt where he belonged.

'She's my wife,' he hissed as he opened the door. 'Mine!'

He shut the door and the muffled sound of Mark's whining was abruptly cut off.

14

THE FOLLOWING MORNING A woman turned up at the police station asking to speak to Geraldine. Joining her in an interview room, Geraldine recognised one of the volunteers who worked at the second resettlement centre she had visited. An anxious-looking woman with curly greying hair, keen to help with the investigation, she said she had been asking around at the centre to see if she could find out anything about the recent murder. Geraldine nodded and listened to her rambling account without interrupting her.

'Anyway, the point is, I spoke to everyone there, even though it wasn't really necessary, and you want to talk to Tommy,' she said at last, her eyes bright with some kind of personal triumph.

'Thank you, we've already questioned him,' Geraldine replied gently.

She never liked to disappoint members of the public who had taken the trouble to come forward with genuine information, even when it was no longer needed.

'Yes, I know that. I mean you want to talk to him again.'

'Do you think he knows more than he's already told us?'

The woman nodded. 'I think he knows a lot more.' She leaned forward and lowered her voice. 'He told some of the other residents that he killed Bingo. Apparently they had a fight and Tommy killed him. That's what he's telling everyone. Except you, that is. If he'd told you about it you would have arrested him then and there, wouldn't you?'

Geraldine listened closely to what the woman told her. She was clearly convinced by what she had heard, but whether Tommy had been telling the truth or not had yet to be established. Geraldine thanked her and tasked a constable with taking down the woman's statement. Eileen was away at a meeting in another police station, so Geraldine discussed the latest development with Ian, and together they drove to the New Start Centre to find Tommy. They found him shuffling along a corridor, and he greeted them with a lopsided grin.

'Come to arrest me, have you?' he asked cheerfully. 'What took you so long?'

'He did it,' another man called out as he walked past them. 'Tommy's your man. Take him away and lock him up, for fuck's sake. We don't want him here.'

Tommy's smile never faltered.

'Come along with us then and let's hear what you have to say, and you'd better not be wasting our time,' Ian said.

Tommy looked disappointed. 'Aren't you going to arrest me?'

'We need a statement from you first,' Ian replied. 'Now come on.'

'All right, all right, I'm coming, I can't walk any faster than this,' Tommy replied, wincing as he limped along beside them.

'What's wrong with your leg?' Geraldine asked.

'I don't know, do I? I'm not a fucking doctor. Pardon my language, in front of a lady, but I'm in agony with it and it's getting worse all the time.'

He accepted a cup of tea at the police station and appeared entirely at ease with the situation once he was sitting down.

'Yes, it was me all right,' he told them before they had even begun to question him.

Tommy's story corroborated what the volunteer had told Geraldine. He claimed to have been in an argument with Bingo which had gone on for too long and showed no sign of ending.

'So I decided the only thing to do was finish him off.'

'You deliberately set out to kill him?' Ian sounded sceptical.

Tommy shrugged. 'I'm not saying I actually intended to kill him, but that's what happened.'

'Why did you do it?' Geraldine asked.

'Because he was bugging me, that's why,' Tommy replied, his casual good humour briefly replaced by a flash of anger. 'You'd have done the same thing if you had to share a room with that stinking tosser for longer than five minutes. He got on my nerves, that's what. And that's why I did it.'

Geraldine frowned. 'He wasn't even sleeping at the centre on the night he was killed, so what could have prompted you to kill him then?'

'Ah, but he would have been back soon enough once the weather turned. It ate away at me all summer, the resentment and loathing. And now the winter's coming on, I knew he'd be sleeping at the centre again, and bugging me whenever I saw his face. So I did what I had to do.'

'You could have gone to another centre. You weren't tied to him,' Ian pointed out.

'No, but he would have followed me again. He had a thing about me. He just wouldn't leave me alone.'

'He left you alone all summer,' Geraldine muttered.

'I had to get rid of him,' Tommy insisted. 'He would have followed me again, I know he would.'

'Why?' Ian asked.

'I don't know. He just did. He's been following me around for years. I'd just had enough. So I topped him.'

'Really? You killed him? Just like that?' Geraldine shook her head as though to indicate she did not believe him.

Tommy shrugged. 'He was easy enough to get rid of. He was half dead already.'

'But why would you care if he followed you?' Ian asked. 'You've just told us yourself that you were friends.'

'That's what I thought, but he wouldn't leave me alone. At first I didn't want you to know,' Tommy explained, leaning forward and gazing earnestly across the table. 'I thought I could get away with it. But it all got too much for me. The pressure. I couldn't keep it to myself. I had to confess and take my punishment. You'd have caught up with me in the end. I just couldn't bear the waiting. For all I knew, someone had seen me do it and had already spilled the beans. I felt as though I was sitting on a ticking time bomb. I just cracked.'

'Very well, I'm arresting you for the murder of Bingo,' Ian said. 'You do not have to say anything but anything you do say may be taken down and used in evidence –'

'I just told you, I killed him. What more do you need?'

Geraldine turned to Ian as soon as the suspect had been led from the room. They heard him out in the corridor, grumbling that he could not walk any faster as he was taken to a cell.

'Do you believe him?' she asked.

'Why would he lie about it and get himself locked up?'

She shrugged. 'Attention, maybe, or to get his leg tended to.'

'That would be a bit drastic, wouldn't it?'

'Innocent people have made false confessions for more spurious reasons,' Geraldine said.

'Or even no reason at all except they were barmy,' Ian agreed.

'So have we just arrested a man for taking drastic measures to get medical attention for his hip or sciatica, or whatever it is that's troubling him?' Geraldine asked.

Ian looked troubled.

Researching establishments where Tommy had been sleeping, Geraldine was able to confirm that he had stayed at the Fishergate Centre for a few months. Some time after he left there he had moved into the other resettlement centre in York. When Geraldine asked a staff member at the Fishergate Centre why Tommy had moved, the woman replied that the homeless often moved around.

'We're only a temporary measure,' she added, 'and not everyone is willing to avail themselves of our services. Don't ask me why, when we do everything we can to support them. It's not like they have anywhere else to go. Oh, I know it's not exactly a home here, but we offer them a bed for the night and food, and washing facilities, no questions asked, well, very few, and we keep them safe. You'd think it was vastly preferable to sleeping rough, but mostly they don't stay long. Tommy moved out and later he was referred to the New Start Centre. That's typical. They move around. It's just what they do. It's what they want. It suits them. We do our best to make them comfortable and fed –' she was beginning to sound plaintive.

'What about a man called Bingo?' Geraldine interrupted her.

'Bingo? He was the one that was murdered in Coney Street a week ago, wasn't he? Yes, he stayed here. We were all sorry to hear what happened to him,' she added. 'He was a harmless character. He didn't deserve that.' She sighed.

'No one does.'

'No.'

'Was Bingo staying with you at the same time as Tommy?'

'He could have been.'

Geraldine waited while the woman went to check her records. When she came back on the line she confirmed that Tommy had stayed at the Fishergate Centre at the same time as Bingo.

'They shared a room,' she added.

'And did they leave you at the same time?'

'No, Tommy moved into a single room. They all prefer to have their own rooms. But Bingo left us. Why do you want to know about Tommy?'

Geraldine did not answer. So far Tommy's story seemed to check out. They had enough on him for a formal charge to stick, and the investigation was considered resolved. It had taken them only a week to find Bingo's killer. As a detective sergeant, Geraldine was reluctant to challenge the opinion apparently held by everyone else in her team on the basis of her vague suspicion that Tommy's confession was all lies. Even Ian seemed willing to go along with the general consensus that Tommy was guilty.

'So you don't think he was lying to us after all?' Geraldine asked Ian as they were leaving the police station that evening.

'Let's see what the CPS makes of it,' he replied evasively. 'In the meantime, Eileen's satisfied we've got the right man.'

'And what if she's wrong?'

'Then the case will fall apart, and we will have wasted the court's time.' He sighed. 'Let's hope Eileen's called it right. She usually does.'

15

AFTER YET ANOTHER ROW with her mother, Molly went to her boyfriend's place for the night. It was not lost on her that he did not seem pleased to see her. He stood in the doorway, in his grey underpants, arms crossed, scowling at her.

'Molly? What the fuck are you doing here?'

'Well, it's nice to see you too,' she replied sourly, tossing her long blond hair off her face. 'So are we going to stand here like this all night, or are you going to let me in?'

As he hesitated, Molly heard someone calling his name.

'Who's that? Is someone else here?'

It was a stupid question. Obviously there was a girl in his room. Shoving the door wide open, Molly came face to face with a skinny slapper he must have picked up for the night.

'Who the fuck is she?' the other girl asked, scrambling into a tight dress that barely covered her arse.

'"*She*" is his girlfriend,' Molly replied coldly. 'So why don't you get lost?'

'Don't you tell me what to do, bitch. You get lost. Who do you think you are?'

'More to the point, who the hell are you and what do you think you're doing here?'

The girl in the tight dress sniggered. 'Isn't that obvious, you stupid cow?'

'Get the fuck out of here before I throw you out!' Molly yelled, her voice shrill with anger.

She turned to her red-faced boyfriend, only to discover that what she had mistaken for embarrassment was actually fury. He had never hit her before, so she did not see it coming, but her face stung and her ear rang with the impact of his slap. If he had punched her he would probably have knocked her off her feet, if not laid her out cold. She had no intention of hanging around to listen to his stammered apology. Her mother might be prepared to put up with behaviour like that, but Molly had made up her mind a long time ago that she was never going to be knocked about by anyone, whoever they were. It was bullshit to pretend that kind of aggression was any kind of love.

For years she had watched her mother suffer bruising and worse. Only once had she bothered to ask her mother why she put up with violence from men. It had been like talking to a blank wall.

'Why do you let him get away with it?'

'What are you talking about?'

'The way Baz treats you. Why do you put up with it?'

'I've no idea what you mean. And I don't like the way you're talking about Baz. Show some respect.'

'He's a monster. I would never let anyone treat me the way he treats you.'

Her mother had given her a withering look. 'You don't understand.'

'You're dead right I don't understand. That's why I'm asking: why do you put up with the way he treats you?'

'Baz is good to me.'

'How can you possibly say he's good to you? You can lie about it to other people but I live here. I've seen what he does to you.'

'Oh shut up. You're too young to know what you're talking about.'

Her mother had refused to discuss the matter any more, and that had been the end of Molly's efforts to persuade her to stand up for herself. And now she had been hit by her own boyfriend, who had once told her that he loved her.

'Wait,' he cried out, seizing hold of her arm as she turned to leave. 'Don't go. Not like this.'

Molly turned away, shaking and resolute.

'I can explain,' he said.

'Get your hands off me,' she hissed.

'Ooh, listen to her,' the other girl jeered. 'Thinks she's too good for you.'

The girl paused as she was pulling on her heels, sensing that she might be staying the night after all. Molly did not wait to hear any more. Slamming the door behind her, she was off.

'And don't bother coming after me!' she yelled over her shoulder as she marched away.

She need not have bothered. The front door remained shut.

Her mother's reaction on hearing the news the following morning was equally disappointing.

'What do you mean you've split up with him?' she asked, her eyes dark slits of suspicion.

'He threw you out, did he?' Baz asked, with a nasty laugh. 'Well, that's hardly a surprise. Who in his right mind would want to shag *you*?'

'We split up, like I said,' Molly replied, ignoring the interruption. 'And before you ask, *I* left *him*.'

'But where are you going to live?' her mother asked, with an anxious glance at Baz who was shovelling greasy fried eggs into his mouth.

A cold feeling crept down Molly's back. 'Here,' she said. 'This is where I live.'

'But – you – you can't stay here,' her mother stammered.

'What do you mean? This is my home.'

'No, you can't stay here,' her mother repeated.

'We need your room,' Baz explained, wiping his mouth on the back of his hand. 'So you can bugger off back to that boyfriend of yours and beg him to take you back because you can't stay here.'

'What do you mean?'

'Just what I said. We need the room.'

'What for? It's my room! Mum?'

'I'm sorry,' her mother bleated, with a quick glance at her boyfriend. She sounded anything but apologetic. 'Baz pays the bills, and he wants the room.'

Baz smiled.

'So you keep saying, but –'

'It's for my boy. He's coming home.'

'You mean they've let him out? That's a shame. They should have thrown away the key when they locked him up.'

'Well, we won't have to listen to your stupid bitch of a daughter any more,' Baz snapped at her mother. He turned back to Molly. 'There's no room for you here, not now my boy's coming home.' He smiled again, too pleased to remain angry for long.

Reluctant to give Baz the satisfaction of feeling he had won the row, Molly struggled to conceal her dismay. Wretchedly she wondered whether her mother had put up any sort of a fight to keep her. Knowing how feeble her mother was, Molly suspected she had caved in as soon as Baz had made his demands.

'Fine,' Molly said, moving towards the door. 'That's just fine with me.' She turned her back on Baz and spoke only to her mother. 'I wouldn't want to live with a pair of losers like you and him anyway. I hope you're very happy living with a vicious sadist and an ex-con, mum. Just think, your precious boyfriend's going to have an accomplice now. They can both beat you up.'

'Baz pays the bills,' her mother repeated lamely.

Baz stood up and his burly figure towered over her.

Fear lent Molly the courage to stand her ground. 'Don't you dare raise your hand against me!' In spite of her attempt to remain calm, she was vexed to hear herself squealing in alarm. 'You can terrorise my mother, but you don't scare me.'

'Get your things and go,' Baz replied, sitting down abruptly, as though she was not worth the effort of an argument. 'Just fuck off out of my house.'

'Don't worry, I'm going. I wouldn't stay here if it was the last place on earth.' Reaching the door, she added under her breath, 'And it's not your house.' It might as well have been.

Racing upstairs to her room, she threw some things into her rucksack: a T-shirt, underwear, and some toiletries. She gazed helplessly around, wondering what else to take, but she did not want to hang around and let them see how upset she was. Despite strenuous efforts to control her emotions, she had to wipe tears from her eyes more than once. Grabbing her jacket, she ran downstairs and fled from the house without stopping to say goodbye. What was the point? They were throwing her out. No one else cared what was happening to her, so why should she? In any case, she did not want them to see she was upset. They did not care about her. She had to show them the feeling was mutual. In a way, it was.

She had never done anything wrong, yet her own mother had chosen a violent criminal over her. She did not need evil people like her mother and Baz in her life. She was better off without them. They could do what they liked. Nothing they did meant anything to her. She did not even want to live there any more. Out in the street, she realised that she had no idea where to go. Her few friends had all dropped her when she had taken up with her boyfriend, and she had no idea where her father was living so could not turn to him, even if she had wanted to. There was no one in the world who cared about her now that her mother had rejected her.

It began to rain as she hurried along the street, letting her tears flow unchecked. She did not bother to wipe her eyes. The rain fell more heavily so she took shelter at the bus stop while she considered her next move. She could not stay in the village and let the local people witness her humiliation. Some of them knew her, even if none of them were her friends. Standing at the bus stop she decided to catch a bus, any bus, and go somewhere else. The first bus that turned up was going to York. It was as good a place as any. Alone in the world, and homeless, it made no difference to her where she went, and besides, there would be jobs in the city, and accommodation. She could start again there. Fate had decided her destination for her. Her mother would never know what had happened to her only child. Molly smiled. She hoped the old bitch would be sorry.

Sitting back in her seat, she watched green fields speeding past the window. She was on her way to a new life.

16

LYING ON DUSTY FLOORBOARDS, trussed up in a stinking pool of his own piss, Mark had no idea where he was, or why he had been brought there. His head was thumping, and his memories were muddled and disjointed. He wondered whether he had been drugged, or had fallen sick. Perhaps he had suffered a mental breakdown. Whatever the reason for his plight, something was very wrong. He had a confused recollection of a man locked in a cell for many years counting off the days with scratch marks on a wall. It could have been a character in a book. He could not remember the circumstances in which the makeshift calendar was devised. At times he thought he was that character, marking off the days with black marks, only his hands were tied together so that could not be him. He wondered why he had been targeted for this torment.

His eyes flickered around the room, trying to make sense of the pitted floorboards and rough-textured white walls. After a while he realised the streaks of grime on the walls must have some significance. If he could only work out what those marks meant, he might break out of his prison. With flashes of lucidity, he knew the marks were just random dirt on the walls. It was pointless trying to make sense of his incarceration. Then the conviction returned and he began studying the marks closely, searching for a meaning. But as he stared at them, the marks moved around and he realised they were only there to lead him further from the truth. As his confusion cleared, he remembered that all of this had something to do with a woman he had been seeing. He could not remember who she was, or what she had looked like. In any case, however beautiful she was, no woman was worth this acute physical suffering.

He allowed his mind to wander in an effort to stop thinking about his situation, but every time he began to drift off, physical pain recalled him to his plight. His shoulders were not designed to remain immobile for long and had both frozen, sending daggers of pain along his neck and back as soon as he stirred. Even when he kept perfectly still they ached horribly. His head continued to pound like a ticking bomb. He imagined his skull exploding, splinters of bone and brain matter spraying around the dimly lit room. His back felt as though it had been brutally pummelled, and his left side was sore from lying on the bare floorboards. Trying to control the distress caused by his physical pain took up most of his conscious attention, but he decided that was preferable to thinking about his imprisonment.

There seemed little doubt that the man who had brought him here had no intention of releasing him alive. Apart from anything else, his captor had made no attempt to conceal his face from Mark. He was crying with pain and self-pity when the door opened and footsteps approached. He heard low breathing as his gag was removed, and then a voice shattered the silence that seemed to have lasted throughout all eternity.

'He's still alive then.'

'Help me,' Mark rasped, his throat as dry as desert grass. 'Water. Please.'

Laughter rang around his head, but it was not his own. Someone else was laughing. The sound spun around in his mind like a whirlpool. From a long time ago, he remembered what it was to laugh. He tried to join in but all he could manage was a low bleating sound. His lips felt swollen from the pressure of the gag and his tongue was so raw he could scarcely move it.

For all his terror of his captor, he was grateful not to be alone.

'Stay with me,' he croaked. 'Water.'

'He wants us to stay here. He wants us to give him water,' the man echoed the words in his curious singsong voice. 'But he knows we can't do that.'

'Water,' he pleaded, desperate to cling on to the shred of life slipping from his grasp. 'I don't want to die.'

'Oh, he doesn't want to die. Well, that's all right, because he's not going to die. Not yet. That would be too easy, wouldn't it? We're not going to let him off so lightly. He has to suffer a while longer before we let him go.'

'Why?' Mark asked. 'Why are you doing this to me?'

The other man's face creased into a grin but his eyes were implacable. 'He knows why we're doing this. He knows all about it. He knows he's been brought here to suffer the most terrible pain imaginable, just like he made us suffer.' His features twisted with loathing. 'He's not going to die yet. That would be letting him off too lightly.'

'No, no, you can't do this,' Mark begged.

'That's enough,' the man said as he replaced the filthy gag.

And Mark knew this must be the end. Shuddering, he closed his eyes. 'I don't want to die. I don't want to die.'

All around him was silence. The words existed only in his mind. No one would ever hear his voice again. Somewhere beyond his reach he was dimly aware of movement. The man had grasped him under his arms and was dragging him across the floor, towards the door and freedom.

'Where are we going?' he asked, in his mind. 'Are you taking me home?'

With a tremor he realised that he did not know where his home was. Did he even have a home? A brilliant light shone on his face but he did not blink. His eyes remained closed.

'Where are we going?' he asked again, in a silent cry. 'Where are you taking me?'

Something was fiddling at his neck. He thought his gag was

being removed but he could still feel it between his teeth. And then he began to choke.

'Help me!' He tried to cry out but he could not utter a sound.

Terror swept through his chest, clutching at his lungs until he could not breathe. Blood spurted behind his closed eyelids and a roar reverberated in his ears. Then the pumping blood grew still and the roaring in his ears fell silent as the light drifted away from him and hovered on the edge of his consciousness, forever out of reach.

17

'WELL DONE,' EILEEN SAID to the team who had gathered for a final debriefing meeting. 'With Tommy's confession, we've as good as wrapped this one up. We just need to press him for some more details, and we're finished. So let's get this done and dusted as soon as we can.' She grinned. 'After our last case, it's reassuring to know we can still track down a killer this quickly. Brilliant work, everyone.'

With the case resolved to the satisfaction of the detective chief inspector and her superiors, there was nothing left to do apart from finalise the paperwork. For once that was straightforward because Tommy was co-operating fully. There was not even any real need to take statements from all the people sleeping and working at the Fishergate Centre and York New Start Centre, because Tommy's confession was so lucid. He had explained his motive for killing Bingo, which was about as logical as might be expected from any murderer, because of course although his motive made sense, it was nonetheless insane. Put simply, his annoyance with Bingo had grown into a rage that had led to the fatal attack on his victim.

'I still don't understand why you killed him,' Geraldine said, reiterating the point she and Ian had made several times during the course of their interviews with Tommy. 'He'd already left the centre. Why did you go after him like that? You must have known you were risking your own liberty. You'll go down on a murder charge.'

Tommy shrugged, seemingly careless of his predicament.

'I told you, he was doing my head in,' he replied.

'But he'd left the centre,' Ian repeated.

'He would have been back as soon as the weather turned,' Tommy told them. 'I knew he'd be back. Once I decided to kill him, I couldn't wait for him to come back to the centre, could I? Not if I was going to be in with a chance of getting away with it. Surely you can understand that?'

Geraldine thought there was something odd about his eagerness to persuade them of his guilt, but her colleagues seemed happy to accept his confession. She wondered if there was something wrong with her, she was so out of step with the rest of the team. Not only was Tommy adamant that he was responsible for Bingo's death, but he had been able to describe the nature of the attack quite accurately. Admittedly, all the information he gave them was readily available in the public domain. In an ideal world, the means by which Bingo had been killed would have been kept under wraps. In reality, it was almost impossible to keep anything from the media. With the advent of the internet, information spread faster than wildfire in the outback. The media had not yet learned that a red tie had probably been used to strangle the victim. That was the only detail Tommy had been unable to supply, along with the whereabouts of the noose.

'I chucked it,' he said simply.

'Chucked it?'

He nodded. 'In one of the bins in town.'

The street bins had all been emptied since the night of Bingo's murder. Even if they searched every bin in the town, they would have very little chance of finding the tie Tommy claimed to have used to kill Bingo. It would have been shredded along with tons more litter. The bins were not going to be subjected to scrupulous forensic examination, looking for any minute traces of the tie too small to be seen by the naked eye, because Tommy had confessed. Even without forensic evidence to back up his statement he would be convicted. In any case, he claimed not to remember the exact location where he had disposed of the noose, so finding any such evidence would be almost impossible.

Geraldine reread the interview notes for the twentieth time, searching for any clue that Tommy was lying.

'I crept up on him while he was asleep,' Tommy had told them. 'I put the noose round his neck and twisted the ends together until he stopped moving. It didn't take very long.'

'Where did you get the noose from?'

Tommy barely hesitated. 'It was already round his neck. He was wearing it.'

'Can you describe it?'

He shrugged. 'I didn't look at it closely. It was some scrap of material, something like that.'

'And where it is now?'

'I don't know. I don't remember. I threw it away.'

It was hopeless. She might as well give up and accept that they had found Bingo's killer, unlikely as it seemed.

Geraldine's latest visit to her sister in Kent had been postponed, due to the investigation. Now there was nothing to prevent her from seeing her family so she called Celia and arranged to go and see her the following day. Saturday dawned bright and crisp and Geraldine set out early intending to spend a whole day with her sister, but her journey was slow and she did not arrive until late morning.

'Sorry,' she said, when Celia opened the door, 'the traffic was horrendous.'

'Come on in, you're here now, and we've got time for a cup of tea and a natter before lunch. Oh, there he goes,' she added as they went into the kitchen where the baby had just begun to wail. 'He was fast asleep a moment ago.'

'I hope the doorbell didn't disturb him.'

Celia laughed. 'No, don't worry. Once he's asleep nothing wakes him up until he wants a feed. Here, do you want to hold him while I get his mush ready?'

'Mush?' Geraldine queried, watching her sister contentedly bustling around. 'That sounds appetising.'

Celia laughed. 'It's what Chloe calls it. Milk and mush is what we feed the baby. Here,' she added, thrusting a pot and a little plastic spoon at Geraldine, 'you can feed him if you like.'

Geraldine laughed nervously. 'I'm not used to feeding babies.'

'I thought it would be part of your training?'

Geraldine did not reply that she was used to dealing with those whose lives had recently ended, not with those whose lives were just beginning. The baby was protesting loudly now, his tiny face puckered and resembling a gigantic pink raisin. Celia worked quickly and within minutes Geraldine was carefully spooning food into the gaping little mouth. The baby stopped crying immediately and sucked eagerly at the plastic spoon loaded with a dollop of beige purée.

'What on earth is he eating?' Geraldine asked. 'Is it porridge?'

'It's chicken and potato,' Celia replied and they both laughed.

As soon as Geraldine stopped feeding him, the baby began to yell.

'It's all right, little man,' Geraldine reassured him. 'There's plenty more. He's like a baby bird, isn't he?'

'If you say so.'

Absorbed in inserting food into the gap between her nephew's tiny gums, Geraldine forgot about everything else and for a few moments her life ceased to exist. All that mattered was feeding the little boy in her arms.

'He's so tiny, isn't he?' she murmured.

'He's doubled his birth weight,' Celia replied, a trifle sharply.

'Oh, I didn't mean he's not growing exactly as he should. He looks really healthy and he's certainly got a good appetite. But he's still so small, isn't he? Look at his tiny little fingers! He's beautiful, Celia.'

'I know,' her sister agreed, appeased and complacent. 'He's

adorable.' Celia let out a little sigh. 'I wish he could stay like this forever.'

'No, you don't.'

'They're so sweet when they're babies.'

'I bet you can't wait until he starts talking.'

Celia laughed. 'He's only six months old.'

'I know. It's so strange to think he'll be walking around and talking in a few years. Oops,' she added. 'I think he just did something in his nappy.'

As her sister took the baby from Geraldine, she felt an unexpected sensation of loss as the small bundle was lifted out of her arms.

18

MOLLY HAD NEVER BEEN to York before, although she had been to London, so going to a big city was not exactly a new experience for her. But she had never been homeless before, and she was not quite sure where to go or what to do. Once she had found a toilet in a pub, her most pressing needs were food and shelter and, most importantly, staying safe. She was not sure whether to be pleased or worried to discover she was by no means the only homeless person in the city. She passed several rough sleepers as she walked around, and saw that most of them had sleeping bags and blankets, as well as backpacks. She was thankful she had brought her padded jacket but that was not enough protection and on her first night, although the weather had been dry, the cold had forced her to keep moving. She stayed in the side streets, scared of the noisy drunks and raucous women out on hen nights who travelled in packs and were too drunk to reason with. As a girl on her own, it was definitely best to avoid them, and she kept away from other people as far as possible, aware that a solitary man could pose just as much of a threat as a gang of revellers.

Crossing a quiet square she spotted a bench but before she could sit down, a group of men fell out of a pub across the way, singing and shouting. In a panic, she slipped into a narrow alleyway, out of sight. Just then it began to rain and she clambered into a recess with a raised step where she could shelter, hidden from view. She was too cold to sleep, but if she could only get hold of a sleeping bag this might be a place where she could spend the night, at least until she sorted herself out with a job and a proper place to live. Drawing her knees up to her chest and wrapping her arms around them, she pulled her jacket around her and allowed herself to relax for the first time since she had left home. Her situation was as dire as before, but at least she was safe for the night, alone at last and hidden away in an alcove in a deserted alleyway.

And then, in the darkness of the alleyway, she heard someone cough.

Instantly alert, she froze, straining to listen for any other sound of life. Someone must be walking along the passageway, but however attentively she listened, she could not hear footsteps. She held her breath, afraid to stir. There could be a drunk in the alleyway who might attack her. Whoever it was, she had no way of escaping, enclosed as she was on three sides by brick walls. Her ledge had become a trap. Minutes passed like hours, stretching the silence. Whoever had coughed near her hideout must have gone. After a while, Molly began to relax.

And then she heard it again: a faint cough.

It came from the same direction as before, along the alley towards Back Swinegate. Whoever was coughing there was not moving, which suggested they were injured or else hiding, like her. Either way, knowing that made their presence seem less intimidating. Holding her breath, she shifted forwards, inching towards the edge of the alcove where she was hiding. Peering out, she saw only the empty passageway but on the wall opposite, a few feet further along, just on the bend, she saw the outline of a second recess. Another rough sleeper had taken refuge in the alleyway. She hoped he – or she – would not object to sharing the quiet passageway at night. Faintly uneasy, she pulled herself to the back of her alcove, out of sight, and waited for the morning. In spite of her circumstances, she was so tired that she nodded off a few times. There was little point in listening out for anyone approaching. If someone did come along, she could only try to keep perfectly still and hope they went away without discovering her cowering there, out of sight.

Once the sun came up, everything seemed very different. Pulling herself forward she slipped down off her ledge. Instead of returning to St Sampson's Square, she continued in the other direction, walking towards Back Swinegate. It was time to face the other occupant of Nether Hornpot Lane. When she reached the alcove in the opposite wall, she saw an old man pulling himself into a sitting position. Oblivious to her approach, he was clearly startled to see her. An expression of fear flickered across his wizened face. Encouraged, she stepped forward and he held out a hand.

'I haven't got any money, more's the pity,' she told him.

'Who are you?' the old man asked in a quavering voice. 'What do you want? Go away, go away.'

'It's OK,' she replied. 'I'm not going to hurt you. I'm the same as you. We're neighbours.'

The old man frowned, and shook his head.

'I slept in the alcove over there last night,' she explained. 'My name's Molly.'

'Go away, go away,' he repeated, scowling at her.

She did not mind. If he wanted to be left alone that suited her. As long as he did not bother her they could coexist quite peacefully in Nether Hornpot Lane, at least until the really cold weather set in. When that happened, with any luck the old man would know where they could go to find shelter. At his age, he could not be intending to sleep rough through the winter.

Making a mental note of the place where she had spent the night, Molly set off to hunt for a sleeping bag. Several shops sold them, but she did not have enough money to buy one, so she settled for a thick navy blanket that she found in a charity shop. It was not ideal, but it was better than nothing and she was cautiously pleased with her purchase. Not only would the blanket keep her warm, but it was dark enough to conceal her at night. Having spent the last of her money on food and water, she climbed into her alcove and settled down for the night. The next day she would pluck up her courage and talk to some of the rough sleepers she had seen as she walked around, and learn where they found their food. She had seen some of them begging on the street, but that was not for her. She was going to find a job. In the meantime, while she was looking for work, she still had to eat.

19

THE SECOND OCCASION WAS not as exciting as the first. For a start he had done this before, so this time there was no sickening fear that he would be unable to see it through. It was amazing how differently he felt about everything, once he knew he was capable of killing. It was like stepping through a door into a new world of possibilities where he could do whatever he wanted, and no one could stand in his way ever again. Acknowledging his new identity as a killer, it was hard to believe how rapidly the shift had occurred from planner to perpetrator. Whatever happened from now on, that change could never be reversed.

Apart from his newfound confidence in his own abilities, the task was also less daunting because his next victim was old. The risk of him fighting back was negligible. Even so, despite the frailty of his quarry, he took nothing for granted. It was important to keep his wits about him. The old man might yet surprise him but even if he turned out to be as feeble as he looked, someone else might appear at just the wrong moment, when the noose was already in place and tightening around the scraggy neck. It would be impossible to pass that off as a prank. If he was caught in the act of killing and could not eliminate the witness, he would have no option but to leg it. For months he had been running along the river bank every morning, training for just such an eventuality. But after selecting his next victim so carefully, he thought he would be unlucky to get caught.

He followed the old man through lightly falling rain, keeping a reasonable distance behind him. From Spurriergate they went along Feasegate and diagonally across St Sampson's Square. It was growing dark. The streets were more or less empty of people scurrying home along wet pavements, and only a few cars went by, their drivers staring straight ahead through falling rain and swishing windscreen wipers. No one paid any attention to a decrepit old tramp, or to a figure in a hooded jacket walking not far behind him. Just before Finkle Street the old man vanished into Nether Hornpot Lane, a curved snickelway running north from St Sampson's Square to Back Swinegate.

Slipping into the narrow lane, the old man stopped by a covered alcove where he had been sleeping for the past few weeks. Having lowered himself gingerly down on to the wide step, he glanced around. He did not notice a figure pressed against the brick wall just out of sight around a bend in the lane. Unaware an attack on his life was imminent, the old man leaned back against the locked door behind him and lifted his legs on to the step, using his hands to assist him in raising them, one at a time, and letting out a breathy 'ouf' sound with each movement. Once in the shelter of the recess, he set about making himself comfortable, removing his battered boots before wrapping his threadbare sleeping bag around him and wriggling inside it until he was satisfied.

Meanwhile the watcher waited, pressing himself against the wall, as the old man settled himself for the night. It was a quiet place, protected from the wind and all but a hard driving rain, and secluded from prying eyes so the old man could get up and piss against the wall during the night. There was no artificial lighting along the lane, which was bordered by brick walls on both sides, and it was illuminated only by the moon overhead. In the absence of any street lamps, under an overcast sky the lane was dark.

The square had been deserted as he crossed it on his way to the lane, but he was not going to take any chances. The element of surprise was vital to his success. If his victim yelled loudly enough, the outcry might attract the attention of people passing by at either end of the passageway, along Back Swinegate or out in St Sampson's Square. Although the pub was closed, and it was too late for many people to be wandering around, revellers were sometimes out on the streets of York until the small hours. Even in the rain there was no guarantee that the streets around the alleyway would remain empty for long.

As soon as the old man's eyes closed, without making a sound the hidden figure darted forward from the shadows to crouch beside him and slip a red noose around his scraggy neck. If the old man had seen it coming maybe he would have put up a show of resistance. In his younger days perhaps he would even have proved a worthy opponent. But now he could barely shuffle along the street unaided, let alone put up a fight. If he had not been intending to end his life, the strangler might have felt sorry for the old man. He was a pathetic apology for a human being.

'What –? What –?' was all the frail victim managed to grunt as the noose tightened around his neck.

As if the attack was a cue, just at that instant the moon emerged from behind a cloud, lighting up the scene. Staring into the old man's watery eyes, he tugged the noose tighter. Even his victim's dying gurgles were feeble, and he only managed to scrabble at the noose with his gnarled fingers for a few seconds before his arms flopped down at his sides, his head rolled forwards and he lay still. It was over very quickly.

The killer could not afford to linger there for long. The lane appeared deserted but someone else might come along at any moment. Meanwhile, the light, bright blue sheen of the sky was turning navy, making it easy for him to move around the streets unobserved. Sliding the noose from around his victim's bruised neck, he slipped it in his pocket and straightened up. There was no need to panic. The body was unlikely to be discovered until the next day and even then no one would pay much attention to the scruffy corpse. He stood perfectly still for an instant, gazing down at the results of his handiwork: a shapeless mass, black in the darkness. With a scowl, he turned and strode away, towards Back Swinegate. The job was complete and, thanks to his planning, everything had gone smoothly, as he had known it would. A man's life had just been snuffed out, and no one even knew about it.

20

WRAPPING HERSELF IN HER blanket, Molly wriggled around trying to get comfortable. Luckily, she had managed to find her way back to Nether Hornpot Lane before the rain had started. With her knees pulled right up to her chest, and the edge of her covering tucked underneath her buttocks, she was able to keep her blanket dry. She was actually quite snug beneath it. The blanket had a musty smell, but she was only using it as a temporary measure until she managed to find a job and somewhere to live. Her immediate problem was going to be finding food. What little money she had brought with her had all gone. Somehow she had to find a job where no one asked questions about who she was or where she was living. She had a few ideas, but there was nothing she could do until the morning so she tried to focus on getting some rest.

Suddenly she sat up. For a second she had no idea what had disturbed her, but her heart was pounding and her skin was prickling as though she had received an electric shock. Assuming she had been woken by a nightmare, she tucked her blanket under her out of the rain before lying down and closing her eyes again. All at once she heard a strange noise. She could not work out exactly what it was. It sounded as though an animal was choking nearby, a dog, or a rodent. It occurred to her that her elderly neighbour might be ill. He had hardly looked healthy when she had seen him close up. Perhaps he was having a heart attack. Whatever was wrong with him, he sounded in need of assistance.

Dithering about whether she ought to go and see if he was all right, she sat up cautiously and considered her options. She would not know what to do if the old man was ill, and her phone had run out of charge so she could not even summon help. She could try and find someone who *was* able to call an ambulance, but on balance she decided it was probably better not to get involved. The old man was not her responsibility. They had not even met, not properly, and when she had tried to approach him, he had told her to go away. He might not appreciate her interference.

But she could not stifle her curiosity. Cautiously, she inched her way to the edge of her ledge and peeked out. In a shaft of moonlight she spotted a hooded figure crouching on the ground beside the recess on the opposite side of the alleyway. His arms were waving, twisting something, while in front of him the gurgling sound grew fainter. She waited, scarcely daring to breathe, and at last the noise stopped. The figure straightened up and glanced around, shoving something in his pocket as he did so. Unnerved by his furtive manner, she pressed herself against the wall of her recess out of his line of vision. In the pale moonlight she had been able to see enough to know that he was not a rough sleeper. His shoes were shiny, and his jeans looked new. Beneath his hood, she had caught a brief glimpse of a clean-shaven face as he looked around.

If he had happened to glance over at her alcove, he might have spotted her shrouded in darkness while she peered out along the passage, but he did not look in her direction. Moving only her eyes, she looked out again and saw that the hooded stranger was striding away towards Back Swinegate. Shaken and confused, she gulped in a lungful of air before bursting into tears. She was used to living in fear but at least she had known where Baz was most of the time, and had been able to avoid the worst of his tempers. This stranger striking in darkness was an anonymous threat, and far more menacing.

She did not sleep again that night, but sat watching for the hooded man to return. He did not reappear, and no one else disturbed the quiet of the alleyway. As soon as the sun rose, she rolled up her blanket and forced it under the flap of her backpack so she could carry it with her. Some of the rough sleepers left their sleeping bags on their steps, but she was not confident her blanket would be safe from thieves. She had no money to buy another one, and the weather would soon turn cold. Besides, after what she had seen, she had no intention of returning to Nether Hornpot Lane. Scurrying along the passageway, away from St Sampson's Square, she glanced into the alcove on the opposite wall and felt her jaw tighten as her fears were confirmed.

The old man lay very still, his tongue sticking out between his lips and his pale eyes gazing blankly up at her. She stared at him in terror. Specks of blood dotted the whites of his eyes that seemed to bulge from their sockets as though he was searching for a breath of life. She wanted to run away, but she could not tear her gaze from the disgusting face lying motionless at her feet. With a trembling finger she reached down to the old man as though to make sure he was really dead. Just in time, she jerked her arm back to avoid touching the body and leaving a trace of her own DNA. She had seen a dead body once before, but that had been a very different occasion. Her grandmother had looked composed, neatly dressed in a long white gown, with her hair brushed back off her white face and her hands neatly folded over her chest. After an orderly passing, an air of serenity had hung over her coffin. The death of the old man had been a violent disruption of natural order, more shocking than the fact of death itself.

Baz hit her mother whenever he lost his temper, which happened with sickening regularity. He had only once hit her in the face. As a rule he was careful to punch her where the bruises would be concealed by her clothes. But Molly had known exactly what was going on. It would be impossible to live under the same roof as Baz and her mother, and remain oblivious to their frequent yelling and whimpering, or fail to witness the repeated physical assaults. By contrast, the attack on the old man in Nether Hornpot Lane had been unexpected and silent. Molly had heard no raised voices, and had witnessed no sudden rage resulting in loss of control. The stranger had simply and deliberately assaulted a rough sleeper, seemingly without any provocation. And while Baz had tormented her mother for what had felt like a long time, leaving her bruised and battered, the attack on the old man had been swift and deadly.

Realising the implications of what she had seen, Molly began to shake. The horror extended beyond the death of one old man. The victim might have been chosen simply because he was homeless and vulnerable, like Molly. Grabbing her bundle, she fled from Nether Hornpot Lane, resolving never to return. As she ran, she felt a surge of hatred for Baz. She and her mother had managed fine until he had come along to ruin their lives. Now, nowhere was safe. Sprinting out of the lane, she slowed down, her breath coming in painful gasps. Her mind was spinning, making it difficult to think clearly. Whatever happened, she could not report what she had seen to the police and risk them sending her home. It began to rain again and she took refuge in a doorway, shivering and crying. She was alone in the world and did not know what to do.

21

JASPER WAS ALREADY IN trouble with his boss for having turned up half an hour after the restaurant opened on Saturday morning.

'Consider this a warning,' the boss had fumed. 'You pull a stunt like that again, and you'll be looking for another job. Now get to work, and you can make up the time at the end of your shift or you can walk out of here right now and don't bother coming back.'

Jasper was pretty sure he could not be fired without due warning, and without the correct legal procedures being followed, but he was rattled all the same. He could not afford to upset the boss again, not so soon after a reprimand like that. As a result, he was up and out early the following morning, determined to set up before the boss arrived. Scurrying around the kitchen, he emptied the dishwasher and set out the menus. He even swept the floor again, although it was not necessary. The bins stood just outside the back door which opened into Nether Hornpot Lane. Emptying the rubbish, he almost stumbled over a figure lying on the step. The mound of fabric bore so little obvious relation to the shape of a human being that Jasper did not register straight away that a person was lying there, blocking his path. Just in time he stopped himself from tripping over.

'Hey!' he yelled, more in surprise than annoyance that anyone would be stupid enough to fall sleep on the step like that. 'I nearly tripped over you, stupid git.'

He spat on the ground in disgust. There were too many

homeless tramps sleeping on the streets, cluttering the place up and making it look lousy for tourists who made up the bulk of the restaurant's customers. Shifting sideways, he stepped over the sleeper and shouted, but the man gave no sign that he had heard.

'Hey! Get up. Move out of the way, will you?'

The man did not stir. Clearly he had drunk himself unconscious. It was beginning to drizzle and Jasper shivered, wondering what to do. He bent down, yelled right by the man's ear, then grabbed him by the shoulder and shook him. Still the man did not respond. Jasper tried to shift him and froze with one foot on either side of him as he caught a glimpse of the man's face. The skin looked mottled and faintly blue on one side, although that could have been shadow, and the eyes were wide open, staring up at the sky. Only then did Jasper understand what he was dealing with. It occurred to him that he ought to call the police, but that would mean he would be questioned and the restaurant might be closed. The boss would be furious. He could just imagine what the boss would say if he brought this trouble to the business which was already struggling to survive.

'Sorry, boss, I found a dead body out the back and had to close the restaurant while I waited around for the police to come and investigate.'

Some rough sleeper dropping dead in Nether Hornpot Lane was not his problem, unless he chose to become involved. He did not. Apart from his concerns over his job, the police were hardly his favourite people. Only a year ago he had been cautioned for brawling and had narrowly escaped being prosecuted for common assault. He had no wish to be involved with them again in any way. What he had chanced to find in the lane had nothing to do with him, and it was not his problem. The stiff was hardly hidden away. Someone else would be along the lane soon enough, and they could deal with this hobo who had probably drunk himself to death. Jasper was not about to risk losing his job over it. Clambering around the body, he hurried to the bins and was back inside with the back door shut before the boss arrived. They were busy at work that day, and Jasper soon forgot about the man on the step outside who had no doubt died of an overdose or alcohol poisoning.

Although he had no reason to keep away from the spot where he had stumbled on the body, Jasper avoided going out through the back exit when he left that evening. Not until the next morning did he cross the square, approaching the lane directly. He did his best to hide his agitation on seeing a white forensic tent, while the area at the entrance to Nether Hornpot Lane was cordoned off. The sight of two uniformed policemen standing guard outside a white van parked in the square, flanked by police cars, did nothing to calm his nerves. Seeing so much police activity, a horrible thought occurred to him. The man might not have been dead the previous morning. Perhaps if Jasper had summoned an ambulance straight away, the man's life might have been saved. Dismissing the disturbing notion he hurried on his way, averting his eyes from the forensic tent hiding the body from view.

His shift was nearly over when the boss summoned him. Wiping his greasy hands on a cloth, he made his way to the small front desk where the waitress, Holly, was staring warily at a uniformed policewoman.

'Jasper Parker?'

He nodded. Although he had done nothing wrong, he felt a sick feeling in the pit of his stomach. Whatever the police wanted, it could not be good news that they were interested in him.

'We'd like you to accompany us, please,' the policewoman said.

Involuntarily, Jasper took a step back, and a uniformed policeman moved to stand between him and the outer doorway. As if he was going to try and make a run for it.

'What's this about?' he asked, speaking as calmly as he could.

To give himself time to think, he made a show of wiping his hands on the cloth he was holding. The police remained irritatingly vague in their answers, merely insisting they would like him to go with them to the police station to answer a few questions.

'Do I have a choice?' he grumbled. 'Can I at least go and wash?'

'You can leave your apron here,' the boss said, holding out a hand in an impatient gesture.

It was humiliating, peeling off his greasy blue apron in front of the boss, Holly and the police officers, but he made the best of it.

'This must be a mistake,' he muttered. 'There's no reason why the police could possibly be interested in me.'

Holly was watching him, her blue eyes wide with alarm.

'Don't worry,' he told her, 'this is all a mistake. I haven't done anything.'

She lowered her gaze and stood staring at her feet, blushing faintly.

Jasper turned to the boss. 'See you later,' he said with a show of confidence. 'I'll be back as soon as I can.'

The boss's beady eyes seemed to burn with rage, and Jasper could almost hear him thinking, 'You're nothing but trouble, Jasper Parker. I should never have given you a second chance.'

That was not fair, any more than it was fair for the police to turn up and insist on dragging him off to the police station. Jasper had done nothing wrong, and he was a good worker. Admittedly, he was occasionally hungover on a Sunday morning, but that was hardly a serious offence.

Miserably he handed his apron to the boss. 'See you later,' he repeated, doing his best to sound cheerful. 'Come on, then,' he said to the police. 'I'm ready. But I'm telling you, this is all a mistake. I haven't done anything.'

Actually, he was far from ready to go with them, but he could hardly refuse their request that he accompany them to the police station.

22

THE IMPLICATIONS OF THE second murder were not lost on anyone. Two rough sleepers had been killed in less than two weeks. With a sinking feeling, Geraldine followed Ariadne into the incident room where the detective chief inspector was waiting to address them.

'This is a tragedy for the victim, and his loved ones,' Eileen said.

'If he had any,' someone muttered.

Ignoring the interruption, Eileen continued.

'It's a tragedy on a personal level, as any murder is, but we must also all be aware that this places us under additional scrutiny. People are bound to be asking how this could have happened again, so soon after the first fatality, and in almost the exact same location. This isn't the nineteenth century. We have officers on patrol, we have security cameras, SOCOs and pathology labs. The forensic tent hasn't yet been taken down from the last crime scene and already we're dealing with another one.' She was almost incoherent in her indignation. 'The morning papers are accusing us of negligence on account of the first victim being homeless and disenfranchised. We know that's a load of bunkum, but more accusations are inevitably going to follow, and we have to maintain a dignified and united message that these murders are being meticulously pursued. Our procedures will be open to appropriate scrutiny and in the meantime we must ignore all the fuss and flapping in the media and get on with the job. I know I can rely on every one of you to carry out your allotted tasks with your customary professional commitment.'

Geraldine zoned out of the pep talk, and stared at images of the second tramp which had been posted on the wall behind Eileen. He looked elderly and frail, and was unnaturally pale, even for a corpse. His cheeks were sunken, as though he had lost all his teeth, and marked with liver spots. There was something painfully pathetic in his frailty, as though he had only been clinging on to life by a tenuous breath anyway. How clumsy and pointless it seemed that someone had snuffed out that feeble existence.

'Really, what is the point of all this?' she muttered.

Eileen glared at her. 'The point is that a man has been murdered, and we need to find the killer. The point is that justice must be served regardless of the circumstances of the victim.'

'Yes, of course, I know, I know,' Geraldine replied, returning Eileen's glare. 'That's not what I meant.'

'Good.'

Geraldine was glad she had not been challenged to explain exactly what she had meant. It was too complicated, and too depressing, to try and explain that if an old man's death seemed pointless, that only served to highlight the meaninglessness of life itself. In any case, this was no time to indulge in existential angst. A suspect had been brought in for questioning.

Behind his bravado, the young man looked frightened as he faced Geraldine and Ian across the table. That was not necessarily significant. Many people were intimidated by the police, and he had been arrested before. He was in his early twenties, with light brown hair and dark eyes that blinked frequently, never quite meeting Geraldine's gaze.

'What's this all about then?' he demanded loudly, before she had said a word.

Instead of answering, Geraldine and Ian sat in silence and let him talk. People sometimes let things slip in an unguarded moment when they were given free rein to rant. Geraldine listened closely as indignation intermittently overwhelmed his attempt to sound reasonable.

'I can tell you, I don't take kindly to being dragged out of work for no reason and brought here to answer your questions without being told what's going on. If you'd like to tell me what you want with me, I'm sure we can clear up this misunderstanding without too much trouble. But you had no business coming to get me from work. I can't imagine what the hell my boss is going to think. So let's get this sorted out, shall we? I don't intend to stay here any longer than is absolutely necessary.'

For the most part Jasper's words sounded rational enough, but his expression was tense and he fidgeted constantly with the cuffs of his sweatshirt. At last, after a great deal of posturing, he fell silent.

'A man was discovered on a doorstep in Nether Hornpot Lane yesterday morning,' Geraldine said softly.

'Well?' Jasper butted in, a little too promptly. 'What's that got to do with me? You still haven't told me what I'm doing here. Am I being charged with something? Because if not, I'd like to leave right now. I'm an innocent man. I'm not obliged to sit here and listen to your crap.' He leaned forward and added plaintively, 'You know this could cost me my job.'

'Yesterday morning a man was discovered on a doorstep in Nether Hornpot Lane, behind the restaurant where you work in Back Swinegate,' Geraldine said. This time she added, 'He was dead.'

For a second, they were all silent while he digested this.

'Who was he?' Jasper asked at last. 'Was it someone I know? Is that why you brought me here?'

'We're hoping you'll be able to tell us what happened to him,' she replied.

Registering the implications of her words, Jasper straightened up almost imperceptibly in his chair and scowled.

'I don't know what makes you think I might know anything about this.'

'We have evidence that places you at the scene,' she said quietly.

'What evidence? That's bullshit. You can't prove I was there, just because I happen to walk along that stretch of pavement on my way to work every day. So what? And yes, I was accused of assault last year – a charge that didn't stick – but that was a fight in a pub and it wasn't my fault. I was the victim. And that's got nothing to do with any of this. So if you think you can frame me for –' he paused, his eyes glaring wildly at her. 'I'm not saying another word until I have a lawyer.'

'We can arrange that for you, if you like.'

'Good. Yes, I demand to have a lawyer.'

Ian nodded and Geraldine followed him out of the room.

'Do you think he's hiding something?' she asked Ian.

'He certainly looked nervous,' he replied. 'Not that that means anything.'

'No, it doesn't mean he's guilty of murder.'

Jasper was left with a uniformed constable for company while the duty brief was summoned. Eventually he arrived, a slick young lawyer with black hair and very thick eyebrows from beneath which his narrow eyes peered at Geraldine and Ian.

As soon as Geraldine began to question Jasper, the lawyer interrupted her.

'Has my client been charged?'

'No,' Geraldine replied.

'Not yet,' Ian added.

The lawyer turned to Ian, his thick eyebrows lowered in a frown. 'I must protest at this clear attempt to intimidate my client –'

'We have evidence that places him at a crime scene,' Ian said. 'We can charge your client now, or he might prefer us to hear what he has to say first.'

'A crime scene?' the lawyer repeated with a note of scepticism in his voice.

Geraldine was mesmerised by his eyebrows, one of which had risen quizzically as he challenged Ian.

'A murder,' Ian said.

Jasper half rose to his feet, and Geraldine noticed he had begun to sweat.

'No,' he spluttered. 'That's bullshit. I wasn't involved in any murder. I don't know what the hell you're on about but you can't pin this on me.' He turned to the lawyer. 'They haven't got anything on me. They're bluffing. This is bullshit. I want to go home.'

The lawyer nodded. 'My client denies any knowledge of the crime he is alleged to be implicated in.'

'We have evidence which places him at the scene,' Ian repeated calmly.

'What evidence?'

Geraldine explained that Jasper had left a sample of his DNA on the body.

'What are you talking about? I never touched him!' Jasper blurted out. 'I never touched anyone,' he corrected himself, glancing frantically at the lawyer. 'This is bullshit.'

'Left a sample of his DNA?' the lawyer queried. 'What exactly do you mean by that?'

'He appears to have spat on the body,' Geraldine explained.

Jasper shook his head, momentarily unable to speak.

'I may have spat on the pavement. I walk along there every day. But that's not a crime, is it?'

'Would you like to start telling us the whole truth?' Ian asked. 'Because when you spat on the pavement, a few drops of your saliva landed on a dead body.'

'If you lie about it, that won't help you,' Geraldine said. 'We know you were there when he died.'

'Or after he died,' the lawyer pointed out quickly. 'And my

client has already told you he did not see the body.'

Jasper stared, aghast, from Geraldine to Ian and back again, before turning to the lawyer and grabbing him by the arm.

'Get me out of here,' he muttered in a panic. 'This is bullshit. Get me out of here. I never touched the guy. I spat on the pavement, that's all. I knew someone would be along soon and I couldn't – I didn't – I couldn't be late for work. So I just left the stiff for someone else to find. But I didn't kill him, I swear I didn't. He was already dead when I saw him.'

It was concerning that another tramp had been killed so soon after Bingo's murder. They had all seen photographs of the second victim. In a ripped and filthy long coat, if anything he had looked even dirtier than Bingo. Unshaven and unkempt, there seemed little doubt that he was homeless. At this point the lawyer stood up, insisting he needed to speak to his client, and they had to take a break.

'This does raise the question of whether Jasper could have killed Bingo as well,' Geraldine said. 'Because if he killed one tramp, he might have killed both.'

'Yes. It's a bit too much of a coincidence otherwise, isn't it?' Eileen agreed.

Ian nodded at Geraldine. 'You never believed Tommy's confession, did you?'

She frowned. She had not told anyone about her scepticism over Tommy's guilt.

'What makes you think that?' she asked.

'I'm right, aren't I?'

'Well, yes, you are, but –'

'I know you, Geraldine,' Ian said with a curious smile.

Eileen merely raised her eyebrows.

'Well, at least we have the right killer this time,' the detective chief inspector said firmly. 'His lawyer can wriggle as much as he likes but it was only ever going to be a matter of time. With Jasper's DNA on the body, he can hardly deny he was there. And unless he comes up with a plausible explanation, I think we'll have our killer. We still have Tommy's confession, of course,' she added thoughtfully. 'But that might be a pack of lies.'

'Being present doesn't prove Jasper was responsible for the victim's death,' Geraldine pointed out. 'Shouldn't we wait and see what he has to say before we reach any conclusions?'

Ian nodded. 'You're right. But it seems to me we've got Jasper bang to rights, at least for this second case. The good news is, he's an idiot, spitting on the body like that, so it won't take us long to crack him.'

'I just don't think we should rush to assume he's guilty,' Geraldine muttered, speaking more to herself than anyone else.

They all knew that appearances were not necessarily reliable but having questioned Tommy's guilt, she hesitated to do the same about Jasper. She didn't want to get a reputation for challenging her superiors at every possible opportunity, even if she did think they were sometimes misguided.

'What makes you think Jasper could be innocent?' Ian asked Geraldine as they sat in the canteen over a coffee while the suspect was speaking to his lawyer.

'I don't, not necessarily,' she replied. 'But he insists he didn't kill the victim, and the evidence only proves he was there. We can't build a case on circumstantial evidence, even if he is our killer.'

'Yes, I know,' Ian replied. 'We mustn't speculate. You taught me that years ago.' He smiled at her. 'I learned most of what I know from you, Geraldine,' he added quietly.

She laughed, embarrassed by the compliment. 'No more than I've learned from you,' she replied.

Before they could continue, Ian's phone buzzed. 'The suspect is ready to continue with the interview,' he said.

Having spoken with his lawyer, Jasper seemed relatively calm and confident as he insisted he was not responsible for anyone's murder. However hard Ian pushed, Jasper remained steadfast in his account of what he had done.

'My client acknowledges he was responsible for spitting on the pavement, and he admits he was wrong in failing to report the body, but he did not murder the victim,' the lawyer summed up Jasper's position.

23

MOLLY SPENT THE MORNING wandering around York in a daze. She had left her mother's house thinking her life could not get any worse. Although she was furious with her ex for letting her down just when she needed him, she did not give a toss about him cheating on her. It was not as though they were exclusive. They had only known each other for a few weeks, and she did not even like him that much. What with his bad breath, flatulence and smelly feet, every part of him stank. If he had not been living in his own place where she could stay whenever Baz was on one of his drunken benders, she would never have carried on seeing him after their first night together.

What had happened with her mother was another matter altogether. When Molly's father had walked out on them, she and her mother had agreed they would always look out for each other.

'It's just the two of us now, Molly,' her mother used to say. 'Just you and me against the world.'

They had muddled along quite happily until Baz had forced his way into their house to undermine the life she and her mother had built together. Molly had done her best to challenge her mother about the situation.

'We got on well enough before he came along, didn't we? Why have you let him move in? It's me or him, mum. I won't live under the same roof as that brute.'

Her mother had pointed out that Baz paid their bills, as though that was the end of the discussion.

'So what? We managed just fine before he turned up. We're not dependent on him. Tell him to get lost. You can get another job. I can get a job. We don't need him.'

Her mother insisted she could not work. 'My nerves are all shot to pieces, Molly. I can scarcely leave the house any more.'

'That's because of the way he treats you. Anyone would be embarrassed to go out looking like you do sometimes, and when you do go out you have to cover up your arms. Bloody hell, no wonder you're a nervous wreck. He's destroyed your confidence. You used to have a job before he came along. You're the same person now as you were then.'

Her mother refused to listen to reason. When Molly pressed her, she became tearful.

'Baz pays the bills,' she kept bleating, like a mantra. 'Baz pays the bills. He takes care of things. I don't know how we'd manage without him. He pays the bills.'

'Mum, he knocks you about. He's vicious.'

At the mention of Baz's violence her mother would start to cry in earnest.

'Please, Molly, don't talk like that. You don't understand.'

'What don't I understand?'

'He looks after me.'

'Oh, please. How can you say that? He hits you.'

It was hopeless. Still, in spite of everything, Molly had never expected her mother to throw her out of the house, and when she thought about Baz's son taking her place at home, she struggled to control her rage at the injustice of it all. Molly had always supported her mother who had repaid her by offering Molly's room to a man who had just served a prison sentence for violent assault. Like father, like son. One day her mother would realise she had made a terrible mistake. But whatever happened from now on, Molly would never forgive her mother. She was never going home, and she would not contact her mother again. She had no mother.

'I hope you rot in hell for what you've done,' she muttered.

It was hard to shut her resentment out of her mind and concentrate on her immediate problems, although they were pressing. In her present state of exhaustion, it was difficult to focus on anything. The image of the dead man she had seen in Nether Hornpot Lane kept flashing across her mind. She might have been the last person to see him alive. Even more disturbing than that was the thought that the same fate might befall her if she continued sleeping on the street. Unpleasant as it had been living with Baz, the death of the old tramp made her fear for her life. She felt no safer now than she had been with Baz threatening to beat her if she crossed him.

It was possible the killer had been harbouring a personal grudge against that particular old man, but it was equally possible he had picked his victim simply because he was homeless and vulnerable. If that was the case, then anyone sleeping on the street might be in danger. The killer might attack her next. Terror and hunger made it difficult for her to think clearly. She had to force herself to concentrate on her plight. She was homeless, friendless, and broke. Without an address she would not be able to find a job, and if she continued living on the street, she risked being murdered in her sleep. She had to find shelter somewhere before night fell. She could not even go back to her stupid boyfriend, because she had no money for the bus fare home.

Wandering around aimlessly, she grew increasingly conscious of hunger gnawing at her insides. Seeing signs for the station, she followed them and found the Ladies Room where she was at least able to use a toilet, and have a cursory wash. It was not much, but it was better than nothing. Splashing cold water on her face made her feel slightly less forlorn, until the sight of her bloodshot eyes in the mirror reminded her of the old man she had seen in Nether Hornpot Lane. With a jolt, she recalled the hooded killer. For all she knew, he was prowling the streets, waiting until darkness fell so that he could attack his next victim. But somehow the knowledge no longer seemed so terrifying. She would soon be dead anyway. It was all Baz's fault.

She had witnessed a murder, and she was too tired and hungry to care. She knew she ought to go to the police and tell them what she had seen, but she had no idea how they treated homeless minors. She did not think she could be locked up for sleeping on the street, but they might contact her mother, and force her to return home, or else shut her up in some institution that was little better than a prison. On balance, she decided it was best to avoid any contact with the authorities. Her life was challenging enough without having to contend with the police and social services, and possibly being sent back home to Baz and his son, and her ineffectual mother. She could just imagine how that would end.

Leaving the station, she returned to the city centre where she had seen several people with sleeping bags. Worse than the fear of being sent home was the thought that her mother might not have reported her missing, and would refuse to take her back. Baz had told her she had to leave the house, so her mother would probably refuse to allow her to return, even if the authorities sent her back. Had another rough sleeper not told her about a church hall where breakfast was served to homeless people, she might have gone to the police and given herself up as a runaway anyway, she was so hungry.

She found herself in St Helen's Square. There was a smart café on the corner. Through the window she could see people seated at tables drinking tea and eating cakes. Her mouth watered and she could have cried with longing. Her relief when she learned that the church served fry-ups to rough sleepers until midday was almost unbearable. She followed another rough sleeper to the church and gorged herself until she felt sick. But the breakfast renewed her strength. It was only her second day living on the street and she already knew where she could find a meal at least once a day, and where she could find a toilet, and even have a wash of sorts. It was amazing what a difference a full stomach made to how she was feeling about her circumstances. All she needed was a safe place to sleep and her immediate problems would all be solved.

24

DON SWORE OUT LOUD. He distinctly remembered leaving the van parked around the corner, outside a house with a spindly tree growing in the centre of a small patch of grass to the side of the front door. He had specifically noted that tree, growing above the height of the house, so he would have no trouble finding the van again. He had easily recognised the tree and reached the house, only to find himself standing in an empty parking space. He swore again. There was no way he could be mistaken. He was sure he had locked the van but, fishing in his pockets, he could not find his keys.

A horrible suspicion crept through him. If he had left the keys in the ignition, and some bastard had gone and nicked it, the insurance company might refuse to pay up. Not that the van was worth much anyway, but anything was better than nothing. He looked around helplessly, as though he might spot the van in a different parking space. It was possible kids had taken it for a joy ride and dumped it somewhere nearby. In fact, when he thought about it, that was the most likely explanation for the disappearance of a battered old van like his. He could not imagine anyone would actually want to steal it.

He ran back home and phoned his insurance company straight away but he already knew it was hopeless. Even when he told them he had left it securely locked, he knew he might as well not bother. The list price was hardly worth the cost of the keys, let alone the van itself. It was a good runner, but it was pretty ancient. It had been old when he had first purchased it, and now it was even older, and battered. Every year since he bought it the old thing had limped through its MOT on a wing and a prayer. If Don had not been mates with the foreman of the garage, it would probably have failed.

'As long as you get the tyres changed,' his friend would say, or 'You really need to sort out your suspension.'

And every year Don would promise to deal with the problems, and promptly forget about them until the next MOT test. The van went. He only used it for local trips around the city, delivering gardening tools for a local outlet. There was always a risk the engine would pack up, but he felt safe enough driving it around town. As long as the brakes and the steering worked, he was not going to kill anyone. The worst that could happen was that he might fail to deliver an order.

He searched everywhere for the keys, but could not find them in the house. As he had expected, the value the insurance company put on the old vehicle was nowhere near enough for him to replace it. He was left with a payout of a few hundred quid and no transport. Talk about bad luck. Except that it was not bad luck, it was his own stupid fault for leaving the keys in the van, which only made it worse.

'At least it wasn't full of gear,' his girlfriend said. 'You could have ended up losing a load of stuff that didn't even belong to you.'

That did not help. Things could not look much bleaker.

'How the hell am I going to replace it?'

'Can't you tell the insurance company it was full of tools?' she suggested. But he could not claim for contents, only for the vehicle itself, and that was almost worthless. Only it had not been worthless; it had given him a means of earning a living.

'What the hell do we pay insurance for?' he grumbled. 'And what the fuck am I supposed to do now?'

'You'll have to get on to the police and report it stolen,' she replied. 'Maybe they'll be able to recover it for you.'

'Fat chance.'

But he had to report it anyway, if he was to get anything at all out of the insurance company. Without wheels, he had nothing better to do, so he decided to catch a bus to the police station in Fulford Road and report the theft in person. That way, he might stand a better chance of getting something done, although he doubted anyone was going to pay much attention to his problems.

The desk sergeant barely glanced up when Don announced he had come to report the theft of a vehicle.

'I've got the logbook and everything,' he said.

'That's bad luck,' the policeman said, with a surprising flash of sympathy. 'Can you fill this out please?'

Don wrote down all the details. He felt quite pleased with himself for knowing exactly where he had left the van, and the registration and even the chassis number. The time the theft had taken place was necessarily vague as it had disappeared at some point during the night.

'If you ask the people living nearby, someone might have heard it driving away?' he suggested. 'Then you could find it on CCTV and follow it to wherever it was taken?'

'We'll do what we can, sir,' the desk sergeant replied briskly.

His tone suggested that the last thing the police were going to do was conduct a door-to-door investigation to discover whether anyone in the street had heard a vehicle driving past, looked out of the window, and jotted down the registration number of a dirty white van as it drove off.

'It's my livelihood. You have to do something.' Don blustered, but he knew when he was defeated. 'Is there nothing you can do?'

'We'll be keeping a lookout for it, sir. The registration number will be circulated to all our patrol cars and it's possible we'll spot it somewhere. It could have been joyriders taking it for a spin,' he added.

He looked dubious. Don could almost hear him thinking that a seventeen-year-old van was hardly likely to attract the attention of kids out for a spin. Still, it was possible. Thanking the policeman, Don turned to leave.

'I take it you've reported it to your insurance company?' the policeman called out.

'Oh, yes, thank you for reminding me. They asked me to give them a crime number when I'd reported it.'

The policeman gave him the number and Don left. Short of hiring a car and driving around York searching for the van himself, there was nothing more he could do. Cursing his bad luck, his life, his own stupidity, and everything else he could think of, he walked all the way home to save the bus fare, as though that was going to make any difference to the rest of his life.

25

'YOU DO KNOW IT'S only two weeks since you were last here?' Jonah greeted Geraldine as she entered the room.

She waited for a quip about how they had to stop meeting like this, but Jonah just stared down at the body for a few minutes without speaking.

At last he broke the silence. 'I'd guess he was in his late seventies.'

'He looks older than that,' she replied. 'He was found in a doorway, his lower half still inside a tattered sleeping bag, so it seems we're looking at another rough sleeper. Does that make a difference to your estimate of his age?'

Jonah shrugged. 'The lifestyle took its toll. It's hard to say how old he was.'

They both stared at the body. It looked skeletal; a delicate layer of white flesh stretched like tissue paper over the bones. Pale eyes stared up at the ceiling as though surprised by the brightness of the light, after a life spent in the shadows.

'Was he strangled?' Geraldine asked.

Jonah merely grunted. The answer was obvious from the dark line of bruising around the dead man's scrawny neck, and the way his eyes bulged unnaturally in their sockets.

'He's not a very pretty sight, is he?' Jonah asked. 'I wouldn't fancy his chances in a beauty pageant.'

Geraldine smiled fleetingly. She was relieved at the return of Jonah's customary good humour, without which her visits to the mortuary would have been unbearably depressing.

'What about the murder weapon?'

She hoped it had not been a strip of red fabric, although the circumstances in which the victims had both lived, and the manner in which they had been killed, pointed to a single killer. She was not surprised when Jonah confirmed the second victim had also been strangled by a strip of red fabric, probably a tie.

'Was it the same piece of cloth as was used on the previous victim?' she asked.

After listening to Jonah's reply, Geraldine returned to the police station to pass on what she had learned. The forensic report on the red fabric used in the second murder had not yet been completed, so it had not yet been proved that the same strip of material had been used on both victims. However, the details of the red fabric had been kept from the press, so no one outside the police investigating team knew the material or even the colour of the noose. In view of that, it was virtually impossible that more than one killer was involved, which also meant that Tommy could not have killed both victims since he had been in a cell on the night of the second murder. It seemed his confession had been false.

'He could have been working with an accomplice,' Eileen said, 'or have told someone about the red noose when he was boasting about having killed Bingo.'

But for the time being, at least, they had to release him, and Geraldine was sent to share the news with him.

'Tommy, new evidence has come to light.'

Tommy's eyebrows rose slightly, but he did not say anything.

'Tommy, we know you didn't kill Bingo.'

'What do you mean? I confessed, didn't I? So what's the problem? I told you I did it. Why wouldn't you believe me?'

'The problem is, you were lying. We can prove it wasn't you.'

Tommy sighed. 'So you've caught the real killer? Oh well, I had a few nights with a roof over my head here. It made a change.'

'We could charge you with wasting police time.'

'Go ahead,' Tommy smiled.

They both knew that, short of prison, there was no punishment the courts could mete out against Tommy. He was in no position to pay a fine, however derisory the amount, and he would seemingly welcome the chance of being locked up in a warm, dry cell for the winter.

'Why did you confess to a crime you hadn't committed?' Geraldine asked him.

He sighed. 'I thought you'd tumble to the truth long before now,' he replied. 'But I did think I was in with a chance, at least for a while.'

'What if we hadn't been able to disprove your confession? You would have gone down for years.'

'And if that happened, maybe something would have been done sooner about this wretched hip of mine. Oh, well. Never mind. It was worth a try. But you know what, Sergeant?'

'What's that?'

'The honest truth is, I would never have touched a hair on Bingo's head. He was my mate. I'm going to miss seeing him around.'

'He was your friend, yet you were perfectly happy to be convicted of murdering him,' Geraldine said. 'Some friend you are!'

Tommy shrugged. 'Makes no difference to him now, does it? He's well out of it.'

'Don't you ever consider that you might be able to turn your life around?'

'And do what, exactly?'

'Oh, I don't know, get a job, find a room somewhere, make a life for yourself.'

'A life? What kind of a life? You tell me. You think I want to spend my time in a shit job being told what to do by some jumped-up young imbecile throwing his weight around, just so

I can live in a squalid little room somewhere, sitting around waiting to grow old and die? What's the point of that?' It was the first time Geraldine had seen him at all animated. 'I had a life once,' he added, his anger subsiding as rapidly as it had erupted. 'I had a life. A good life. And now it's gone. All I'm left with is an aching body and a bottle to dull the pain.'

It was not clear if the pain he referred to was physical or mental. Geraldine suspected it was both.

'There are people who can help you,' she began, but he interrupted her.

'Yes, there's an army of volunteers and key workers, busy salving their consciences by giving a leg-up to poor sods like me who are down on our luck. I've met them all. And at the end of the day they go back to their comfortable homes to parade their virtue, while we're cooped up in communal centres. Oh, I'm not saying they don't perform a useful function. God knows what we'd do without them in the bad weather, and they do get a few rough sleepers back into a decent life. At least some of the do-gooders do their good work for the best of reasons. But some of us are no-hopers, beyond help.'

'No one's beyond help.'

'A bottle of whisky and a sleeping bag is the only help I want. Sorry to disappoint you, Sergeant, but if you want to make me a better man, you can fuck off. I was an upright citizen once, a pillar of the community, with a home and a wife and a good job. You might not believe it, but I worked hard. And where did it get me? Look at me. Go on, go home to your cosy bed where you can sleep well at night, knowing you're doing a good job, and save your lectures for people who want to listen.'

26

SINCE JASPER HAD BEEN unable to provide an alibi for the time of either of the two deaths, he now became a suspect for both murders. A search warrant had been issued for his apartment, every inch of which had been carefully examined, but no sign of a red tie was discovered, not even a microscopic thread of red fabric.

'He kept the tie after the first murder, so why didn't he keep it after the second one?' Eileen asked. 'What has he done with it?'

'It's a tie,' Ian replied. 'It could be anywhere.'

Geraldine and Ian questioned Jasper again and this time Ian wanted to put pressure on him to confess.

'Don't give him any wriggle room,' he muttered as they approached the interview room. 'We need to catch him out. Once we establish he's lying he'll crumble. You can see he's not strong.'

Looking at Jasper facing them across the table, Geraldine understood exactly what Ian had meant. The suspect was pale and looked as though he had not slept for days. In stark contrast to Tommy, who had been completely relaxed about his arrest, Jasper showed signs of extreme stress. The interview room was cool, but he was sweating and seemed incapable of sitting still. Fidgeting with the edge of the table, he kept shifting in his seat and was unable to look either of his interlocutors in the eye.

Ian started by questioning Jasper again about the second murder.

'I keep telling you, it wasn't me,' Jasper insisted, his face taut with apprehension. 'I was at home in bed fast asleep when that tramp was killed. I just happened to stumble on the body on my way to work, and that's when I spat on the pavement, which was stupid of me, I know, and disrespectful, but I didn't know he was dead then, did I? I mean, it's not the kind of thing you expect to find on your way to work, is it? A stiff, lying on the pavement. I nearly fell over the guy. I mean, it wasn't his fault, but I thought he'd just crashed out there, and he nearly tripped me up. When I realised he was dead, that's when I should have called you, but I didn't. I admit that. If it's a crime not to report a dead body then I'm guilty, sure. Like I said, I admit that. It was wrong of me. I was afraid of losing my job if I made any trouble for the boss by having the police traipsing all round the restaurant. But I'm telling you, I didn't kill anyone. I just found him. You can't accuse me of something I didn't do, just because I was there. I don't even know who the guy was. Why would I want to kill a complete stranger? I was in bed that night, all night.'

'Can anyone corroborate that statement?'

As Ian continued quizzing him Geraldine listened with growing concern, conscious of the irony of the situation. After believing the false confession of a liar, they were now querying the words of a man who might well be telling the truth. Meanwhile, Ian turned his attention to the first murder. Without any preamble he enquired where the suspect had been on Tuesday evening two weeks earlier. Jasper looked baffled. Turning to his lawyer, he asked what was going on. The lawyer merely shrugged and looked at Ian in silence, waiting to hear where this was leading. Ian repeated his question.

'I was at home in bed,' Jasper replied, with growing alarm in his expression.

'Another tramp was murdered that night,' Ian said quietly.

The lawyer's expression did not alter, but his eyes narrowed almost imperceptibly as he understood what was being implied. Jasper understood too, and his reaction was explosive.

'You can't pin any of this on me!' he yelled, losing all his self-control. 'I never touched anyone! I'm not a violent man!'

He was sweating profusely, and his eyes had taken on a strange wildness. Fear could change a man almost beyond recognition, and Geraldine felt a frisson of pity for the suspect who, for all they knew, might be innocent. Still, unfortunately for Jasper, he had a record for GBH.

'That was years ago,' he protested when Ian brought it up. He lowered his voice and his tone became pleading. 'I was a kid. I did community service for it. That's got nothing to do with any of this. I was only a kid.'

In desperation he turned to his lawyer, who sat impassive at his side, listening.

Returning to the office, Geraldine and Ian joined Ariadne and a young constable, Naomi, who were discussing the case. Naomi thought Jasper must have been killing tramps for some bizarre reason of his own.

'We need to question him about what he thinks of rough sleepers,' she was saying. 'He might give himself away.'

Geraldine was faintly irritated that Ian promptly agreed with Naomi. Blond and petite, and undeniably efficient, Naomi blatantly fancied Ian who seemed completely unaware of her interest in him. Geraldine wondered if he could really be as oblivious to his young colleague's interest as he appeared, when just about everyone else seemed to have noticed how Naomi trailed around after him, fetching him coffee and laughing at his jokes. Geraldine had known Ian for a long time, and was aware he was vulnerable after the breakdown of his marriage. She held back from commenting, for fear of being accused of prying, but she was concerned he might enter into a new relationship on the rebound. Still, Geraldine told herself, it was none of her business. Naomi was young, attractive, and smart. What Ian chose to do in his personal life was his own business.

For her part, Geraldine needed to stamp on her own affection for Ian. They had worked together closely for such a long time, it was inevitable that an intimacy had grown up between them. But there was nothing more to it than a close professional relationship. When Geraldine had first moved to York, she had allowed herself to hope their friendship might develop into something more romantic. The realisation that she was deluding herself had been painful, but thankfully she had avoided the humiliation of betraying her feelings.

Ariadne's curiosity did not help. 'Do you think Naomi and Ian are going to get together?' she had asked Geraldine. 'You know Ian, don't you? You knew him before you came here, didn't you? What do you think?'

'I'm not interested in idle gossip,' Geraldine had snapped.

Now she watched Ian and Naomi, standing side by side, discussing the possibility that Jasper could have killed both victims for no other reason than that they were homeless. The two officers made a good-looking couple, Ian tall and attractive, and Naomi petite and pretty.

'But why on earth would he want to kill rough sleepers? And if he thought they were potentially dangerous, what made him pick on his second victim? He was so old and weak, he was hardly going to pose a threat to a young man like Jasper.'

No one had an answer to that. They just had to try to establish the second victim's identity in the hope that it would enable them to solve the case. In the meantime, the absence of any evidence placing Jasper at the scene of the first murder was proving problematic. An unknown killer seemed to have struck twice. Neither attack appeared to be a crime of passion, or a one-off loss of control. Both murders had been carefully planned and executed to ensure the killer's anonymity was protected, and where two victims had been so skilfully dispatched, there could be more. They had to establish whether Jasper was guilty and, if he was innocent, they needed to find the killer, and they needed to do so quickly. A killer who had already claimed two victims could not remain at liberty to strike again.

27

THE PROPERTY WAS RENTED under a false name, and he could leave no clue as to what he had been doing there. That had been a secret known only to him and Mark. Now that Mark was dead, he alone knew the truth, and he was going to make sure it stayed that way. It had taken a week, but Mark's life was finally over. Towards the end, the self-appointed executioner had looped a red noose around his victim's neck and tightened it. By then Mark was as good as dead already, and was too weak to even try to remonstrate when his gag was removed. If anything, it was disappointing that he had succumbed so easily. He might even have been unaware of what was happening. But it was important to strangle him to death. That was how it had to be done, or the other two would have been killed for no purpose, and he hated wasted effort.

Mark's body was still lying on the floor of the cellar but it could not stay there indefinitely. Apart from anything else, after a while it would start to smell. Before that happened the corpse had to be moved somewhere sufficiently public for it to be found, yet secluded enough for it to be deposited discreetly. Following the news, it was obvious the police had no inkling who was carrying out these murders. That was not going to change, unless someone saw the body being dumped. That would be it. Game over. Up until now he had been playing the game so well. He was not about to throw away his liberty for a stupid blunder like that.

It was easy enough to roll the body up in a length of old carpet, but securing the bundle tightly proved extremely difficult. At last he had the roll tied up in six places, and was confident its contents would not slither out on to the street at either end. Carefully he rolled the carpet across the floor and manoeuvred it through the door. Hauling it up the stairs was heavy work, but he managed it, mainly because he had no other choice. It could not stay where it was.

It had been a stroke of luck finding an old van with the key still in the ignition. That had made his life easier. He wondered if the owner had left the key there deliberately, hoping someone would come along and steal the rusty old heap. But he did not really believe in luck. To be fair, it had taken him a long time to find what he needed. He had been looking out for just such a vehicle for months. If he had not come across that particular one, he knew where others were kept out on the street at night. He had spent months earmarking them for use when the need arose. Having the key was not essential, but it certainly helped.

The house he had rented at the end of a badly lit cul-de-sac had an internal door to the garage. He had been very particular about that. With the van backed up into the garage, he rolled his weighty bundle a short distance across the hall, over carpet covered in plastic sheeting, until at last the body was in the garage. All that remained was to hoist it up into the back of the van. He worked slowly, wary of hurting his back and ending up in serious trouble, but eventually he completed the arduous task. With false number plates attached to the van, front and back, he drove slowly out of the garage without turning the lights on. It was a pity the van was white. He would have preferred a black or navy one, but he had to work with what he could get.

Turning out of the side street to the main road, he put his lights on and went in search of an isolated spot. No one paid any attention to a battered old van cruising along the street. Whistling, he drove along Gillygate to Union Terrace where he parked the van in a corner of the car park. Glancing around to make sure there was no one else about, he slipped out of the driving seat and made sure the van was unlocked. Originally he had planned to dump the body in the city where it might be mistaken for another rough sleeper, but trying to deposit it there would be too risky. In any case, left in the car park the body would be discovered soon enough. Crouching down out of sight, he took the false number plate off the front of the van, but decided against going around the back to remove the other plate, for fear of being spotted. The van would be found sooner or later. What mattered now was for him to leave the car park swiftly, without being seen.

Stealing away, he kept to the shelter of the trees, avoiding any cameras. At a safe distance from the car park, he dropped the key to the van down a drain, and made his way home. Already he was regretting having left the false number plate on the back of the van in case it was traced back to the house he had rented but, having left the scene, he was not going to risk going back. He would visit the rented property once more to clear away the plastic sheeting and check he had not left any mess. After that, he had no further use for the house. It was a pity in some ways. He had turned out to be rather good at killing people. But he was not stupid enough to tempt fate by carrying on for too long. So far he had easily escaped detection, but every murder increased his risk of being caught. The rental agreement on the house was due up in a week. He would not renew it. The killer could now vanish without trace, satisfied that he had achieved his purpose. There was no further need for him. At least, that had been the plan.

Thinking over the excitement of the past few weeks as he walked home, he realised he was not ready to give up his new pastime. Admittedly, killing Mark had been the whole purpose of his attacks in the first place. The tramps had been strangled only to conceal the motive behind Mark's murder, so his killer could never be traced. But he had not anticipated the thrill he would experience as he squeezed the life out of a total stranger. Now that it was all over, he felt compelled to repeat the experience. Every time he killed, he imagined it was his wife's lover who was struggling frantically against the noose, and the intense gratification he felt turned out to be addictive.

He was going to have to take a break in order to be properly prepared before his next venture. Instead of a house, next time he might rent a lock-up garage under a false name. There were many ways in which to improve his operation. But the red tie would stay. He had become quite attached to it. He smiled, because no one else could possibly have thought up such a simple plan, to use an innocent item of clothing to strangle the life out of his victims. And it meant he could never be caught.

28

MOLLY PASSED A NERVOUS night in the doorway of an empty shop around the block from Coney Street. Over breakfast the next morning she learned that another homeless man had been murdered along there shortly before her arrival in York, but that did not seem to deter a number of rough sleepers from returning to their customary haunt.

'Shouldn't the police be examining the area?' Molly asked one of the volunteers serving breakfast.

The woman shrugged. 'They put up a cordon and wouldn't let anyone go there for a few days.'

'It was two weeks ago,' another volunteer chipped in.

'It must have been longer than that,' the first volunteer said. 'They closed the road for weeks.'

A rough sleeper disagreed. 'It wasn't as long as that.'

'The shops complained,' the first volunteer said. 'That's why they relaxed the cordon.'

'That wasn't the reason. The police would have been there for longer if anyone else had been killed,' a rough sleeper called out, and a few others nodded and called out in agreement. 'No one cares about a couple of homeless men being murdered.'

'I'm sure that's not true,' one of the volunteers replied, but she did not sound convinced.

By the time it began to grow dark, Molly was feeling hungry again. It helped to know that she would be given a good breakfast in the morning. In the meantime, she had to try and ignore the pangs of hunger stabbing at her guts. And there was another night ahead of her. With nowhere else to go, she made her way to St Sampson's Square, but there was a policeman standing at the entrance to Nether Hornpot Lane in front of a cordon blocking off the alleyway. Several police vans were parked in the square and the pub was closed. Apart from the police presence, the square was deserted. Molly turned and slunk away before any of them noticed her loitering nearby.

Back in St Helen's Square, she hung around, uncertain what to do.

It was busy there, with groups of Japanese tourists gabbling in excited voices, and well-dressed people entering smart restaurants that bordered the square. They seemed to belong to a different world. Seeing them made Molly feel hungry again, but there was nothing she could do about that until the morning. Right now her priority was to find somewhere safe to sleep. She decided against looking for another deserted alleyway. With a killer seemingly targeting rough sleepers, it was safer to be with other people. In any case, Nether Hornpot Lane was closed and she did not know where else she might find a doorway concealed from view.

'Are you OK?' a girl's voice asked suddenly, right by her ear.

Startled, Molly spun round. She had not been mistaken in thinking the girl was speaking to her.

'What?' she asked stupidly. 'What did you say?'

'I asked you if you're all right. You look lost.'

On the point of retorting that she was not lost and the other girl could mind her own business, Molly hesitated. The girl who had addressed her was little more than skin and bone. Thin blond hair hung to her shoulders and her eyes looked huge in her gaunt face. If she had not been so thin she would have been pretty but, as it was, her skull-like face made her look ill. Her limbs stuck out of her T-shirt and skirt like twigs that could be snapped with ease, adding to the impression of physical vulnerability. Molly had noticed her at breakfast that morning, but she doubted the other girl ever ate much. Molly relaxed. The girl hardly looked threatening and in any case she was clearly also homeless.

'I asked you if you're all right?' she repeated, with more than a hint of impatience.

'Yes, yes, that is, well, no, not really.'

'Have you got somewhere to sleep tonight?'

'No,' Molly admitted.

The girl studied her for a moment, before saying, 'You do know there are hostels in York where you can stay, don't you? You have to be referred though, and you need to be from York. You can't just parachute in and expect to be supported by the local council, you know. They're all bastards like that.'

'Are you living in a hostel?'

The girl gave a twisted smile. 'No way.'

'Why not? Aren't you from York?'

'It's not that. It's just that they have their rules, you know.' She shook her head vigorously. 'Fuck that shit. I need my freedom.'

Freedom to shoot up, Molly thought.

'No alcohol, no skunk, no nothing,' the girl explained, rolling her eyes. 'Like a fucking prison. I'm Rose,' she added.

Without thinking, Molly gave her mother's name. 'I'm Laura.'

She was not sure why she lied, but it hardly mattered. Rose was probably not the other girl's real name either. Perhaps she was right to prefer living on the street to being controlled by people running a hostel. At least on the street there was no one telling her what to do. With all her belongings crammed into a bag on her back, there was no need to find her way back to any particular place every night, and she could literally go anywhere. Except that she had nowhere to go. It was a pointless kind of freedom.

'Some of us sleep in Coney Street,' Rose said. 'And they serve a proper cooked breakfast at one of the churches. I could show you the way there, if you like.'

Molly nodded. 'I know where it is. But thanks,' she added.

Rose seemed eager to be helpful and did not appear to have any ulterior motive in befriending her, but Molly was wary of her nonetheless.

'How did you know I had nowhere to go?'

'I didn't. I just thought you looked lost.'

Molly sighed. Rose was right about that. She *was* lost. But at least she was no longer alone. It was growing dark, so she followed Rose to a wide covered shopfront in Coney Street. The shop must have closed down a while ago, because the sign had been taken down and the windows were painted white, but there were still posters in the doorway showing young women modelling summer dresses. Clearly it had once been a clothes shop. The models in the posters were all smiling.

'This is me,' Rose said. 'I can show you an empty doorway, if you like.'

She led Molly a few doors along to another covered shop front where Molly would be sheltered if it rained during the night.

'Someone used to sleep here, but he's gone.'

'Gone where?'

'People come and go,' Rose said vaguely, gazing past Molly along the street.

Molly thanked her and unrolled her blanket. It was as comfortable a place as any, and Rose would be just a few doorways along the street. It was company of a sort. And in the morning, there would be a cooked breakfast. But as she closed her eyes, she shivered, wondering whether this was the spot where the killer's first victim had slept.

29

POLICE CONSTABLE GEOFF JONES was patrolling the area near the university building in York. He had not long been a member of the police force, and this was the first time he had been out on patrol on his own. It was exciting, cruising along in a police car, but for the most part the job fell short of his expectations. He would not have admitted as much to anyone he worked with, but he was bored. Other than dealing with the drunken fallout from stag dos and hen nights, his duties were generally tedious.

'That's a good thing, isn't it?' his mum said when he complained about the monotonous routine.

She was proud of him for joining the police force, although she was concerned that policing was more dangerous now than it had been back when her father had been a police constable. Geoff was not so sure. With instantaneous communication, he would be able to summon backup at a moment's notice, if anything kicked off. But nothing ever did.

'Honestly, mum,' he reassured her, 'it's no different to any other job except that I get to wear a uniform and drive a police car.'

Part of his route that morning took him to the Union Terrace car park. Driving through it, his attention was caught by a scruffy van in the corner of the car park. As he drove by he noticed that not only was the back door dented, but both of the back tyres looked bald. He pulled over to take a closer look. Walking slowly around to the front of the vehicle, he saw the two front tyres were also bald. By now he had spotted something

151

else that was even more interesting: the number plates were not the same, front and back. He went round to the back of the van again to take a proper look, and found he had not been mistaken in thinking the number plates did not match.

Faintly intrigued by his discovery, he bent down to examine the plates more closely and saw that a fake number plate had been stuck over the one on the back. Checking out the actual registration number, he was not surprised to learn that the van had been reported stolen that morning. He had sensed there was something dodgy about it from the moment he set eyes on it. He would not have been surprised to discover it was not insured and had no MOT. It just had that look about it. He was pleased to have been the one to find it, so soon after the owner had reported it stolen. It was a relatively insignificant discovery, but one that would look impressive on his work record, and at least he was doing something useful.

After registering that the stolen van had been found, he turned to have another look at it. It was odd that it had been left there with two different number plates. The van was white, but the original colour was almost lost beneath a film of grime. The bottom of the frame was rusty, and the bumper was scratched and dented. It was hard to understand why anyone in their right mind would bother to steal such a decrepit old heap of scrap metal. Kids out joyriding would surely have chosen a more exciting vehicle than this old van. But the fact that it *was* a van with no windows in the back raised other, more sinister, possibilities. It could have been used to transport stolen goods, or drugs, or illegal immigrants.

Geoff knew better than to get his fingerprints all over it, in case it was being used for illegal purposes, but he could not help wondering whether there was anything inside it. No one would ever know if he took a quick look, just to satisfy his curiosity. The thief might have hidden it in the corner of a car park where no one was likely to spot it, intending to come back for it later.

If Geoff had not noticed it and identified it as a stolen vehicle, the thief might have returned for it and hidden it where it would never be found, in a closed barn, or at the bottom of a lake, for example. Having found the stolen vehicle, Geoff felt a sense of responsibility for it.

He glanced around to see if anyone was watching, then reminded himself that as a police officer he was entitled to examine a stolen vehicle. Even if he was seen, it did not matter. He was acting in an official capacity, in the public interest. After all, there could be something dangerous inside the van, like guns or knives. If he failed to check it was locked, children might come along and injure themselves playing with its contents. So it was his duty to check the van was secure.

Seizing the initiative Geoff pulled on gloves and tried the driver's door. It was unlocked. He peered through the open door but there was nothing inside apart from an empty cigarette carton and a few old newspapers. He went around the back of the van and tried the handle. The door opened with a sharp squeal of protest. Shining his torch inside, Geoff was disappointed to see nothing but a roll of carpet. He stepped back and his attention was caught by the number of lengths of rope that had been tied around it. Secured in so many places, it could be full of drugs. Resisting the temptation to try and untie it, instead he shone a beam of light from his torch right inside the roll of carpet and fell back in alarm. Inside the rolled-up carpet he had seen what looked like a naked human foot. He took a closer look and saw there was indeed a human foot inside the roll of carpet. Someone was using the van to dispose of a dead body. Shaking, Geoff called the police station and reported his discovery.

'You wanted a bit of excitement,' his mother said tartly when he told her about his experience. 'Perhaps you'll be more careful what you wish for in future.'

30

ANN THOUGHT ABOUT MARK constantly in between their meetings. Sometimes they went for a few weeks without seeing each other, if one or other of them was not free on a particular Tuesday, and she missed him when that happened. They never met on a different day of the week, as Ann's husband had a regular meeting on Tuesday evenings, so she was confident she could move around York without any risk of him spotting her travelling to or from her lover's house. But since their last meeting, Ann had been bothered by Mark's odd remarks. On balance she decided it would be best to ignore his strange behaviour and visit him the following Tuesday as though nothing unusual had happened. She hoped his unexpected bout of paranoia would have passed by then.

'Sorry if I came across a bit weird last time,' she imagined him saying, with an embarrassed laugh. 'I was just a bit overwrought.'

Or perhaps he would say he had been exhausted and stressed. It was the beginning of term, after all, and he had been grumbling for a few weeks about having to work too hard.

'Do you want to leave it for a while?' she had asked before she had left his apartment on her last visit.

'Leave what? I'm not sure I understand.'

'I mean, do you want us to take a break from each other? Just until you're on top of things at work.'

But he had been adamant that was not what he wanted at all.

'No way. Seeing you is about the only thing that's keeping me even vaguely sane at the moment. I honestly don't think I'd be able to carry on if you stopped coming to see me.'

You'd find someone else to shag, she thought sourly, but she kept that to herself.

The following Tuesday, for the first time Mark did not answer the door when she went to see him. Remembering how he had told her he was being stalked, she became seriously concerned about his mental state, but there was nothing she could do. He might be ill, but she could not even phone him because they had deliberately agreed to not exchange home phone numbers. That had been a stupid decision which she now regretted, but it was too late to change it now. When they saw each other again, she would insist they at least knew each other's numbers. Even if they resolved never to phone each other, they ought to be able to do so in an emergency. Mark could be lying in bed, sick, and she would know nothing about it. He might have had an accident and be in hospital, unable to contact her. After hanging around helplessly on his doorstep for a few minutes, she scribbled a note and posted it through the letterbox. She wrote in block capitals so the message could not be traced back to her, but Mark would know she had written it: 'I came to see you as usual'. Then she went home, and did her best to hide her anxiety.

On Wednesday evening David brought home a free local paper, as he occasionally did. When he tossed it down on the kitchen table, Ann glanced at the front page and stifled a gasp. Distracted by a headline, she barely heard what David was saying to her.

'Sorry, what did you say?' she stammered.

'I was asking you when dinner will be ready. I'm starving.'

He launched into a complaint about how he had been obliged to cut his lunch hour short and had barely had time to grab a sandwich, but Ann was not listening to him.

'Another Local Man Found Dead. Police are treating the death as suspicious,' she read. It was not the headline that had caught her attention. What had startled her was the photo accompanying the article, because she recognised Mark at once. The photograph itself was a familiar one. She had seen it above the fireplace in his flat many times. There was no doubt in her mind that her lover was dead, and the police believed he had been murdered. Swallowing hard, she forced herself to remain calm and turn her attention to the dinner.

'It'll be ready soon,' she said, and was relieved that her voice sounded normal.

With a grunt, David left the room and, a moment later, Ann heard a blare of voices from the television in the living room. She knew she would not be left alone for long. In a few minutes her family would arrive in the kitchen, clamouring for dinner. Now that she was on her own for a moment at least, her mind seemed to go numb. All she could think about was robotically turning over the potatoes and checking the meat was properly cooked. Peas. She had forgotten the peas. As she fumbled with the frozen packet, her fingers slipped and peas shot out, rolling all over the floor. All at once, she felt sobs bubble up in her chest and she could scarcely stop herself from bursting into tears. Pressing her lips together, she put some peas in the microwave, and swept the floor. She had to keep reminding herself she had no ostensible reason for tears. She had to continue as though nothing had happened. Outwardly, nothing *had* happened. Her loss was a secret, locked away in her private thoughts, and it had to remain there. Whatever else transpired, she had to hide her feelings.

'Supper's ready,' she called out.

'About bloody time,' her daughter Aimee said, coming into the kitchen.

'Don't swear,' Ann replied automatically, without turning round.

'Dad's watching the news,' Aimee complained. 'He won't turn over.'

'It's important to know what's going on in the world,' her father said, following her into the room. 'Do you want to grow up ignorant about absolutely everything?'

Aimee pulled a face. 'I want to live without being bored all the time.'

'Don't argue with your father,' Ann said.

It was more of a warning than an admonition. She knew how quickly he could fly into a rage. They ate in miserable silence. As soon as they finished the meal Aimee disappeared upstairs, and David looked directly at Ann.

'Are you all right?'

'Yes.'

'Are you sure?'

'Yes, why are you asking? Why wouldn't I be all right?'

Doing her best to look baffled, Ann tried to shrug off an uneasy suspicion that David could tell she was lying. Pretending she was fine was a strain, but there was nothing else she could do.

David shook his head. 'You just don't seem yourself. Has something happened to upset you?'

'No, no, I'm fine, really.'

She was rescued from David's interrogation by Aimee who rushed into the kitchen, demanding an advance on her allowance.

'What do you want it for?' her father wanted to know.

'I'm going out.'

'Not dressed like that, you're not,' he said.

Aimee turned to Ann who had turned away, struggling to stifle her tears.

'Mum, Dad won't give me any money. What if I need to get a taxi home? You don't want to put me at risk, do you?'

'Don't be ridiculous,' David snapped. 'No one's trying to put you at risk but you yourself, going out looking like a – a prostitute.'

Aimee glared at him. 'You're always criticising,' she

complained. 'What's wrong with what I'm wearing?'

'Nothing if you want to go around showing your knickers to every Tom, Dick and Harry.'

'I'm fifteen. I can go out when I like and wear what I like.'

'Not while you're living under my roof.'

'Which hopefully won't be for much longer,' Aimee muttered, before appealing to Ann again. 'Mum, will you lend me a tenner?'

But Aimee knew she was beaten. Ann would never contradict any of David's decrees.

'Your father's right,' Ann replied.

'Now go upstairs and do your homework,' David added.

Muttering darkly, Aimee ran from the room, slamming the door behind her and yelling that her parents never wanted her to have any fun. Ann watched her go, relieved to have an excuse for her own tears that she could no longer control.

'It's all right,' David said, with an unexpected show of sympathy. 'She has to learn.'

A moment later they heard the front door slam and, looking out of the window, saw Aimee striding down the front path. Muttering an expletive, David set off in pursuit. As she heard the door close behind him, Ann collapsed on to a chair and began to cry in earnest. Hearing raised voices, and the front door slamming, she pulled herself together, blew her nose and dabbed her eyes with a tissue, all the while listening to David and Aimee arguing. By the time she heard Aimee's footsteps pounding up the stairs and David had rejoined her in the kitchen, she had regained control of herself. Even so, David could see she had been crying.

'There's no point getting upset about it,' he said. 'Teenagers will be teenagers, but I'm not having a daughter of mine running around town dressed like a tramp. Who knows what kind of trouble she might get herself into? Honestly, I don't know what's got into that girl.'

Nodding miserably, Ann breathed a silent sigh of relief that he had misunderstood why she was crying. Whatever happened, he must never discover the truth.

31

THE TUBBY PATHOLOGIST, JONAH Hetherington, looked younger than his fifty or so years on account of his high energy and good humour. Geraldine liked him very much. Not only was he sharp and efficient, he was also obliging. Several times he had made comments off the record that had helped to clarify her thoughts. On occasion he had even offered her a new slant on a case.

'Don't quote me on this,' he liked to say or, 'This is just between us, of course,' as though they shared a guilty secret which, in a way, they did.

'Of course,' she would reply, returning his grin. 'Silent as the grave.'

It seemed an appropriate phrase, given the circumstances.

This particular occasion was no different. Geraldine had gone to speak to the pathologist on her own, as Ian had told her he was too busy to accompany her.

'You get more out of him when you go by yourself,' Ian said.

They both knew the real, unspoken, reason why Ian was not going to the mortuary.

'This chap here is a bit of a puzzle,' Jonah said as soon as Geraldine entered the room.

'In what way?'

Jonah's usually cheery features creased in a frown that made him resemble a comical gargoyle, but his words were anything but amusing. 'Well, it's just that the evidence seems to be contradictory. The victim is certainly emaciated, and severely dehydrated. In fact, if he hadn't been strangled, he would have been dead within hours anyway without medical attention.'

'What kind of medical attention?'

'First and foremost he needed to be put on a drip to hydrate him. But apart from that, and the fact that he was covered in carpet fibres, there doesn't appear to have been very much wrong with him at all. I can find no evidence of any disease, and no long-term problems. In fact, you don't need to scratch very far below the surface to reach the conclusion that he seems to have looked after himself. Granted he's not eaten for days but one of his teeth has recently been capped, and his leg muscles are well toned and, what's strange in someone so badly malnourished and dehydrated, is that his hair's been dyed with what appears to be quite an expensive product, and although his nails are quite dirty, the ends look manicured and his feet are in unusually good condition for someone living on the street.'

Geraldine stared at the unshaven face of the victim. He hardly looked like someone who had taken care of himself.

'And he has a molar implant which would have been expensive and not strictly necessary, I'd say. A lot of people would have simply lived with a gap in their back teeth. It wouldn't have shown. Hopefully you'll be able to discover his identity from his dental records?'

Geraldine nodded. 'We'll follow that up right away. So he hadn't eaten for a few days and was severely dehydrated. Had he been ill, do you think? Or taking drugs?'

'Perhaps, although there's no sign of that. I'll be able to confirm whether there were any substances in his system once we get the tox report. In the meantime, I've cleaned him up.' Catching Geraldine's sceptical expression, he added, 'He was absolutely filthy when he was found. Not just fibres from the carpet he was wrapped in, but his trousers were covered in excrement – his own. Before they were ruined, they were a good pair of trousers, and his shirt was an expensive one as well.'

'He could have been given the clothes.'

'Yes, but I suppose what I'm saying is that if this was another tramp, as he appeared to be at first sight, he seems to have been a very affluent tramp. Look at his feet.'

Geraldine looked at them. Like the rest of him, they were clean and very pale. Although his toenails could probably do with trimming, they were not unusually long, and there was nothing remarkable about his feet at all, as far as she could see.

'They're just feet,' she said.

'Exactly. You'd expect a tramp to have a few blisters or bunions, wouldn't you? The shoes he was wearing had moulded to his feet and show no signs of having been worn by a previous owner.'

'Don't tell me, they were an expensive brand.'

'Not cheap anyway. Oxford brogues, fifty or sixty pounds at least. And appearances certainly suggest he wore them from new. Even his socks were cashmere wool and looked as though they'd hardly been worn.'

'So you're telling me you think this man wasn't homeless at all, he just happened to be soiled and unshaven and malnourished and dehydrated.'

Jonah nodded. 'I'm not able to reach any conclusions, but I am casting doubt on the theory that he was some kind of tramp. His clothes, shoes and teeth make that highly unlikely – but not impossible of course.'

'Was there anything under his fingernails?'

'Nothing useful. Just dirt.'

'So he was well off and had recently lost his income and all his money?'

Jonah inclined his head. 'Yes, it's possible he'd only recently fallen on hard times. Very recently, I'd say, from the look of him. Within the last fortnight. But what is it they say? We're all only two pay days away from homelessness?'

As she drove back to the police station, Geraldine mulled over what Jonah had told her. There were any number of reasons why people might lose their homes. If there was no evidence of drink or drugs, it could be gambling or depression that had ruined his life, or he might have just lost his job and gone to pieces. Perhaps he would have recovered, given time. But he had not been given time. The team were all agreed that a killer was attacking rough sleepers, for some demented reason of his own. She wondered whether it was just bad luck for this latest victim that he had become a target so soon after becoming homeless, but at least he should be relatively easy to identify. All the same, she wondered whether it was significant or just bad luck that this third victim had looked like a tramp, yet had been wearing expensive clothes and had teeth and hair that until very recently had been well cared for. And he had not been killed in the city like the other two victims, but had been left in a rolled-up carpet in a van in a car park. It was looking as though there might be two killers on the streets.

32

JASPER HAD BEEN IN a cell for over forty-eight hours, with a case building against him. Uneasy about his alleged guilt, Geraldine was arguing with Ian about the arrest.

'Why would he wear gloves and then spit on the pavement so close to his victim that some of his saliva actually landed on the body?' she insisted. 'It doesn't make sense for someone to be so careful and at the same time so careless.'

'Well, clearly he didn't spit directly on to the body,' Ian replied. 'He wasn't to know some of the spit would be carried on the wind and land where it did and incriminate him. It was just unfortunate for him that happened.'

Geraldine shook her head. 'And why would anyone be stupid enough to stop and spit near a victim right after killing him?'

'Oh, for goodness sake, there could be any number of reasons. To show his loathing? His disgust? Or perhaps it was an expression of his power over the victim?'

'Where's the power in spitting on someone? I mean, if he'd just killed him, surely that would be proof enough of his power?'

'Well, then, maybe he spat on him before he killed him.'

'It just doesn't add up. In every other detail the killer was so careful not to leave any trace of his presence. He didn't even touch the victim, and he wore gloves and a hood to make sure his face couldn't be seen. And then, after all that, he just left a nice dollop of his DNA behind for us to find. It would be too stupid.'

'Luckily for us, most killers are stupid.'

'Yes, but Jasper doesn't strike me as a complete idiot, and the murder was neatly executed in a way that hid the identity of the killer.'

'In every detail but one,' Ian pointed out with a smile. 'Don't forget we have his DNA on the second body. Surely that wraps it up?'

Initially, Eileen agreed with Ian. 'If the same tie - if it was a tie - was used in two murders, then we have evidence that links Jasper to both victims.'

With Tommy's confession debunked, they were pinning their hopes on Jasper. Either he had killed both men, or the investigation had gone off on the wrong tack altogether. But by now everyone had reservations. Even Eileen, who was keen to see the case resolved, seemed unsure of Jasper's guilt.

'We need to get him to confess,' Ian said.

He was right. A decent defence counsel would be able to destroy their case by claiming the DNA evidence was circumstantial. Jasper had never attempted to deny his presence at the scene of the crime, but he insisted he had only arrived after the murder had been committed. And really, his presence there was all that could be established. They had yet to find a way to prove he had actually killed the victim.

'What if it wasn't him?' Geraldine asked.

'There are other questions we need to be asking,' Eileen said. 'Why was the third victim so malnourished immediately before he was killed? Why would a perfectly healthy reasonably affluent man stop eating and drinking and become so dirty?'

'Maybe his wife left him,' Ian suggested, with a trace of bitterness.

'Perhaps he had mental health problems,' Naomi added.

A team of constables were going door to door questioning Jasper's neighbours. One of them had recently had a security camera rigged up above his front door, and another one along the side of his house. The constable who questioned him explained that the police would like to view the film. The neighbour expressed reluctance, as this entailed disturbing the cameras, but he had no choice. A technical team were promptly despatched to download the relevant footage and take it back to the police station where a constable had the tedious task of watching the film of the street and the approach to the neighbour's house for hours. Only the corner of the frame caught the gate opposite where Jasper lived. He was seen going home at around six in the evening, and there was no sign of him leaving the house again until seven the following morning. His arrival and departure were both outside the time frame when the murder had been committed. At eight fifteen, a pizza had been delivered to his house. The person who opened the front door and took the delivery was out of the frame, which only covered Jasper's gate and front path, but the delivery boy was traced from the logo on the box and the time of the delivery, and he recognised Jasper's photo as the man who had taken the delivery. A next door neighbour confirmed the time when Jasper had arrived home on the Tuesday evening.

'He could have gone out of the back door,' someone suggested. 'If he didn't want to be seen, that would be likely, wouldn't it?'

But the block of flats where Jasper lived had security lights and they had not been triggered all that night. The case against him had all but collapsed.

'So, basically, he appears to be in the clear,' Eileen said, when the team were given the news. 'We'll keep an eye on him, and make sure he doesn't leave the area, but his lawyer is agitating for his release and we don't have enough evidence to keep him any longer. We'll have to drop all charges against him for now.'

With the discovery of a third victim killed with the same red fabric while Jasper was in a cell, the case against the suspect fell apart completely. Geraldine tried not to say 'I told you so' when Eileen announced the disappointing development. Once again they had no suspect.

Jasper glared at Geraldine when she told him he was free to go. He left, grumbling about wrongful arrest and police harassment. Meanwhile, they were doing everything possible to trace other suspects. A team continued scrutinising CCTV from the area in minute detail, searching for the hooded figure which had been sighted near the scene on the night of Bingo's murder. Sophisticated software was in use to analyse the gait of that particular figure, and match it against every other hooded figure caught on camera roaming the streets that night. CCTV from shops in the surrounding area had been requested or requisitioned in an attempt to trace the hooded figure leaving the scene, and the gait of anyone who resembled the figure in question was being studied.

'It's tricky because he's wearing a baggy hooded jacket that masks a lot of movement, but even so there are several distinctive features to look out for,' a forensic podiatrist had advised the team tasked with watching hours of CCTV. 'The suspect is slightly bow-legged, and swings his left leg out to the side when he's walking, and his left arm moves out more than his right one.'

Any video that could possibly match the suspect was sent to the podiatrist for a meticulous frame-by-frame assessment, scrutinising every aspect of the figure's walk, looking at the head, shoulders, arms and hands.

At the same time, a large team of officers had been drafted in to question anyone who lived near Coney Street, and anyone legitimately out on the streets during the night was questioned, as were the prostitutes known to the local Criminal Intelligence Unit. All the other homeless tramps they could track down were questioned. Many of them claimed to have known Bingo, but no one knew anything about his death, and hardly anyone seemed to care. Most of them seemed to be more concerned about their own safety on the streets than the fate of a fellow tramp.

While efforts were being made to find the shadowy figure

spotted leaving Coney Street on the night of Bingo's murder, at the same briefing where Eileen shared the news that they no longer had a suspect, they discussed the surprising identity of the third victim, Mark Routledge, a twenty-seven-year-old music teacher who had lived in Gillygate.

'Everything comes back to Coney Street,' Eileen commented. 'So Mark wasn't a rough sleeper, but he was strangled with the same red fabric as was used on the other two victims.'

'And don't forget he was possibly mistaken for a rough sleeper,' Geraldine added.

Eileen nodded. 'It certainly looks as though we're dealing with one killer.'

'And he's not making himself easy to find,' Ian added.

'Didn't anyone report Mark missing?' Geraldine asked, slightly puzzled. 'He can't have been going into school in the state he was in before he died.'

'Apparently he called in sick,' a constable replied. 'But that's as much as the school secretary knew. She said they were under the impression he had the flu, but she couldn't be sure.'

'So it's not only the homeless who can disappear without anyone noticing,' Geraldine muttered.

'What's that?' Eileen asked.

'Oh, nothing,' Geraldine replied. 'Nothing important.'

33

ANN AND DAVID WERE sitting at the supper table, where he insisted the family ate together every evening. Aimee had disappeared upstairs, having eaten with them in sullen silence, while Ann and David had kept up a semblance of a normal family having dinner together. David was introverted at the best of times and Ann was not feeling chatty, but she had done her best to keep the conversation flowing for Aimee's sake. When she stood up to clear away the plates, David glanced at his watch and announced that he was going into the living room to watch the local news.

'I don't want to miss what's happening,' he added, giving her a sharp glance.

Registering her husband's sudden interest in the local news, a horrible thought occurred to Ann. He had given her no other reason to suppose he might have killed Mark, but as soon as the idea occurred to her, she felt an unnerving suspicion that she could be right. David's behaviour towards her had definitely changed since Mark's death. For no obvious reason he had become very solicitous, and she could think of no other explanation for his concern. He asked her repeatedly if she was all right, which was unusual. The only way he could have realised something was amiss was by knowing about the affair and what had happened to Mark. And if he *had* discovered the affair, the only reason he would have refrained from mentioning it to her would be if he had decided to deal with the situation himself by getting rid of Mark.

It was a wild conjecture, but it was possible that, in an insane bid to save his marriage, her husband had killed her lover. The more she thought about it, the more sense it made. She recalled Mark telling her that he was being stalked. She had been afraid then that David had been following her. He had always been aggressively possessive, refusing to allow her to see any of her friends without him until, one by one, they had stopped calling her. There had never been many of them to begin with. At first, she had not really minded. She had been kept too busy looking after the baby, and tending to her husband's needs, to pay much attention to anything else. Fussy about his food, and fastidious about the house being kept spotless, David expected her to cook and clean every day. For a long time she had not realised his behaviour was peculiar, and she had puzzled over how the married women among her few friends had been the last to stop calling her, as though their husbands had accepted they would want to go out with their girlfriends.

The thought that David could be responsible for Mark's death made her feel physically sick. Her legs trembled. She would never see her lover again, never feel the touch of his lips or his hands on her body, never watch his muscles move as he undressed and walked towards her to take her in his arms. If it was David's fault, she would avenge Mark's death. In that moment she realised she hated him with a passion that threatened to overwhelm her, as though all her love for Mark had been channelled into loathing for David. Alone in the kitchen she leaned against the sink while the room seemed to spin around her and she struggled to control her rage. She breathed deeply and tried to think clearly. She told herself she must be overreacting, allowing her emotions to overrule her sense. There was no evidence that David was guilty. Yet she knew, deep down, that she was right to suspect him.

If it was impossible to accept the loss of the man she loved, it was going to be unbearable living with the man she suspected of killing him. Convinced she would never manage to control her emotions, she was aware that she had to get away from her husband, but she understood David would never let her leave him. It was not in his nature to let her go. In his mind she was a possession, like a dog, only more useful and more malleable. Despite his authority over just about every aspect of her life, he could not control her affections any more than he could dominate her thoughts. She went into the living room, determined to confront David and learn the truth, but her resolve weakened when he turned his head and saw her watching him.

'Look at this,' he said, with a strange smile on his face, 'there's been another murder in York. That makes three in quick succession. Someone's been busy.'

He sounded almost pleased about it.

'What do they know about the killer?' she asked. 'You know you should be careful. If there's a killer on the streets, you could be his next victim.'

'Oh, I won't be,' he replied airily.

Hardly able to breathe, she asked him how he knew. She could hardly believe her voice sounded normal, when David had as good as confessed to being the murderer.

'Because whoever this nutter is, he's only killing homeless people,' he replied.'

'What about me? Could I be in danger?'

'No, I told you, he's only killing tramps. He won't touch you.'

'How can you be so sure?'

He gave a careless shrug. 'Of course, I can't be sure. No one can. But he's only killed men so far, so it seems likely he'll carry on doing just that. The police have no idea who he is,' he added.

She saw his reflection in the window, and his grinning face seemed to confirm her suspicion. Returning to the kitchen, she studied the report in the newspaper David had brought home. The police believed one man was responsible for three murders in York, his victims all strangled with a red tie. She ran upstairs and checked the tie rail in his wardrobe. All his ties were neatly displayed in a row. All but one. The red tie she had given him for Christmas was missing. Reaching for her phone, she hesitated. If the police knew that Mark had been her lover, and David's red tie had disappeared from his wardrobe, they would certainly investigate her accusation. But David was clever, and there might be insufficient evidence linking him to the crime scenes. He would have made sure he would be able to wriggle out of the charges, and her revenge would be incomplete. She put her phone back in her pocket and went back downstairs.

Stacking the dishwasher, she listened to the muffled sounds of the news on the television in the next room and realised that, whatever happened, ending her marriage would not be enough. Her shock hardened into a cold anger against the man who had ruined her life, snatching away her one chance of finding happiness. She would never love anyone as she had loved Mark. Such a loss could never be redressed. In that moment she knew what she was going to do. It was going to take careful thought and she would have to carry out her plans away from the house.

Finishing the clearing up, she joined David in the living room and was just in time to catch a television presenter chairing a discussion between a police spokeswoman and the manager of a homeless shelter.

'That makes two homeless people murdered in recent weeks on the streets of York, and there has been a third murder in the area,' the manager was saying. 'The point is, if these victims weren't homeless and disenfranchised, their deaths would be getting a lot more attention in the media and more public money would be spent on bringing their murderer to justice.'

'More attention than air time for a discussion on television gives them?' the policewoman asked wryly.

'This,' the manager waved a hand irritably in the air, 'this is all just propaganda. What we want to know is, what is being done to find this killer? If innocent householders were being murdered on the streets, there would be uproar.'

'Uproar? How would that help?' the policewoman enquired quietly. She sounded slightly bored.

'The question is surely: what is being done to make our streets safe again?' the broadcaster asked.

The police spokeswoman sat forward and reeled off a list of actions that the police were taking. More police on the beat, helplines open for anyone who had noticed anything suspicious, an unnamed person helping them, and several leads being followed up.

'Oh, yes, someone's helping you with your enquiries, and there are various leads being followed up,' the manager of the homeless shelter said, with a visible sneer. 'But that's exactly my point. It's all just talk, isn't it? The question we want answered is, what exactly is being done and, more importantly, when are you going to make an arrest?'

'We are doing everything possible to reach a swift conclusion, and I can assure you that every murder victim is given the same attention, regardless of his or her background. The victims' identities and circumstances make no difference to our procedures. We investigate any death with equal determination and rigour.'

There was more along those lines, with the two interviewees batting away each other's claims and protests and refusing to change their own views. After a while, Ann stopped listening. What worried her was that the police were increasing their presence on the streets. That was going to make her plan more difficult to carry out. Difficult, but not impossible. She would just have to be extra cautious. But nothing she had heard weakened her resolve. Somehow she was going to find a way to kill her husband and, to make her revenge perfect, David would look in her eyes as he was dying, and he would understand how much she had loved Mark.

34

THE VAN WAS REGISTERED to a man called Don Wilson who lived not far from York St John University in Portland Street, just around the corner from the car park where the van had been found. He had reported it stolen on Tuesday morning, just a matter of hours after the estimated time of death of the victim.

'He could be an innocent victim of theft, but it's equally possible he killed Mark, made a poor stab at disguising the registration number of the van, dumped it in the car park and then reported the van stolen in an attempt to distance himself from the contents of the van.'

'I still don't understand why he only tried to disguise one number plate,' Naomi said.

'Presumably he'd covered both plates, but one of the false ones fell off,' Eileen replied.

'Either that or he was a complete moron,' Ariadne said.

'Or both,' Ian added. 'The false one on the back was only stuck on with gaffer tape.'

'Not much of an attempt to conceal it from us,' Eileen commented.

Geraldine had been listening to the discussion. Now she spoke up. 'It seems as though whoever left the van there didn't care if we traced the owner. Surely that bears out the owner's claim that it was stolen?'

'With the specific intention of disposing of a body,' Eileen agreed. 'Well, let's speak to the owner and see what he has to say for himself, bearing in mind that he could be hoping to trick us into believing he's innocent. Remember, he didn't report the van missing until the day after Mark was killed.'

Geraldine and Ian went to the address where the van was registered, and Don himself opened the door.

'Yes? What do you want?'

The two detectives introduced themselves and his face brightened.

'Are you here about my van? What's happened? Has it been found?'

'We've located your missing vehicle,' Geraldine said.

'So when can I have it back? Only I've not been able to work –'

'I'm sorry, but we can't release it just yet.'

'What do you mean? It's mine. I've got the logbook and everything, and it's insured. I can show you the certificate. Look, I know it's a rusty old heap, but it's how I earn my living. I couldn't even get an old bike with what the insurance company's offering to pay out. I know the tyres are a bit bald, but I'm on it. In fact, I was about to take it along to the tyre and exhaust centre when it was stolen. But I'll get on to replacing them as soon as I get it back. So, where do I collect it?'

'I'm afraid you can't have it back just yet,' Ian said.

'Why not?'

'It's being examined,' Geraldine said.

With a detective inspector and a detective sergeant telling him he could not have his van back, it was understandable that the owner of the van began to look nervous.

'What for? I told you, I'm going to get it fixed. Listen, do me a favour, it's just an old van. So the tyres are a bit bald. I know that. I'm not denying it, am I? If there's a fine, I'll just have to take it on the chin, but it hardly seems fair when I'm willing to sort it out. I want to get it done up. I mean, it's not as if it's unsafe –'

'I'm afraid this is more serious than a few bald tyres,' Ian interrupted him.

'What do you mean? Is it the suspension? If it is, then –'

'Your van is being held in a criminal investigation,' Geraldine told him.

'What do you mean, a criminal investigation? It's not a crime to have a few bald tyres and –'

'We'd like you to accompany us to the police station. We need to ask you a few questions,' Ian said.

'What questions? What are you talking about?'

'Come along, Don,' Geraldine said gently. 'We only want to ask you a few questions. It won't help you if you resist.'

'Resist? Who said anything about resisting? You're putting words in my mouth.'

Still grumbling, Don went with them to the police station. Although Geraldine was almost convinced their suspect was innocent of murder, she agreed it was possible they had just apprehended a serial killer. Ian was more optimistic about the chances they had solved the case.

'If you'd killed someone and wanted to dump the body in your old van, wouldn't you say it had been stolen?'

Eileen decided Don should initially be charged with obstruction, at least until they heard what he had to say. She hoped nerves would help to loosen his tongue. But Don seemed genuinely aghast at the charge, and insisted he had no idea what they were talking about.

'My van was stolen,' he kept repeating. 'I'm not a criminal. You can't charge me just because my van was stolen. I reported it. I told you I was going to replace all the tyres, only someone nicked it before I could get it to the garage. I've got a crime number.'

He had calmed down a little by the time they were all seated in an interview room with a duty solicitor in attendance.

Ian showed Don a photo.

'Who the fuck is that?' he asked.

'Do you recognise this man?'

'No, I don't. I've never seen him before in my life. I take it he's the one who nicked my van?'

Ian shook his head. 'He was found in your van.'

'Good. I'm glad you got the bastard. I couldn't be more pleased. You've got your thief, and I can have my van back.' He hesitated. 'There is just one small problem.'

'I think it's more than a small problem,' Ian said quietly.

'I seem to have lost my keys. I think I may have left them in the van. But don't worry,' he laughed nervously, 'I'll sort that out. Can I go now?'

Ian grunted. 'You're not going anywhere.' He tapped the photograph on the table. 'This man wasn't driving the van. He was left in it.'

Don frowned. 'Left in it? What does that mean? Was he being transported somewhere? Like illegal people trafficking? But how is that even possible? I was driving my van the day before it was stolen, and you told me it was in York when it was found. It can't have gone far. This is ridiculous.'

'We're not investigating people trafficking,' Ian replied solemnly. 'We're investigating a murder. Now, I want you to think very carefully before you answer. Have you seen this man before?'

Don had gone pale. 'A murder? What do you mean? What are you talking about?'

'We're talking about the murder of this man,' Geraldine said, pointing to Mark's photo.

'But what's that got to do with me?' Don asked. His expression altered suddenly. 'The victim... you said he was left in my van? What? Are you telling me there was a body? In my van?'

Geraldine was convinced his shock was genuine, but Ian was not so sure. They discussed the interview with the other members of the team once they had finished questioning Don.

Eileen agreed with Ian. 'He would deny it, wouldn't he?'

'There was no sign the van had been broken into,' Ian pointed out, 'and Don told us he hasn't got the keys, even though he told the insurance company he had left the van locked.'

'So he's asking us to believe he lost his keys after he locked the van for the night, and it was stolen?' Ariadne asked.

'And however clumsy his attempt was to conceal the registration number, he did try to hide it,' Ian concluded.

Eileen nodded briskly. 'Charge him.'

Geraldine understood why Eileen might think that, but she had an uneasy feeling about the accusation.

'What if he's not guilty?' she asked.

'Then we're back where we started, only with one more victim,' Eileen replied. 'No one's happy about this, Geraldine, and it may well turn out that Don Wilson isn't our man, but the likelihood is that he's guilty, so until he can prove otherwise, we're not letting him walk out of here.'

Geraldine nodded, satisfied that the investigation had to continue, at least until Don's guilt could be confirmed. But she was concerned that after Tommy and Jasper, now Don had been arrested, and the case against all three had been incomplete. She had to follow the orders of her superior officers, but it was frustrating to find herself powerless to influence the decisions of the detective chief inspector who appeared to be settling for the easiest option again.

'Is everything OK?' Ariadne asked her, seeing Geraldine scowling at her screen.

Geraldine grunted. 'Everything's fine.'

'Well, I'd hate to see you on a day when it was all going horribly wrong,' Ariadne replied with a grin.

Geraldine did not respond.

35

AT NINE O'CLOCK THE next morning, Geraldine arrived at the school where the third victim had worked, and waited half an hour for a fleeting and pointless meeting with the headmaster who was able to confirm only that Mark had been employed in the establishment as a peripatetic guitar teacher.

'Of course I know all the full-time staff personally,' he explained, 'but I only meet the peripatetics at their initial interview, after which I don't really see them unless any problems arise. They're not required to attend academic staff meetings, and the music block isn't part of the administration corridor, or even the main teaching block. It's on the far side of the campus, beyond the science labs and art studio. This young man didn't have any problems as far as I was aware, so there was never any call for him to come and see me once he'd been appointed. So I'm sorry I can't help you any more than to say that he seemed a pleasant young man. Our head of music will have seen him regularly and will be able to tell you more. I've alerted him to your visit and he's waiting for you in the music block. The school secretary will escort you there. I thought you might like to see where Mark worked.'

The school secretary was similarly unable to tell Geraldine much about Mark. The head of the music department on the other hand was visibly upset, and eager to help.

'Mark was a gifted teacher,' he said, sounding almost tearful. 'He'd only been with us for a couple of years, but he was well liked by his pupils. He's a great loss to the department. He was so young. It's terrible, what's happened. Just terrible. I still can't believe it.'

But for all his dismay, the teacher was unable to help Geraldine. According to him, Mark had been reliable and pleasant to work with.

'There was no problem with him. He was always in on time and he got on well with the kids.'

'What about the rest of the staff?'

'What about them?'

'Did he get on with his colleagues?'

The head of music more or less reiterated what the headmaster had said, about the peripatetic teachers not spending much time with the rest of the staff.

'They just come in and see their pupils, eat in the staff dining room if they're here at lunchtime, and leave. They're not really part of the permanent set-up here. They work on the periphery.'

'But you saw him regularly, didn't you?'

'Yes. Although he was off sick for the week before we were told what had happened to him.'

'Off sick?'

'Yes, he was in on the Monday, the week before he was killed, and he seemed fine. But he called on the Wednesday morning to say he had flu. He sounded terrible.'

'Did you speak to him?'

'Yes, he called the department.'

'And are you sure it was Mark who called you?'

The head of music frowned. 'It was his mobile. I have all the peripatetic staff in my list of contacts so I can see who's calling. But I couldn't swear it was Mark speaking. He said he had lost his voice and honestly he could barely talk. He sounded awful.'

'So it could have been him, but it could equally have been someone else calling from his phone?'

The music teacher shrugged. 'I guess so,' he agreed miserably.

'But how was I to know? I mean, there was no reason to suspect it wasn't him.'

'And I suppose he had your number stored, as "head" or "school" or something similar so someone else could have identified which number to call, if they wanted to make sure no one noticed he was missing for a while,' Geraldine said, speaking more to herself than to Mark's colleague.

'Yes, I suppose so. If he was on the regular staff, questions might have been raised sooner, because other teachers would have needed to cover his lessons and the head would have wanted to know how long he was likely to be off. But the peripatetic teachers work one to one, and if they miss lessons they're expected to make thcm up, if possible, but no one else is involved.'

There was nothing else the music teacher could tell her that moved the investigation forward, so Geraldine thanked him and left.

Back at the police station, Geraldine wrote up her notes before going to the cantccn for a quick lunch. Ian was already there but she ignored him. She was fond of him, but he distracted her and she wanted to be alone to think about the case. Although she did not think there was a sound reason for it, Ian's attitude towards her had definitely changed since she had joined him in York, and he seemed almost hostile towards her. Thinking about Ian more than their relationship warranted, she concluded that he had become distant towards her since he had started divorce proceedings against his wife. But his marital difficulties were no concern of hers. Losing his friendship was more painful for her than he could possibly realise, given his ignorance of her growing affection for him. More than ever, she realised that she had overestimated the strength of their friendship, and she wished she had never agreed to join him in York. It was an uncomfortable regret.

Geraldine was shaken out of her reverie by a voice calling her.

Looking up she saw Ian standing beside her table.

'Sorry,' she replied, without inviting him to join her. 'I was miles away. What was that you said?'

For the first time in a while she watched his smile spread from his lips to his blue eyes, which had lately been looking sad.

'I was just wondering if I could join you.'

She could hardly refuse. She was less than thrilled when Naomi turned up and sat down next to Ian without asking.

'So, it's looking like you were right about Jasper all along,' Ian remarked, slightly ungraciously. 'Geraldine Steel's instincts hit the mark again.'

Geraldine shrugged. 'It was just the spitting that didn't seem logical.'

Naomi raised her eyebrows. 'You can't assume the behaviour of someone who goes around killing people is going to make sense.'

'We have to assume that or we're just casting around in the dark.'

'We have forensic evidence,' Naomi pointed out. 'That's the only reliable information we have. Anything else is just speculation. Anyway, we've got him now, haven't we? And if you ask me, it's obvious Don's the killer. It was his van, wasn't it? So now it's just a matter of finding the proof. I think we've done a great job.' She smiled at Ian.

Geraldine refrained from pointing out that, just a moment before, Naomi had said that forensic evidence was the only information they could rely on.

'Why do you think he did it?' Geraldine asked.

Naomi shrugged. 'Who cares? He's obviously insane.'

'Not everything that seems obvious is necessarily true,' Geraldine said gently. 'We need to have more than that. We can't produce convenient theories and then look for the proof to support them. We have to start with evidence.'

She was irritated when Ian agreed with Naomi. 'It had to be

the owner of the van,' he said. 'Otherwise how do you explain his conveniently losing the key?'

'Perhaps he left the key in the ignition, and that's how the killer was able to drive it away. And then he might well have lied about leaving his key in the van so he could claim on the insurance. They wouldn't pay up if he admitted he'd left the key in the ignition, would they? That seems to make sense.'

She stood up, and left them sitting together. She thought Ian looked forlorn as he watched her leave, but that had nothing to do with her. She had given up hoping he might regard her as anything more than a useful member of his team. When she glanced over her shoulder he was no longer watching her. He had turned to Naomi and they were laughing together. It seemed a long time since he had laughed with her.

That evening, with an unaccustomed feeling of loneliness, she called Celia.

'Geraldine, lovely to hear from you,' Celia said. 'I can't chat now, we're going out this evening. A work do for Sebastian. If you lived nearer, you could have come round to babysit,' she added, with only a touch of bitterness.

She had come to terms with Geraldine moving so far away from Kent, where she had lived near her sister before moving away to London, but Celia could not resist making the occasional barbed comment when the occasion presented itself. Celia thought Geraldine had chosen to move even further away, but that was not the whole truth. Geraldine had been given a stark choice when she had been demoted from her post in London: relocate to York or leave the force altogether. Somehow Celia had gathered that something had gone wrong in her sister's professional life, but she had generously refrained from challenging Geraldine about her demotion from detective inspector to detective sergeant, merely raising her eyebrows in an interrogative expression which Geraldine had ignored.

One day Geraldine would tell her adopted sister what had

happened, but it was complicated because Celia did not know that Geraldine had discovered the existence of a birth twin. At first Geraldine had kept quiet about Helena because she had not wanted to upset Celia while she was pregnant. Now so much time had elapsed since the momentous discovery, Geraldine did not feel she could easily share what she had been keeping from Celia. If she confessed her secret now, Celia might never feel able to trust her again. So Geraldine remained silent about Helena, and with every passing week the truth became more difficult to share.

After tidying her already tidy living room and emptying her dishwasher, she put some dinner in the oven and switched on the television. There was nothing worth watching. She hesitated to open a bottle of wine. She was trying to cut down on her drinking so she put the kettle on and settled down to read a book, but her thoughts kept wandering. Somehow she was convinced they had not yet found the killer and, as long as he remained at liberty, there was a danger he would strike again.

36

HATRED GREW INSIDE ANN like a monstrous embryo, but she had to control her impatience until she had worked out how she was going to kill her husband without being caught. Other than her own impatience there was no immediate reason to hurry; her revenge could wait for as long as it took to devise a foolproof plan. Still, given that she had unlimited access to him, it should not be too difficult for her to come up with a way of getting rid of him. Her main worry was that David might die of natural causes before she had a chance to exact her vengeance on him. She desperately wanted her husband to know that in killing her lover, he had sealed his own fate at the hands of the woman he loved. It was the only way she could live with the knowledge of what had happened to Mark. Every time she saw David, she wanted to tear at him with her bare hands, and feel her nails dig into his flesh, scratching until she drew blood. Never before had she experienced a feeling as strong as this. Even her love for Mark paled into a dim memory beside the power of her hatred for David. She gloried in the assurance that she was going to kill him. And all the time he remained oblivious to her feelings, as he had always been.

'Are you feeling all right?' he asked her one night, when she rejected his advances in bed.

She did not tell him that the thought of his body touching hers made her feel physically sick, or that such a betrayal of Mark was unthinkable. Instead, she told him she was fine. It was true, because there was nothing physically wrong with her.

'I've got a headache, that's all.'

The next time she made that excuse, David suggested she go to the doctor.

'I'm sure it's nothing,' she replied. 'I just need to get my eyes tested, or something.'

'Go and see the doctor,' he insisted. 'I know it's probably nothing, but you can't be too careful with your health.'

She promised she would book an appointment. 'But stop hassling me about it.'

'I'm not hassling you,' he answered. 'I can't help worrying about you if you're not feeling well.'

She turned her back on him, mumbling that she was tired and wanted to get to sleep. After that she lay perfectly still with her eyes closed, trying to work out how to kill him. In any murder case, those nearest to the victim were always top of the list of suspects, especially when money was involved. As it happened, David's death would not leave her particularly well off although she would inherit the house. She knew where he kept his documents and made a point of checking the details of his personal circumstances. It was as well she did, because he had a small pension fund that specifically excluded suicide. That was annoying. It would have been relatively simple to fake her husband's suicide, but she would be stupid to forfeit a tidy little pension from the insurance company by acting rashly. Having decided that the best option would be to fake his suicide, she needed to rethink her plans.

She would have expected that killing her own husband would be easy but the more she thought about it, the more she realised that was not the case. When she stopped to consider what she was planning, her whole mindset felt unreal and she could not believe she was really contemplating committing murder. But then she remembered that David had killed Mark, and she knew that prison was too good for her husband. He had to die, and it had to be at her hand. Only the thought of her revenge kept her from falling apart. She needed to witness the shocked expression on David's face when he realised she was killing him. Mark was dead, and someone had to pay for taking him from her.

Whatever happened, she had to avoid the police coming along and asking too many questions, so the next best plan, after suicide, was to make David's death look like an accident. The trouble was, an accident was not necessarily going to prove fatal. If she pushed him down the stairs, for example, and he survived, the game would be up. He would make sure she never had a second chance. She could try to damage his brakes, but the police were bound to discover someone had tampered with them. She had no illusions that she would be clever enough to escape detection if there was a full-scale murder enquiry, with forensic examination of the body and all the evidence.

There was no point in lying to the police and telling them David had been ill, because a medical examination would easily disprove that, and then everyone would know she had lied. But it was imperative the police believed either that his death was an accident, or that he had died from natural causes.

She could try and read up about different poisons but she would have to be discreet. Researching poisons on the internet at any time before her husband was poisoned would be a bit of a giveaway. The only other possibility she could think of was to hire a hitman, but she had no money of her own. Even if she could persuade David to give her however many thousands of pounds it would cost to have him killed, there would be evidence that she had spent a lot of money, and questions would be asked.

She seemed to have reached an impasse, when she had a brainwave.

'You're looking a bit more cheerful,' David said to her that evening as she served dinner.

She nodded, hesitating. If she admitted she was feeling better, she might be expected to resume her conjugal duties. But she supposed she could put up with his attentions, knowing it would not be for much longer.

'Yes, I'm feeling a bit better,' she replied and he smiled.

'That's a relief,' he said. 'I was beginning to worry about you.'

She returned his smile without answering; he was right to be worried about her.

37

A SEARCH TEAM WERE going through Mark's flat. Interested in seeing where he had lived, Geraldine went along to see how they were getting on. The rooms he had rented were located above a shop in Gillygate. The staircase leading up to it was poorly lit and dingy, but the interior of the flat was clean and neat. She took a quick look around. It did not take long as the flat was small and compact, comprising one square living room, a single bedroom, a kitchenette and a bathroom. The rooms were a curious combination of slovenliness and cleanliness, with a pile of soiled laundry on the floor of the bathroom, and a kitchen sink full of dirty dishes, while the carpets looked as though they had been recently hoovered, and there were no cobwebs, and no sign of dust anywhere.

'Either he was obsessed with cleaning, or else someone has tried to remove their prints from all the surfaces,' a scene of crime officer replied when she commented on the state of the flat.

'Or he had a cleaner who came in once a week,' she muttered.

It looked to her as though he might have been leaving the laundry and the washing-up for someone else to do.

'We found this under the sofa,' another scene of crime officer told her when she went into the living room.

He held up an evidence bag containing a bright pink bra.

'And there was women's hair in the plug hole in the bathroom, from more than one source,' he added, with a grin. 'By the looks of it he was seeing several women here, at least three, from what we've found so far. And who knows if there were more? He was a busy boy.'

Geraldine nodded curtly. 'Send off whatever you find for analysis and keep searching.'

'Yes, Sergeant.'

There was nothing to suggest the women Mark had been seeing had anything to do with his death, but there might be a lead somewhere in the evidence they had found in his flat. Leaving the search team to continue their work, Geraldine went to see Mark's doctor.

'He rarely came here,' the GP admitted. 'I can't say I knew him personally, but he saw a couple of my colleagues when he had the flu, and other ailments relatively minor in a healthy young man. I'm afraid I have no explanation for why he had been starving himself before he was killed. Certainly there's nothing in his history to point to any mental instability or depression. That's not to say there wasn't anything,' he added, covering himself. 'When it comes to illnesses like depression, we only know what patients choose to tell us.'

Thoughtfully, Geraldine returned to the school where Mark had worked. A stream of pupils were leaving and she threaded her way through the noisy throng as quickly as she could, hoping the head of music had not yet left for the day. He was in his office and greeted her with a worried smile.

'Any news on who did it?' he asked.

Geraldine was struck by how awkward members of the public felt when talking about the dead. She and her colleagues were accustomed to the language of death and spoke about it as openly as they would talk about the weather, but other people talked about murder in the vaguest of terms.

'Did Mark ever mention any personal problems?' she asked.

The teacher shook his head. 'Quite the contrary. I'd say he seemed very happy with his personal life. He didn't talk about it in any detail, but I know he had a girlfriend. Possibly more than one. And as far as I know he was on good terms with his family. He visited his parents at Christmas and over the summer, and he seemed to quite like them, so I don't think there were any problems there. I certainly wasn't aware that anything out of school was bothering him.'

'What about in school?'

'No, he was fine. He seemed to like teaching here. I never heard him complain anyway.'

'What about his mental state? Did he show any signs of depression?'

'If he was suffering from depression, I knew nothing about it. Nothing at all. He was regular in his attendance here, kept his records up to date and, well, he seemed perfectly sound in every way possible, really.' He pulled a face. 'It's terrible, what happened to him. He was the most unlikely victim, if anyone can be an unlikely victim of murder. I mean, I'd be astonished if this was anything other than a tragic case of being in the wrong place at the wrong time. I don't know what else to say. If he *was* unstable, we didn't see any evidence of it here. He always seemed cheery enough, without being over the top, you know. I mean, he wasn't one of those over-excited happy blokes who make you think he must have his darker moments.'

The teacher glanced at his watch. Remembering that the school day had finished, Geraldine thanked him and left.

'Do you think he was killed by one of the women he was seeing?' Ian asked.

He and Geraldine were discussing what they had discovered that day with a group of their colleagues while they waited for Eileen to arrive for a briefing.

'It's possible,' Geraldine said. 'But I don't think we can draw any conclusions from what we've found so far.'

'Anything's possible,' Naomi said. 'He could have been killed by a jealous lover.'

'You mean a crime of passion?' Ariadne shook her head. 'It

LEIGH RUSSELL

seems to have been a bit too carefully planned for that.'

'Passion can be a slow burner,' Ian replied.

He looked at Geraldine as he spoke and she dropped her eyes, hoping he had not guessed how she felt about him. They had been friends for a long time and she would hate to jeopardise their relationship by betraying her true feelings for him. The discussion was interrupted by Eileen's arrival.

They all agreed with her view that Mark's murder had not been a one-off crime, sparked by jealousy, but part of a campaign targeting rough sleepers. Mark had been mistaken for a tramp after somehow starving himself and getting so filthy that he looked homeless.

'That's a shame,' Naomi said. 'A crime of passion is much more understandable. And how unlucky for Mark that he was mistaken for a rough sleeper when he had a perfectly good job and somewhere to live.'

'Whichever way you look at it, there's something odd about all this,' Geraldine said.

Eileen agreed with her. 'Mark was killed with the same kind of noose used on the two rough sleepers, but he was a very different kind of victim. Why was he targeted?'

'That's obvious. The killer made a mistake,' Ariadne said. 'He thought Mark was homeless.'

Eileen nodded. 'That's what we thought too, to begin with, before the victim was identified.'

'We thought that because Mark was dehydrated, starving and dirty when he died,' Geraldine said. 'But the real question is: why had he got himself in such a bad way? He wasn't suffering from depression, as far as we've been able to ascertain.'

'I think you might be making more of this than it warrants,' Eileen replied. 'He must have had mental problems. Just because there was nothing recorded in his medical history, doesn't mean he didn't have issues.'

Geraldine nodded. 'You could be right, but it's odd that there's no record anywhere of any issues like that, and everyone we've spoken to seems to think he was perfectly stable.'

'No one knows you have mental issues if you don't choose to share them,' Eileen replied, echoing what the doctor had told Geraldine.

Although Geraldine knew her colleagues were making sense, it was hard to believe that a man could be so close to the edge that he would leave home and forget to eat and drink, while no one who knew him had the faintest suspicion that he was ill or in trouble, and there was no evidence of drugs in his system. Her sister had not sat around covered in her own excrement, even after she had been using heroin for years.

'I just can't believe he would deteriorate to such an extent in so short a time,' she said.

'So what are you suggesting?' Eileen asked.

Geraldine shook her head. 'Only that we need to give this a lot more thought before we go jumping to conclusions.'

Eileen gave her a worried frown. 'Very well,' she replied. 'Why don't you go away and think about it?'

38

WHILE MARK'S FLAT WAS being searched, the van his body had been recovered from was also being examined. So far, as well as finding Don's fingerprints, hair and skin cells, the forensic team had found evidence of a woman whose fingerprints and hair matched those found in his flat. As well as fingerprints on the door and a few long hairs on the back of the passenger seat, a tissue with lipstick on it had been picked up off the floor, as had a woman's earring. In addition to the evidence of a female passenger, several other sets of fingerprints had been detected. Most were unidentifiable, but one set matched the prints of a man called Guy Sampson who had been convicted of shoplifting seven years earlier. He was easily traced and was now working as a mechanic at a local motor repair workshop.

Geraldine was sent straight to the garage to question him. His fingerprints on the van meant he was a potential suspect, even though there was nothing else to link him to the case. The manager of the workshop wiped his hands on a rag blackened with oil and grease before leading her into the small makeshift office. Without mentioning Guy's name, Geraldine enquired about the van and he checked their records and found that the van had been brought in there for an MOT three weeks prior to the murder. When she asked to see the certificate, the manager gave her a filthy look. For a moment she thought he was going to refuse, but he handed it over and she saw the test had been carried out by Guy Sampson. With no trace of his prints or DNA in the interior of the van or anywhere on the body or carpet,

Geraldine had to accept this was probably a false lead and on balance decided not to stop to question Guy. If any other evidence turned up that pointed to him, the police had his address. In the meantime, if he did have something to hide it was best to avoid alerting him to the fact that the police might be interested in him in relation to a murder investigation.

'Thank you,' she said to the manager. 'That's been very helpful.'

'He was told quite clearly that his tyres needed replacing,' the manager said.

His belligerence had evaporated now that she was preparing to leave but he still looked anxious, clearly under the impression that she had been sent to query why a certificate had been given to a vehicle that blatantly should have failed its MOT. Geraldine did not disabuse him but left him to stew, hoping her visit would deter them from giving out dodgy MOT certificates in future. Just to be sure, she made a quick call to the traffic department and alerted them to what was going on at the garage.

Meanwhile the carpet had been sent off for forensic examination. They had no clue yet where it had come from, but it looked like the end of a roll, and was a common enough brown colour. The pile had been analysed but although it was possible to be fairly sure where it had been manufactured, there was no way of establishing where it had been bought. A few threads from other carpets found on the surface had probably been there since the carpet left the warehouse or shop it came from. They had been unable to find any of Don's prints or DNA on the carpet itself, although they were all over the van. The absence of evidence was not conclusive, but it was frustrating to find nothing that could definitely pin the murder on the suspect.

Leaving the garage, Geraldine set off to speak to Don's girlfriend. Jessica worked in a picture framing shop that sold all sorts of prints and greetings cards, as well as original artwork by local artists. A sample of her shoulder length blond hair had been taken from the flat and matched with the ones found in the van. She was a short dumpy woman, with a face that would have been beautiful had it not been scored by a scar that ran from below her left eye, across her rounded cheek, down to her chin. The scar itself was not unsightly, but it pulled her eye out of shape which gave her whole face a slightly grotesque twist when she smiled.

'What's happening to Don?' she demanded the moment Geraldine introduced herself.

She sounded angry, but Geraldine could tell she was frightened.

'Don needs your help,' she replied. 'Can you remember where he was on these dates?'

She showed the woman a list of the dates when the three murders had been committed. Jessica was vague about where Don had been on the night of the first murder.

'He was at home with me, I suppose,' she said. 'That's where we always are at night. We might have been in the pub for the evening, I don't know, do I? I don't keep a record in my head of everywhere we go.'

'And what about Saturday night?'

'Last Saturday?'

'Yes.'

Jessica screwed up her face and her scar puckered. 'We were in Leeds, weren't we? Didn't Don tell you?'

Surprised, Geraldine kept her face impassive. 'In Leeds? What time did you get home?'

'We got back about midday on Sunday. We stayed there overnight. It was a birthday bash for Don's cousin. We spent the night at their place.'

'Do you have any witnesses who can confirm where you were?'

'Are you joking? Only about twenty people who were at the pub, and Don's cousin and his wife. We stayed there because we knew it was going to be a late one and we thought it might be an all-nighter.'

'Did you drive there?'

She shook her head. 'We got the train.' She paused. 'Don only uses the van for local deliveries. He doesn't like to take it far.'

Geraldine nodded. Given the state of the van, she could understand why.

She reported back to Eileen who arranged for local constables to question Don's cousin and his wife, who were both able to corroborate Jessica's story. With nothing to link Don to the bodies and confirmation that he had been in Leeds on the night of the second murder, it seemed that once again the wrong man had been arrested. What no one could understand was why Don had not told them he had been in Leeds that night.

'So, Don – why didn't you tell us?' Ian asked.

Don, a suspect no longer, shrugged. 'I didn't want my cousins to get involved. Now they've been questioned all my family are going to know about it. Being accused of murder isn't the sort of thing you want people to hear about, is it? You know, it's going to be all around the family by now. And Jessica's mother's bound to hear about it. Even though it's not true, some people are only too happy to believe the worst of you, aren't they?'

Remembering how Ian used to complain about his former mother-in-law, Geraldine glanced at her colleague who was sitting at her side, rigid with anger.

'We could charge you with wasting police time,' she said. 'This is a murder investigation. I don't think you appreciate how serious it is.'

'You could have been locked up for weeks, months, while you were withholding the truth from us,' Ian interrupted her. 'For what? So your girlfriend's mother didn't hear that you'd been charged with a crime you didn't commit?'

'Yeah, I can see I was an idiot, but I wasn't thinking clearly.

It's not every day you get banged up on a murder charge. I didn't know what I was doing.'

There were actually tears in eyes.

'Oh, let him go,' Ian said crossly.

'What about my van?'

'You'll get that back when we've finished with it, and not before.'

It was irritating having wasted so much time on another false lead, but there was nothing they could do about it. They just had to keep looking and hope a witness would come forward with new information, or the forensic search would throw up a new lead.

39

NEARLY A WEEK HAD passed since Molly had witnessed the fatal attack on another rough sleeper. During the day she managed to forget about it, preoccupied with the business of surviving: eating, washing, and begging when she could. But huddled in her shop doorway at night, she was afraid to close her eyes in case the killer came for her. There had been no mention of any further attacks, but she knew from talking to the rough sleepers at the breakfast centre that the old man was the second recent victim. She tried to banish the image of the killer from her mind, telling herself the memory would fade in time. But when she went along for her free breakfast on Friday morning, she found the hall buzzing with chatter about another death. No one was sure who the victim was. All they knew was that there had been another murder on the streets of York the previous night.

'It was Andy got himself killed,' a stout woman announced. She folded her thick arms and glared around, as though daring someone to challenge her. 'Serves him right. He was a tosser.'

'Bullshit,' a man replied. 'I saw Andy this morning, as alive as you or me. I asked him if he was coming to breakfast and he said he'd already eaten somewhere else.'

'Yeah, he told me he breakfasted at the Hilton this morning,' a woman said.

'I heard it was the Marriott,' another voice piped up.

Although the discussion was good natured, it was clear that they were all edgy and the conversation soon moved on to the topic that was uppermost in everyone's mind.

'I don't know about you, but I'm going to put my name down for a room in Fishergate as soon as I've finished here,' one of the men said.

There was a murmur of agreement.

'Fat chance of getting in,' someone else chipped in. 'They'll be inundated.'

'True, they can't take us all.'

'Well, I'm not sleeping on the streets again until all this has blown over,' the stout woman said.

'Blown over?'

'Until they've caught the killer and put him behind bars where he belongs.'

'Prison's too good for him.'

'So which hotel are you planning on staying at then, Bess?'

The woman shrugged her ample shoulders. 'It's back to sofa surfing for me. It's starting to get cold anyway.'

'That's all right if you've got friends who'll put you up,' one of the men said.

Molly did not join in the chatter. She felt as though a net was closing around her. When she had finished her breakfast she left, still keeping quiet about what she had seen. Walking back towards Coney Street, she bumped into Rose.

'You OK?' she asked.

Rose's face looked pale and grey, and she seemed to have difficulty focusing on what Molly was saying. 'Yeah, yeah. I'm good. You?'

'Can I ask you something?'

Rose nodded, her eyes staring past Molly's shoulder.

'What would you do if you knew something?'

'What?' Rose laughed, rocking unsteadily on her skinny legs. 'I don't know anything.'

'No, that's not what I meant. What I mean is, what would you do if you knew something about the killer?'

Rose drew back in alarm. 'It's not you, is it?' When she tried to speak quickly, her speech became slurred to the point of incoherence.

'Don't be stupid.'

'It started when you turned up.'

'Listen, Rose, it's not me. That's a stupid thing to say. But the thing is, I may know something about it.'

Rose's eyes were focused on Molly now and she spoke in a hushed tone. 'Do you know who did it?'

'I don't know who it was, but I saw him.'

Carefully, Molly described what she had seen.

'Holy shit!'

'Do you think I should I go to the police and tell them what I saw?'

Rose nodded and then, without a word, she turned and walked away.

'Wait,' Molly called after her. 'Don't tell anyone what I said.'

She was not too worried; the chances of Rose remembering what she had just heard were remote. Having shared her secret with her new friend, Molly decided to tell the police as well. With so many rough sleepers being murdered, she could no longer remain silent. She nearly lost her nerve when she stepped off the bus outside the police station in Fulford Road, but she could not afford to spend money on a second bus fare. If she did not go in now, she never would. She owed it to the poor old man who had been killed, and to all the rough sleepers she had met, to tell the police what she had seen. And she owed it to herself to try and make the streets safe. But she would make sure they did not tell her mother where she was. Taking a deep breath, she marched into the police station.

A sergeant behind the desk looked up at her with a blank kind of smile, as though he had attended a training course on how to look friendly but had not yet mastered the technique.

'Yes?'

'I have – I may have – I think I might have some information about the killer who's killing people,' she babbled, conscious of how stupid she sounded. 'I mean, about the killer.'

After taking her name, the policeman asked her to wait while he called someone.

'Please, take a seat, Miss,' he said.

If he had not spoken so respectfully to her, she would probably have run out of there without a backward glance. As it was, she sat down on one of the chairs that were lined up against a wall. There was no one else there but, even so, she was kept waiting for a long time before someone arrived. At last a tall woman with short dark hair emerged through an internal door and approached her.

'Laura Frost?' the tall policewoman asked.

Molly nodded.

'Hello, Laura. I'm Detective Sergeant Geraldine Steel. The desk sergeant tells me you might have some information for us?'

Molly nodded again, and the detective gave her an encouraging smile. She was not wearing a uniform and carried herself with an air of confidence that suggested she was in a position of authority, so it looked as though the police were taking Molly's claim seriously.

'Please, come with me and you can tell me whatever it is you know. Any information at all could be important.'

'OK.'

There was something reassuring about the woman's composure, and the way she spoke to Molly, as though what she had to say really mattered. Perhaps it did. After all, she had witnessed a murder.

'Before we begin, Laura, can you please tell me how old you are, and where you live?'

'I'm fifteen, that is I'm sixteen. I can't tell you where I live because I haven't got a home and I don't live anywhere. I've got a shop doorway, in Coney Street, and that's where I sleep.'

202

She stared defiantly at the detective, who smiled at her.

'You don't need to feel frightened here,' she said kindly.

'I'm not frightened,' Molly lied.

She had the impression the woman's black eyes could see right through her.

'Would you like someone else to be present while you talk to me?'

'Like who?'

Molly glanced at the female constable standing silently by the door, as though to point out there was already someone else in the room with them.

'Would you like to have someone you know and trust here?'

'No. I don't want anyone else here. And I don't trust anyone.'

'You can trust me, Laura. And we don't have to ask anyone to join us if you don't want to. What was it you came here to tell us?'

'I saw him,' Molly blurted out. 'I was sleeping – well, that is, I wasn't asleep, but I was in one of the alcoves in Nether Hornpot Lane for the night, and I heard a weird noise.' She paused, reliving the experience, and was grateful to the detective for waiting until she was ready to resume her account. 'So I heard this weird noise, like a kind of choking sound. I thought it was an animal or maybe someone was sick. Anyway, I looked out and saw a man squatting down by the old guy who sleeps on a ledge in the opposite wall. He used to sleep there, anyway. The noise went on for a bit, not very long, and before I could do anything to help the old man, the other man got up and left.'

'What happened then?' the detective prompted her after a moment.

'I stayed where I was, because it was all over. But in the morning I saw that the old man was dead.' She hesitated, struck by a sudden fear. 'Am I going to be arrested?'

'What for?'

'Because I didn't tell anyone what happened. I just ran away.

I was so scared. But he was already dead, so it didn't make any difference to him if he waited a bit longer to be found, did it?'

'No,' the sergeant agreed gently, 'it didn't make any difference to him, but we do need to find this killer, and it might have helped if we had reached the crime scene earlier. But no one's going to blame you for running away. You were sensible to leave the site. And it was very brave of you to come and see us now.' She leaned forward slightly. 'Laura, I want you to think very carefully. Can you describe the man you saw?'

Molly nodded. Screwing up her eyes, she told the detective the man had been wearing a grey hoodie.

'He wasn't a rough sleeper,' she added. 'I'm sure of that.'

'What makes you think he wasn't another rough sleeper? Tell me everything you can remember about him.'

Molly told her about the man's smart shoes and his jeans that looked new.

'Did you see anything of his face?'

'Not much.'

'But you did see something? Can you tell me if he was white or black?'

'He was white, and clean shaven, and his eyes looked black. His nose was quite pointy and I think he might have been quite tall and he wasn't fat or thin, really, just normal.' She hesitated. 'Normal in his size, I mean. I don't think it's normal to kill people. That's not what I meant. He turned round but he didn't know I was there,' she added, with a shiver. 'If he'd seen me...'

The detective nodded, suddenly brisk. 'Would you recognise the man if you saw him again?'

'I don't know. Probably, yes, because he had a funny walk.'

The detective's expression did not alter but there was a faint air of excitement about her after Molly mentioned the killer's awkward gait.

'In what way was it funny?'

Molly frowned with the effort of remembering. 'He had – it

was like a limp, but not a limp. Just a funny way of walking. I'd recognise him if I saw him walking. One of his arms kind of waved around more than the other one when he was walking.'

She stood up and tried to show the detective what she meant, and was rewarded with a broad smile.

'Thank you, Laura. That's very helpful. You've been brilliant, and very brave.'

40

THE DETECTIVE ROSE TO her feet. 'Now, you must be hungry. Would you like something to eat?'

Molly nodded, and the detective left her with a female constable while she went to organise some food. It seemed to take a long time but at last she came back with a mug of tea and a plate of chocolate biscuits.

'We can offer you somewhere to stay for the night,' the detective said, as Molly began tucking into the biscuits. 'We can't put you up here, in a cell, of course. Those are reserved for people who have been arrested.' She gave a little laugh. 'But we *can* find you a bed in a hostel for young women, just until tomorrow,' she added quickly, seeing Molly's reaction to her suggestion. 'You'll be able to have a shower there, and wash your hair, and they'll give you supper tonight and a really good breakfast in the morning, and then you can have a chat with them about your future plans.'

'I don't have any plans,' Molly replied crossly. Somehow things were spinning out of control. 'I'm happy as I am. I don't need anyone else to get involved.'

'That's fine then. You can be on your way after breakfast tomorrow. Now, why don't I find out whether you can stay there just for tonight? I think they said they have fish and chips and chocolate pudding on the menu tonight.'

The prospect of fish and chips and chocolate pudding did it.

'OK,' Molly agreed. 'But just until tomorrow.'

The detective smiled again. Suddenly, Molly was afraid she

had been an idiot to trust her. After all, she was a policewoman and trained to lie in such a way that people would believe everything she said. But it was too late to change her mind and, besides, the thought of having a hot shower followed by fish and chips and chocolate pudding was hard to resist. The detective had said she could leave the hostel the next day, so there really was no downside to the arrangement.

The hostel itself was nothing like she had expected. For a start the building looked as though it had been recently decorated. There were a lot of windows and stairs, and although the door was locked behind them there were no bars in sight. The other girls did not seem to mind being there. It reminded Molly of school. She was not keen on the woman in charge who was bossy, and spent ages telling her all the things she was not allowed to do. Molly recalled Rose telling her that the hostels were no better than prisons.

'I don't smoke, and I don't drink,' she fibbed at last in the hope that the litany would come to an end, and the woman's stern expression relaxed a little.

Molly showered and changed into clean clothes that were too big for her, before she was given fish and chips followed by chocolate pudding. She hardly spoke to the other girls staying at the hostel, and they ignored her, but that did not bother Molly because she was only staying there for one night. In a narrow bed in a narrow room, she slept well for the first time since she had left home. She had forgotten how comfortable it was to sleep on a mattress with a pillow under her head instead of a bundle of old newspapers, not smelling of piss and sweat, and above all not listening out for trouble.

When Molly finished breakfast the following morning, one of the key workers summoned her to the manager's office for a chat about what she wanted to do. Molly followed her submissively enough, although she had already told the detective and anyone who would listen to her at the hostel that she wanted to return to the anonymity of the streets. But no sooner had she taken a seat with the manager than the office door opened and she was shocked to see her mother walk in.

'What's she doing here?'

'The police officer you spoke to yesterday identified you and told us how we could contact your mother. You don't have to go back with her, but you should at least listen to what your mother has to say. After that, if you still decide not to go home, we can make arrangements for you. Either way, we have a duty of care towards you as a minor, which means we can't just let you go back on the streets.'

Molly frowned. 'I don't understand. I told the police my name's Laura so how did they find out who I am?'

'Yes, you gave your mother's name. Fortunately for you, the detective you spoke to realised what had happened.'

'But how did she find out who I am?'

'She checked with the Missing Persons Bureau, and she must have looked through photos of missing girls until she recognised you.' The manager paused. 'She must have spent hours looking through thousands of pictures. She sent us your details and we called your mother. Now, the least you can do is listen to her.'

Molly turned to her mother. 'I don't understand. Why did you report me missing?'

'Because you vanished, and I thought something must have happened to you. I've been looking everywhere for you.'

'You needn't have bothered. It was a big mistake, you coming here. I don't ever want to see you again. I'm leaving right now.'

'Wait,' her mother cried out.

'You can't just walk out of here,' the hostel manager said.

'You can't stop me. And I'm definitely not going home with her.' She turned to her mother. 'It's not my home any more, is it?'

Thinking about Rose, she wondered how many rough sleepers would be pleased to have a mother who wanted to put a roof over their heads.

'At least talk to me,' her mother begged, with tears in her eyes. 'Baz has gone.'

'How come?'

'I threw him out after you left.'

Molly was not sure whether to believe her.

'Once I knew it was going to be him or you, it had to be you. I've been searching everywhere for you. I went to the police. I went to the papers, and the Missing Persons Bureau. I want you to come home, Molly.'

Molly interrupted her mother. 'Did you get rid of him because of his son?'

Her mother shook her head, but she looked uneasy. 'All that matters is that they've gone, both of them. It'll be just you and me again, like before.'

Molly nodded. 'OK. But he's not coming back. The minute he walks through the door –'

Her mother interrupted her in tears. 'He threw me down the stairs. He could have killed me. I was wrong about him, about both of them. I promise you, things are going to be different from now on. But I need you to come home. Please. I can't do this on my own.'

'If he comes back, I'm off.'

'He won't come back. He can't. I've applied for an injunction which means they won't be allowed anywhere near me again. If they do, they could be arrested. I mean it, Molly. I'm serious about this. The only person I care about is you. Come home with me.'

Molly was crying as well now. 'OK, mum. Let's go home. But you'd better not be bullshitting me.'

As she followed her mother out of the room, Molly wondered what would have happened to her if the dark-haired detective had not searched for her photo in the records of the Missing Persons Bureau. She wished she had thanked her for her help, but it was too late now.

41

LEEDS POLICE OFFICERS WERE sent to the pub where Jessica claimed she and Don had been drinking on Saturday night. The landlord recognised Don's photograph as one of a party who had been carousing there on Saturday evening. If any additional proof were needed that Don had been there, he had paid for a round on his credit card. The intelligence unit in Leeds identified two people recorded on the pub security camera leaving the premises with Don and his group around midnight. After that, Don would conceivably have had time to get back to York and kill the old tramp, Alf, and return to Leeds early the next morning in time to catch his train home again mid-morning, in order to give himself an alibi for the time of the murder in York in the early hours of Sunday morning.

But although a team scrutinising CCTV from the station spotted Don and Jessica arriving in Leeds on Saturday afternoon and leaving again late Sunday morning, there was no sign of Don returning to York and going back to Leeds again between those times. When the local police questioned Don's cousin and his wife, both corroborated Jessica's story, as did another friend of theirs from London who had also stayed the night with Don's cousin. This last witness alleged never to have met Don before the night of the party, and she seemed credible as well as independent.

'So it seems Don's in the clear, and we're left with three bodies and no suspect,' Eileen announced to the team who had assembled in the Major Incident Room. 'Three bodies,' she repeated, as though anyone present could have missed that. 'And we're back to the drawing board.'

'It's better to discover we had the wrong suspect, than waste time building a case that was bound to collapse,' Geraldine said.

There was a muted murmur of consent.

'Now we can devote all our resources to looking for the real –'

Before she could complete her sentence, Eileen interrupted her sharply. 'Thank you, Sergeant.'

Not for the first time, Geraldine hoped Eileen wasn't going to berate the team for their lack of results. It was hardly the fault of the officers working on the case if they had no leads. If anything, they needed to be encouraged, not reprimanded. For once, the detective chief inspector seemed resigned to the situation and the team dispersed to their various tasks without being subjected to one of her lectures. Given the tension between them, Geraldine felt a flutter of dismay when she was summoned to the detective chief inspector's office. Eileen was evidently disappointed when they had to release Don, but it was hardly fair to vent her feelings on Geraldine.

'You wanted to see me?' she asked as she entered the detective chief inspector's office.

Eileen nodded. 'Come in and pull up a chair.'

Geraldine did.

'I just wanted to throw a few ideas around. To be frank with you, I'm struggling. I haven't said anything about this to anyone – and this is in confidence – but my brother's going through a rocky divorce and I'm afraid I may have taken my eye off the ball.' Eileen heaved a sigh. 'I know my family situation has got nothing to do with work, but he's staying with me which makes it difficult to ignore what's going on. He's in pieces. He keeps me up half the night wanting to talk about it, and it's not as if there's anything I can do.'

Geraldine could feel the tension in her shoulders relax as she realised she was not in trouble with her senior officer.

'You're an experienced officer,' Eileen went on more briskly. 'I wonder what you make of this mess, only it seems to me every time we have a suspect, by the time we work out we've got the wrong man, there's been another murder.'

'It's early days,' Geraldine began, but Eileen interrupted her.

'Yes, yes, I know, spare me the platitudes, please. Don't tell me it's unreasonable to expect the answer to drop into our laps. Believe me, I'm well aware of that. But the Powers that Be are putting pressure on us to put a stop to this killing. We've had so many resources thrown at us, we could start an army. Three victims. The media are going insane about the "Tramp Murders!" It's all over the national press, and questions are being asked.'

Geraldine thought she understood Eileen's drift, but she wanted to make sure.

'Questions are being asked?' she repeated.

'Yes, yes, questions,' Eileen snapped. 'Questions about the team, and about my competence.'

Uncertain exactly what Eileen was asking for, Geraldine remained silent.

'Do I take it by your silence that you agree I'm not up to the job?'

'No, absolutely not. That wasn't in my mind at all. We've been investigating the first death for less than a month, the second death was only a week ago, and the third victim was killed just three days ago. He's barely cold. They can't expect miracles.'

'No one's looking for a miracle – except me, perhaps. But we seem to be getting no closer to a resolution. What if we never find him?'

Geraldine felt a flicker of anxiety, seeing the fear in her superior officer's eyes. Now, more than ever, they could not afford to lose their focus even for a moment.

'We just have to keep going and it will all work out,' she

replied, trying to sound confident. 'And with so many officers following up so many different threads, it's just a matter of time before something comes up. You have some good officers working the case. I've never known Ian to fail. It's almost inevitable that we'll find this killer –'

'Almost,' Eileen cut in sharply. 'That's not good enough, is it?'

'I'm a hundred per cent certain that we'll find him,' Geraldine fibbed, correcting herself. 'What I was going to say was, it's almost inevitable we'll find him *soon*. He can't be that clever or he wouldn't have used the same noose on more than one of his victims. He's clearly got some kind of emotional reason for using the same noose, because it's not rational or sensible. Once we nail him for one, we'll have him for all of them. We just have to keep going and we'll get him. That's all we can do.'

Eileen sighed. 'I wish I had your self-assurance. You should be sitting here, Geraldine, not me. You've got the mental resilience to see this through.'

Geraldine was too startled to respond.

'I know you've had your problems, but you've never let that stop you powering on through, doing your job. You'd make a better DCI than me. No, don't, please.' Eileen held up her hand as Geraldine began to remonstrate. 'I've been watching you more closely than you may have realised, and I misjudged you. When you first arrived here, I found you – oh, I don't know – distant, and I thought because you'd been demoted, you resented being a sergeant again, and that was making you difficult to work with. Ian thought the same for a while. But I see now that the colleague I mistook for an insolent subordinate was actually a strong-minded woman voicing an opinion. I should never have tried to silence you.'

'You didn't silence me,' Geraldine retorted, although it was true that Eileen had undermined her confidence.

'No, I didn't,' Eileen agreed, smiling. 'So, Geraldine, where do we go from here?'

'We keep going,' Geraldine replied, and Eileen sighed.

Geraldine returned to her desk.

'You look cheerful,' Ariadne greeted her.

'You never really know what someone else is thinking or feeling,' Geraldine replied.

'OK,' Ariadne said, with a faint smile. 'Now I'm intrigued. What are you talking about?'

'Nothing. That is, it's too complicated to explain. Come on, let's finish off here and go for a drink.'

'I'm up for that. No point in letting all this get us down.'

'No, we'll get him, sooner or later. Wherever that demented scum is hiding, we'll find him.'

'I'll certainly drink to that!' Ariadne agreed, returning Geraldine's smile.

When she reached home, Geraldine mulled over what Eileen had told her. It had been uncomfortable hearing that Ian had been critical of her, because he had always been her most ardent supporter at work. For the first time she acknowledged that she had probably been unpleasantly surly when she had arrived in York. Facing a painful transition from detective inspector to detective sergeant, she had allowed herself to wallow in her personal feelings of disappointment instead of focusing on building relationships with her new colleagues. A detective who failed to work as a member of a team was simply not up to the job, and her lapse in focus had been unprofessional as well as immature. It could have been chance, but she suspected Eileen had held back from criticising her until she judged Geraldine was ready to accept the censure. Eileen may have erred in underestimating her sergeant, but Geraldine had been equally guilty of misjudging her superior officer.

42

THREE MEN HAD BEEN killed, which gave her a perfect opportunity, but she had to act quickly before the culprit was caught. Ann took to reading everything she could find in the papers, she watched the news and even kept the radio on all day while David was out. It was imperative she learned everything she could about the recent 'Tramp Murders', as one local paper was calling them. While she carried out her research, a plan was forming in her mind. If she could pull it off, not only would she avenge Mark's death and be free of her hated husband, but she would avoid any possible risk of detection. It was a brilliant plan, in theory, but it was going to take some doing. She was not worried about the police finding her DNA on the body of her husband, but she would have to be extremely careful with certain elements of her plan.

As soon as David left for the office on Monday morning, she set to work on her first task. Putting on her sunglasses and a reversible mac she had bought for the purpose, she left the house with a bulging rucksack slung over her shoulder. The weather was still mild so David would not miss his winter coat yet; by the time the cold weather came, he would no longer be needing a coat of any kind. She smiled to herself. It was a pity her husband would not be around to appreciate just how clever she was. On her way to the city centre she stopped in a deserted side street to turn her coat inside out and tie a silk scarf around her head. She had decided against driving or taking the bus into town, in case her trip was recorded along the way. Cameras were everywhere these days. But with her simple disguise, she was confident no one would be able to trace her journey afterwards even if they wanted to. In the meantime, a woman in a beige mac and navy scarf was hardly likely to attract attention.

Reaching the minster, she sauntered around the city centre pretending to window shop. The streets were crowded with pedestrians, even on a Monday morning. Apart from local residents, groups of tourists clogged the Shambles and queued outside Betty's Tea Shop. Ann did not mind. It was easy to feel anonymous in the crowds. But it did mean she would need to be discreet when she began, because she could not risk being seen or overheard. She was beginning to despair of ever finding what she was looking for when at last she spotted a likely target, an old tramp shuffling along Coney Street. He looked very frail, barely able to put one foot in front of the other. Ann followed him to a quiet side street before approaching him.

'Excuse me,' she said, forcing a smile.

'Eh?' The old man leered suspiciously at her. 'What?'

It was difficult to tell quite how old he was. His face was wan and gaunt beneath his beard and moustache, and his hands shook. In addition to that, he seemed hard of hearing, and every time someone else walked by she had to lower her voice, so it took a while to explain what she wanted.

'You want my coat?' he asked at last, scowling.

'Yes, but please keep your voice down. We don't want everyone to know, do we? Or they might all want this.' She pulled David's coat out of her rucksack. 'Look at this. How would you like to swap your coat for this lovely warm one? You'll be pleased with it in the winter. You don't want to freeze to death, do you? It's almost new. It – it belonged to my husband but he's – he died and I want his coat to go to someone who needs it, someone who will appreciate it. '

For a second the old man hesitated, squinting his suspicion, before snatching at the coat she was holding. Surprised by the unexpectedly swift movement, she almost let go.

'I need yours in exchange,' she said, clinging to the sleeve of David's coat. 'It's – it's for a play. Amateur dramatics, you know? We're putting on a play. It's *Waiting for Godot.*'

That last comment was inspired, but the tramp did not seem to be listening. He had probably never heard of the play she mentioned anyway.

'You want my coat?' he asked her.

'Yes, in exchange for this one.'

For a moment she was afraid he was going to accept David's coat and refuse to give her his own in return, but he was hardly going to run off with it. He was so shaky, he could barely walk. If necessary she could try to take it off him, but that would be difficult while he was still wearing it. No one passing by had taken any notice of her, but a tussle with the tramp was bound to attract attention.

'Please,' she hissed. 'Don't make this difficult.'

Frowning, the old man shuffled out of his filthy coat and dropped it on the ground. Then he retreated with David's coat over his arm. When he was out of reach, he stopped to slip his arms into the sleeves of his new coat. It hung loosely on his thin frame and the hem dragged on the ground.

'It could have been made for you,' Ann mumbled.

With a smirk, the old man turned and scurried away, as though afraid she might change her mind. Trembling with success, Ann shoved her foul-smelling prize in her rucksack and hurried home to hide the old coat before anyone could see it. Her walk home seemed to take forever, but at last she was back in her bedroom where she stashed her rucksack inside a suitcase at the bottom of her wardrobe. With the first part of her plan accomplished, all that remained was to decide exactly how she was going to kill David.

43

'THE BIN'S FULL,' ANN said.

These days she was always complaining about something.

'Do you really want me to empty it now?' he asked. 'It's dark outside.'

'Why don't you just go and do it and then it's done.'

'I was about to go to bed.'

'You know they come and collect the rubbish tomorrow. Are you really going to remember to do it in the morning before you leave for work?

'Oh all right, all right. Stop nagging.' He stood up. 'I'm going, I'm going.'

His wife was right, it was probably just as well to deal with it straight away. If he left the rubbish out the back and forgot to move it in the morning, he would never hear the end of it. Muttering under his breath, he went out through the kitchen door and dragged the first of the two bins along the narrow path that ran along the side of the house. Depositing that bin, he went back for the second one. As he was making his way along the narrow unlit path at the side of the house, he thought he heard a footstep. He stopped abruptly and listened but all was quiet.

'Who's there?'

No one answered.

'Is someone there?'

He turned round and tried to peer through the darkness but he could not see any sign of movement. He carried on, feeling his way with the flat of his hand, the bricks on the side of the house rough against his palm. Still listening, he tried to walk without making a sound; his footsteps reached him like faint whispers. Around him everything looked black. He had almost reached the end of the house when he tripped. By twisting sideways and throwing himself towards the house, he managed to hit his shoulder on the wall and break his fall. He thought he heard someone panting as his head hit the stone path with a sickening thud. If his shoulder had not hit the wall first, he would probably have suffered a serious head injury. The thought made him shiver.

For a few seconds he lay on the ground, trembling with shock. Before he could gather himself and try to stand up, he was aware of something winding around his neck and pulling tight. He tried to cry out for help but, gasping for breath, he could barely utter a sound. His last thought before he blacked out was that he must have got himself caught up in something when he fell.

It was still dark when David regained consciousness. Hauling himself upright and leaning against the wall for support, he staggered back into the house. Ann was standing in the kitchen, fiddling with what looked like a dirty old coat.

'What's that?' he croaked.

She spun round, eyes wide, and screamed. 'What – what happened to you?' she asked at last, seeming to recover from her initial shock at seeing him. 'You look dreadful. What happened out there?'

'I don't know.'

He tried to shake his head, and had to grab on to the worktop as the room spun around him.

'Your head's bleeding,' she said.

'I fell over.'

'Sit down.' She pushed a chair towards him. 'I'll make you a cup of tea.'

'I don't want tea.'

But she was already filling the kettle. Closing his eyes, he listened to her messing about with cups and spoons.

'I put some cold water in it so it's not too hot,' she said a moment later. 'And sugar.'

'You know I don't take sugar.'

'Drink it. Sweet tea is good for shock.' She paused. 'Did you lock the back door when you came in?'

It was typical of her to worry about the back door being secure when he had just tripped and nearly killed himself. After locking the door, she pulled up a chair and sat down opposite him.

'Now, what happened out there? Did you trip or are you ill? Talk to me, David.'

'Something tripped me up,' he said. 'And then I felt something round my neck...'

'What do you mean: you felt something round your neck?'

'It felt as though someone was trying to strangle me,' he said.

Ann laughed but she looked worried. 'You've been listening to too many stories in the news,' she said. 'Weren't those tramps supposed to have been strangled? Perhaps the killer saw you and thought you were a tramp.'

She gave another nervous laugh.

'This isn't funny,' he said. 'I'm telling you, I think someone attacked me out there. We should call the police. Whoever it was might still be out there. And if they are, the police might catch whoever it is.'

'Are you sure you saw someone?'

'No, I didn't see anyone.'

'You probably got caught up in that ivy. I told you to get rid of it. It's growing right across the path. You sit still and drink that tea. It'll help you to relax.'

His head was aching where he had hit it, but his thoughts were clearing. Ann was right. There was ivy growing up the wall along the side of the house. He could conceivably have caught himself in that when he tripped over, and somehow got entangled in a creeper. It was idiotic to suspect that someone had been lurking in the side passage, waiting to attack him.

'Come on, drink up,' she said. 'You'll feel better for it.'

Too tired to argue with her, he took a gulp.

'This tea tastes a bit funny.'

She gave a worried smile. 'I put a drop of whisky in it to help you relax.'

He was not sure that was a good idea but she was so insistent he drank it all, although it tasted strangely bitter and nothing like tea, or whisky.

'Would you like another cup?'

He shook his head which did not hurt quite so badly as before, although he felt dizzy now. 'You're right, it must have been the ivy,' he said.

He allowed her to persuade him to stay indoors and go to bed. She even promised to put the other bin out herself in the morning.

'I think you've had enough of those bins for one night,' she said. 'And in future you'd better put them out the front while it's still light. Either that, or we need to get a light fitted along the side passage. It's no wonder you fell over, really. It's an accident waiting to happen along there.'

'You're right. I could have really hurt myself. I was lucky to get away with just a bump on the head.'

She nodded. 'You're right. It could have been a lot worse. You were lucky.' She hesitated. 'You look grey. Are you feeling all right?'

He frowned. He was not too sure. What with the shock, and the knock on his head, and the whisky, he was feeling quite befuddled.

'I think we ought to get you to the hospital so they can have a look at it,' she went on. 'Come on, let's get you in the car. Here, you can put this on.'

She held out the old coat he had noticed earlier. It looked filthy.

'What the hell is that?'

'It's an old coat I came across in the loft.'

'In the loft? What was it doing there?'

'I don't know. If it's not yours the people who lived here before us must have left it there. I was going to throw it out.'

'Well, it's not mine.'

'You might as well put it on for now. It's cold outside, and you don't want to ruin a decent coat by bleeding on it.'

He frowned, but he really was feeling very drowsy. Too weak to resist, he allowed her to push his arms into the sleeves.

'It smells funny,' he objected.

'That's because you had a knock on the head,' she replied. 'Come on, we need to get you to the hospital.'

'I'm fine,' he said, but when he tried to stand up he would have fallen over if she had not been there to support him.

'Thank you,' he said, 'you're a wonderful wife. You know that, don't you?'

She did not answer.

44

THE SUN HAD BARELY risen and it was raining and chilly when
Geraldine arrived at the scene. Ian was already there.

'Why are we always turfed out of bed?' he grumbled. 'Can't
people ever be killed at a more sociable time of day?'

Geraldine had already been up for a couple of hours, working,
but she did not have the energy to answer. In any case, Ian's
question had been rhetorical. Obviously, people were more likely
to be murdered at a time when there were not many people around
to see what was happening. The sight they had been summoned
to witness in that bleak dreary landscape was depressing. Only
the day before, Eileen had been bemoaning the fact that two
more people had been killed since the investigation opened, and
now they were staring at a fourth body, this one abandoned on
the grass verge along the Tadcaster Road, presumably dumped
there overnight after he had been strangled. Like Mark, this
man was wearing a dirty old coat over a smart set of clothes.

'Oh Jesus, not another one,' a scene of crime officer muttered
as he jumped down from the forensic van. 'Where's the tent? It's
starting to piss it down. We can't have him lying there like that
with God knows what vital evidence being washed away.'

'We're expecting it any minute.'

The road had been closed, and the team were setting up. A
few moments later the forensic tent arrived and was erected with
impressive speed and efficiency. Even so, the ground around the
body was sodden and the body itself had been affected, and no
doubt contaminated, by the rain.

Geraldine watched the SOCOs working in silence for a while.

'You're shivering,' Ian said to her suddenly, with a solicitous glance. 'Are you all right?'

She nodded.

It had taken a while for the traffic division to set up temporary lights but vehicles were now moving slowly in alternate directions along the opposite carriageway.

'A lot of people are going to be late for work today,' Ian said.

At last everything was in place and they were able to approach and view the body which was being photographed before it was removed to the mortuary. The van was already there, waiting for its dead passenger.

'I'll go and see the post mortem this time, if you like,' Ian said.

'Are you sure?'

He nodded. 'Yes. You look cold.'

She smiled. 'It's bloody freezing here. But I don't think Jonah's going to be working outside. Are you sure you wouldn't prefer me to do it?' She lowered her voice. 'I know you don't like going there.'

He laughed. 'Compared to dealing with my wife – my soon-to-be-ex-wife, I should say – viewing corpses is like a walk in the park on a sunny day.'

Geraldine was not sure that was an appropriate comparison. Ian's wife was stunningly beautiful and very much alive.

'All right. But I'll come with you,' she said.

The body had been spotted by a member of the public on her way into York to visit her daughter. Geraldine went over to speak to the woman, who was small and dainty, and looked about seventy.

'I was driving past,' she said, visibly trembling with shock. 'I thought someone had collapsed. I didn't realise he'd been run over.'

Geraldine did not point out her mistake. It would be impossible to hide the bad news from the media, but she was not going to be the first to divulge it.

'I thought maybe he needed help,' the woman went on through chattering teeth.

Someone brought her a cup of sweet tea and she sipped at it gratefully.

'So what happened then?' Geraldine prompted her.

'What? Oh, yes. Well, I pulled over. I mean, I know you're not supposed to stop here, are you, but what if he needed help? I mean, in an emergency, the rules can be waived, can't they?'

Geraldine nodded. 'You won't be in trouble for stopping,' she assured the woman. 'You were right to regard this as an emergency. So what, exactly, did you see?'

The woman drew in a breath. 'I saw him. That man. I thought he might have been knocked out so I went to have a closer look – and that's when I realised he wasn't moving. He was just lying there, staring up at the sky.' Her eyes opened wide. 'So I called 999 and they told me to wait here. So then I had to phone my daughter. I was on my way to her house to look after my grandson because her childminder let her down and she's not best pleased, but what was I supposed to do?' She appealed to Geraldine with tears in her eyes.

The woman appeared to be more concerned that she had annoyed her daughter than upset about stumbling on a corpse. After muttering a few platitudes, Geraldine returned to the body. Lying on his side to begin with, the dead man had been turned on to his back prior to being carried over to the mortuary van.

'Was he killed here?' Geraldine asked.

'No,' a SOCO answered. 'He was killed somewhere else and deposited here after rigor had set in. From the position of his limbs, it looks as though he might have been sitting down when he died,' he added.

The doctor arrived, and declared the man dead. 'He was strangled,' he added in an undertone.

The doctor was young, and he looked sleepy, but he instantly grasped the implications of the cause of death. Geraldine glanced over at the woman who had found the body. Too far away to hear their muttered exchange, she was talking to a female police constable, no doubt relating how she had let her daughter down. The doctor delicately pulled the dead man's collar open to reveal a telltale red line around his neck. And that was the moment Geraldine glanced up and recognised a reporter standing a short distance away, phone in hand.

'Who let her past the cordon?' Geraldine hissed.

She dashed towards the reporter who backed away, a resolute expression on her face. Before she had a chance to remonstrate, Geraldine had seized her by the arm and grabbed her phone.

'Police brutality,' the journalist shouted very loudly, looking genuinely shocked.

'If you don't leave this scene immediately, you'll be charged with obstruction.'

'What? Don't be ridiculous.'

'You have no business to be here, contaminating evidence.'

'What evidence?' The other woman's eyes narrowed. 'Is this a crime scene?'

'That's what we're trying to ascertain. Look,' Geraldine went on, lowering her voice in an attempt to sound as though she was sharing confidential information, 'as soon as we know anything, we'll let you know. In fact, if you give me your card I'll contact you myself. But in the meantime, you really shouldn't be here, and you know that as well as anyone.'

'Someone's been run over and you're treating it as a crime scene,' the reporter pointed out, looking shrewdly at Geraldine. 'Evidently there's more going on here than you're letting on. So come on, what are you hiding under that tent?'

'What can be more serious than a hit and run? If this victim doesn't survive, then whoever ran him over will be facing a murder charge,' Geraldine said.

'I don't believe you. That's bullshit.'

'I thought that was your job. Listen, you'll get the details when we make a press statement. Now, how did you get past the cordon without permission?'

'You can't keep people out. This is a public highway.'

'No, this is a potential crime scene and you've entered it without authorisation.'

'All right, I'm going. Give me my phone.'

'You can collect it from the police station tomorrow.'

'What? You can't keep it!'

'I just found it,' Geraldine said. 'How do I know it's yours?' She glared at the reporter. 'You'll need to bring along proof of ownership before we hand it over to you.'

'That's outrageous! You can't steal my phone!'

'I'll be handing it in at the police station where you can reclaim it any time you want, from tomorrow. Unless my senior officers decide to retain it as potential evidence, that is.'

Still complaining vociferously, the reporter left. Geraldine would have the phone checked, but if pictures of the dead man had been taken they would probably already be automatically stored on the cloud where the reporter could access them. It was just one more irritation for the police to deal with. She stood for a moment, watching the reporter leave, before she returned to the doctor.

'Can you tell us any more about the attack?' she asked.

'It was fatal,' he answered, with a wry smile.

45

'THIS VICTIM IS QUITE different from the other three,' Jonah said.

That much was evident just from looking at the cadaver lying on the slab. David Rawson cut a robust figure in death, broad-shouldered, with huge feet. His skin was pale, but somehow he looked as though he should have a florid complexion. Geraldine pictured him as a brash man in life, red-cheeked like a cherub, with a complacent air, a man who had lived well.

'He was in his fifties,' the pathologist went on, 'but of course you know all about him, don't you?'

'We know his background,' Ian answered shortly. 'His name, his address, where he worked, his family circumstances. We know about his life. What we want to know from *you* is how he died. We're not here to do your job for you.'

'He's cheerful today, isn't he?' Jonah said, casting a sly grin at Geraldine. 'Do you have to put up with this all day?'

'Just tell us the worst,' Ian said, smiling an apology.

'Right you are, then. Here goes. Our man here was well nourished, no scar tissue or evidence of operations or illness.'

'His medical history is of no consequence to our investigation,' Ian pointed out, his gruff temper returning. 'He was strangled.'

'There was a small amount of alcohol in his blood,' Jonah continued, ignoring the interruption, 'which could have been whisky, although it's difficult to be sure. The tox report will confirm that. And then there's this.' He pointed to a mark on the side of the dead man's head.

'That doesn't look too bad,' Ian said. 'Was it a fall or was he hit, do you think?'

'It looks like a fall, because look, there's a graze here on the side of his chin, and his shoulder was also bruised. I agree, it doesn't look like much, especially now I've cleaned him up, but it led to a haemorrhage.'

'So what did he die of? Strangulation or a knock to the head?' Ian asked.

'He was strangled, but he would probably have died of internal bleeding anyway, unless he had received fairly urgent medical attention. And there was this.' He pointed to a picture of a stained coat, slightly torn at the bottom. 'He was found in this.'

'We've already seen pictures of it,' Geraldine said. 'We're waiting for results of the forensic tests on it.'

Images of the coat had been displayed at the police station, and discussed at length.

'So he was strangled,' Ian said, returning to the pathologist's work, 'and I suppose you found fragments of red fibres on his neck?'

Jonah shook his head. 'No, this looks like it might have been a different killer. At any rate, the noose was made of some kind of rough rope, something that might be found in any garden centre or the like. If it was the same killer, he didn't use the red fabric this time.'

'The killer might have lost his tie,' Geraldine suggested.

Anything was preferable to concluding that there might be two people busy strangling rough sleepers. Jonah had nothing more to tell them until the results of the tox report were back, so they returned to the police station to type up their reports.

'It seems pretty obvious that this was a clumsy attempt at a copycat killing,' Eileen said when she addressed the team the following morning. 'For some reason the victim wanted to fool people into thinking he was homeless, and the killer must have mistaken him for a genuine rough sleeper. It's the same as happened with Mark. Only this time it looks as though we may be dealing with a different villain, someone who's trying to imitate the Tramp Killer, perhaps in hopes of concealing his own presence in all this.'

'It would be convenient for a second killer to have his crime blamed on someone who was caught for other murders,' Ian agreed.

'That's the trouble with these high-profile cases,' Eileen said. 'Once the media get hold of them, there's always the risk some lunatic will be attracted by the attention and try to get in on the action.'

'Why would this recent victim have deliberately tried to look like a rough sleeper?' Naomi asked.

'I'm guessing –' Eileen hesitated, because everyone knew guessing was a mug's game in their line of work. 'It's possible David wanted to mix with the rough sleepers, because he was out looking for his next victim.'

There was a brief pause while everyone considered the implication of that suggestion.

Naomi spoke up. 'You're saying that David might have killed three men before he was himself murdered? That would certainly give a motive for David's murder.'

'That presupposes that David deliberately disguised himself as homeless,' Geraldine pointed out. 'Are we getting a bit ahead of ourselves with speculating about what happened?'

'Geraldine's right,' Ariadne said. 'It's just as likely the killer made a mistake in attacking David.'

'Or maybe dressed him in a dirty old coat to disguise the fact that the wrong person had been murdered,' Ian said.

'You mean the right person,' Geraldine corrected him.

Everyone turned to look at her.

'Perhaps this killer wanted to get rid of David, so he strangled him and then put him in an old coat to give the impression he was a tramp, so we'd go off on the wrong tack,' Geraldine explained.

'Except that Jonah seemed to think he put the coat on before he was killed,' Ian reminded her.

'So we're back to the same question: why would David want to disguise himself as a rough sleeper, knowing there was a killer targeting them, unless he himself was the killer?' Eileen asked.

'He could have been a one-man vigilante, hoping to smoke out the killer?' someone suggested.

'Or perhaps the killer knew David and persuaded him to put the coat on before killing him?' Geraldine said.

'Why would anyone do that?' Naomi asked. 'I mean, why would he have agreed to put on the filthy old coat?'

'Geraldine could be right,' Ian replied. 'The killer could have been trying to fool us into thinking this was another tramp murder, when in fact it was something very different.'

Geraldine listened uneasily to the conversation. There was too much theorising going on, without enough evidence.

'Surely the point is that we just don't know why David was wearing that coat. Isn't it fairly obvious that there could be any number of reasons?' Geraldine said, but no one responded.

'I wonder where the coat came from?' Ariadne asked.

'It's being examined now, so we should know the answer to that very soon,' Eileen replied. 'If it wasn't the victim's coat, and we manage to find its owner, he might lead us to the killer.'

46

MALCOLM'S COAT CAUSED QUITE a stir at the church breakfast club the next morning. After he had slept in it for one night it still looked as good as new, not even creased. He stretched out his arms, and looked down admiringly at the camel-coloured woollen cloth. The sleeves were too long for him, but he would appreciate them protecting his hands in the cold, and when he lay down it cloaked him like a long blanket. He grinned and twirled on the spot and then regretted his performance because everyone in the queue turned to look at him. It was a smart coat which felt even better than it looked.

'Where did you get that then?' someone asked, looking up from a plate of beans and toast.

'A woman gave it to me,' he told the other rough sleepers who had gathered round to admire his new coat. 'They can't nick me for stealing, can they? Not when she gave it to me.'

'Who was she? Did she have any more?' someone asked, only half joking.

Malcolm shrugged. 'She didn't say who she was, but she swapped this for my old coat!' He held out his arms to display the coat.

'I reckon you got the best of that deal. Who gave it to you?' one of the regulars asked, eyeing the coat enviously.

'I've got to say, you look bloody good in it,' one of the volunteers called out.

'You're the dogs,' another guy agreed, reaching out to touch the coat.

'Watch it,' Malcolm said, taking a step back from the man who was about to feel the fabric. 'Don't get your filthy paws on it. I don't know who gave it to me,' he added. 'It was just some woman. She said it had belonged to her husband and he was dead and she wanted to give it to someone who needed it, someone who would appreciate it.'

If the woman saw him again, she might deny having given it to him, and demand the return of her dead husband's property. She was bound to have thought better of her generosity by now and be wanting the coat back. It was really too smart for a rough sleeper like him, someone who drifted in and out of homeless shelters. He was going to have to keep an eye out for her. If he saw her, he would have to dodge out of sight and wait until she had gone before venturing out again. Whatever anyone else said about it, he was not prepared to surrender the coat without a fight, especially now that winter was approaching. He had only been wearing it for one night, but he had become attached to it and already thought of it as his own.

Uneasy with so much attention directed at him and his coat, he was relieved when the discussion moved on. His coat had offered a brief respite from the murders that had dominated the homeless community's conversation for the past few weeks. Several of the rough sleepers were angry that the media were calling the deaths 'The Tramp Murders', and to make matters worse, some reporters had been less than complimentary about people living on the streets.

'Calling us tramps! Bloody insult, like we're all fucking trash,' one of the women complained to a chorus of assent.

'Like we're all prostitutes,' another woman grumbled.

'Personally, I'm more worried about being murdered than being called a tramp,' one of the men said, prompting another outcry.

Along with the rest of them, Malcolm was increasingly bothered by the news, especially now that yet another victim had just been discovered. One of the men who had come to the church for breakfast had brought a paper with him, featuring a report of the death on the front page. Like the other two recent murder victims, this one appeared to have been a rough sleeper, although none of them recognised him from his photograph in the papers. They all agreed that was puzzling.

'It must be a shit photo,' one of the men said. 'I tell you, I know everyone from around here, and I've never seen him before. I don't recognise him at all.'

'He must have come from somewhere else,' one of the volunteers agreed. 'Unlucky for him he met the killer while he was passing through.'

'Lucky for us though,' one of the women piped up.

Another woman rounded on her. 'That's a horrible thing to say.'

'I only meant we're lucky it wasn't one of us.'

Glancing at the image in the paper, Malcolm scowled and picked it up for a closer look. As he studied it, his frown deepened.

'I've never seen him before, but I recognise that coat,' he muttered.

'What's that?' one of the volunteers asked him.

'That coat, the one the dead man's wearing.'

'What about it? What are you talking about?' another rough sleeper asked.

The volunteer approached Malcolm and addressed him in an undertone. 'Do you know something about this?'

Malcolm shook his head. 'I don't know anything about anything so you can leave me alone, all of you!'

'He's been on the bottle,' someone else said as several of them laughed, not unkindly. 'You know what he gets like when he's had one too many.'

'Bit early in the day for that,' someone commented.

Malcolm was not rambling this time. On the contrary, he was

perfectly lucid, and he was convinced he was right. His old coat had an oily stain down the front that he now recognised on the coat worn by the dead man. By some dreadful coincidence, his old coat had ended up on the latest victim. The woman who had taken it from him had told him it was going to be used in a play, but somehow it had ended up on a dead body. But he was not about to blab about it. He had learned from experience that it was best to avoid any contact with the police. Strangely disturbed by his discovery, he was only half listening to the conversation taking place around him.

'I just hope he never slept in the same doorway as me,' one of the women was saying. 'The last thing I want is for the police to come sniffing around.'

'How would they know, you daft cow?'

'Who are you calling daft? Haven't you heard of DNA? If that stranger so much as sat down where one of us had been sleeping, our DNA would be all over his backside. And if the police have your DNA on their database, you could be in the shit, is all I'm saying. Bloody hell.'

A cold feeling ran down Malcolm's back as he registered the significance of the discussion. His own DNA would be all over that coat. Cursing the woman who had taken it from him, he hurried away from the group still having their breakfast. As he looked for a place to hide, he considered how he was going to avoid the police who were probably already out scouring the streets for him. If they found him they were bound to think he had killed the stiff for his coat. He should have kept his trap shut at the breakfast club. He hoped no one there would talk. He would go along for breakfast the following morning but if there was any sign of the police at the church, or any strangers there, he would scarper before anyone noticed him.

47

WHILE A FAMILY LIAISON officer was being arranged, it fell to Geraldine to break the news of David's death to his wife. She hated this part of her job, dealing with an outpouring of grief from the recently bereaved. It was by far the worst of her duties. At least the dead were beyond suffering. Miserably she made her way to the victim's address. David lived in a well-maintained semi-detached house. After pausing briefly to admire the neat front garden, she rang the bell and the door was opened by a dainty blond woman, almost waif-like in her figure. Her large blue eyes seemed to shine with unshed tears even before she knew the reason for Geraldine's visit. She looked about twenty years younger than David and could have been either his wife or his daughter.

'I'm looking for Ann Rawson,' Geraldine said, after introducing herself.

The young woman's blue eyes widened in surprise. 'Yes, I'm Ann Rawson. What do you want with me? What's this about, please?'

'Is your husband's name David?'

'Yes, David. That's right. Why? Has something happened to him?'

'I'm afraid I have some bad news. You might want to sit down to hear it.'

Ann's hand flew to her open mouth. 'Is it about Aimee? Has she – has something happened to her?'

'No, this isn't about your daughter,' Geraldine replied. She

237

could hardly say it had nothing to do with Aimee when her father had just been murdered. 'May I come in?'

Ann nodded and led the way into a small living room. As they sat down, Geraldine realised that the shiny quality of Ann's eyes had been merely a trick of the light when she was standing on the doorstep. All the same, she was undeniably beautiful in a delicate kind of way.

'I'm afraid something's happened to your husband,' Geraldine said gently.

'My husband? What about him? Is he all right?'

'I'm sorry to tell you this. He's dead.'

Ann immediately dropped her head into her hands, concealing her face. It was frustrating that Geraldine could not observe her expression, but she had to wait until the other woman regained sufficient composure to speak. As far as anyone knew, David's widow had been robbed of her husband by a violent stranger. There was nothing to suggest his wife might have been involved in causing his death. But Geraldine was aware that in a case of murder, the victim's loved ones were inevitably included on the list of suspects, and were only too often proved guilty of murder, or at least to have been complicit in it. Unlikely as it seemed, even this fragile-looking woman could be a killer.

Ann raised a tear-stained face. 'What happened to him?'

'I'm sorry to tell you he was murdered. Are you going to be all right? Is there someone who can come and keep you company?'

Ann's voice trembled. 'My daughter will be home from school soon,' she whispered.

'How old is she?'

'She's fifteen.'

Ann put her head in her hands again, mumbling. 'How am I going to tell her?' She looked up. 'Oh my God, she's only fifteen. How am I going to tell her? What am I supposed to say to her?'

It did not escape Geraldine's notice that the recently widowed woman seemed concerned only about the impact of her husband's death on their teenage daughter. Making a mental note to mention her impression to the family liaison officer, Geraldine asked her again if she was all right and Ann nodded. Geraldine offered to stay and talk to Aimee, but Ann shook her head and said she would speak to her daughter herself. There was nothing more to be gained from questioning the widow so Geraldine left.

Seated at her desk later that afternoon, Geraldine read through a report which had just been sent in by the pathologist. She was slightly frustrated that the information had not arrived before she had gone to the mortuary, as it was often more useful hearing such details from Jonah in person so that she could quiz him about what it all meant. Now she went through the report thoughtfully, several times, trying to read between the lines and imagine what Jonah might have said to her had he been privy to this new information before she had seen him. Not long after she finished reading, her phone rang.

'I'm writing my report now,' Jonah said, 'but I thought you might want to know straight away that the tox report mentions alcohol and diazepam.'

'Yes, I'm reading it right now. I saw that.'

'Well, it looks as though the diazepam was crushed before ingestion as there were particles lodged in the victim's trachea.'

Geraldine thought she grasped his meaning, but wanted to be certain she had understood him correctly.

'What's the significance of that? Spell it out for me, please.'

'The particles hadn't been broken down by digestion, so they must have been ground into powder before he swallowed them. It's unlikely he would have crunched them with his teeth, because that would have tasted disgusting. Of course it's possible. Alternatively, he could have crushed them into powder himself before swallowing them.'

'But equally someone else could have given them to him, powdered and concealed in food or drink?'

'Yes, that's it, exactly.'

'So you're saying David might have been drugged without his knowledge?'

Jonah hesitated. 'I'm saying that's possible.'

'But we don't know if he was drugged by someone else, because he could have crushed the pills himself?'

'Yes, that may have been the case, although the taste would have been very bitter. But the taste could be masked, with sugar for example, so yes, the drug could have been administered by anyone, the victim included.'

'So you're saying anything's possible.' Geraldine sighed. 'I suppose there's no way of finding out who crushed the pills?'

Jonah gave a short laugh. 'I'm not a magician, Geraldine. To establish that, you would need to travel back in time and see what happened. All I can do is report the facts of an assault insofar as I can discover them after the event, and assess the physical consequences that remain. Clever detection of the truth is your job. And good luck with that,' he added as an afterthought.

'Thanks very much. I value your appreciation of the intelligence that goes into *our* efforts.'

'Well, keep me posted, will you?'

'Sure. And please call me any time if you think of anything else.'

'I certainly will. This is a curious case all right, and I have to say I'm intrigued.'

'Well, like I said, if you do think of anything else –'

'Oh, I'm always thinking of something else when you're around,' he laughed. 'If my hands weren't plastered in gore up to the elbows, you wouldn't be safe anywhere near me.'

'Oh, behave yourself,' she replied as she hung up, still laughing at his idiotic banter.

She supposed Jonah needed to make light of his work. Her sister claimed to be genuinely baffled at how Geraldine coped with murder cases. Now Geraldine found herself wondering, in her turn, how Jonah could bear the horrors he had not only to view, but to handle, on a regular basis. Each to his own, she thought. Jonah was intrigued by the physical puzzle of a cadaver and the answers it could provide. What fascinated Geraldine was what went on inside people's heads. So while Jonah might be satisfied with establishing how a victim had been killed, Geraldine only wanted that information to help her discover why that had happened and, most importantly, who had perpetrated the crime.

'So this time the murder looks quite different,' Ian said, when the team had gathered to discuss the case. 'The killer used a different noose, and the victim wasn't a rough sleeper, although he was wearing a dirty old coat over his decent clothes, and he had been drinking alcohol and taking sleeping pills, whether self-administered or not we don't yet know.'

The noose was not conclusive. It was possible the killer had lost his red tie or whatever it was he had been using, and picked up a length of rope instead. But the sleeping pills, that was a new departure.

'It could be the same killer,' Ariadne said. 'The victim was strangled.'

'After knocking himself out,' Geraldine added.

'So let's say he drank alcohol on top of taking sleeping pills, whether knowingly or not we haven't yet established. He might have fallen over as a result, and been found by the killer who decided to finish him off.'

'And the coat?' Ian asked.

It was decided that David's death would be treated as part of the existing case, since David appeared to have been strangled on the street, although, apart from the manner of his death, nothing about it matched the other recent murders.

'He wasn't a rough sleeper,' Naomi said.

'Nor was Mark,' Ian pointed out.

Somehow the case seemed to be growing more confusing by

the day, and new victims were being added to their load on an almost weekly basis.

All that seemed clear was that this looked like a copycat murder. A second murderer had been caught up in the media hype, and had tried to emulate the Tramp Killer, but not very well.

'We've got to do something,' a young constable said.

'Such as?' Eileen asked, sounding slightly peeved, as though the constable was criticising the investigation.

'Is there anything to link the four victims?' Geraldine asked.

'They were all strangled,' a constable replied.

'All we can do for now is keep gathering evidence, widen the net of potential witnesses to question, and wait for the forensic lab to come up with a new lead. They'll find something,' Geraldine said. 'They have to,' she added under her breath.

'Yes, we'll get him,' Eileen echoed Geraldine's show of optimism. 'Our killer's been busy, but he can't keep this up for long without making a mistake. The chances are he'll become cocky, and that will make him careless.'

'But how many more people is he going to kill before that happens?' the constable asked.

Eileen moved on briskly. 'What about the description of the awkward gait of the man Molly saw in Nether Hornpot Lane? Have we got anywhere with that?'

No one answered. They all knew the description might be useful as evidence once they apprehended the killer, but it was impossible to trace an individual from his gait alone. They needed more information.

'He's bound to slip up sooner or later,' Eileen said. She sounded slightly plaintive.

48

ONE OF THE VOLUNTEERS from the church that hosted breakfasts for the homeless phoned the police station to report that one of their regulars had information that might help the police enquiry. He was referred to the team investigating the murders, and Geraldine took the call.

'What sort of information do you have?' she asked, instantly alert.

She did not add that they were desperate for a new lead in an investigation that currently seemed to be going round in circles, with suspect after suspect being released.

'He said he recognised the coat the victim was wearing,' the caller explained.

He described how an old rough sleeper had turned up for breakfast one morning in an expensive new coat which he claimed had been given to him in exchange for his own dirty old mac.

'He saw a picture of his old coat in the paper. It was the one the latest victim was wearing when he was found.'

'Do you think he was telling the truth?' Geraldine asked.

'I don't know, but he must have got his new coat from somewhere. You can ask him about it yourself if you come along to the church tomorrow morning. Malcolm's one of our regulars.'

'Do you know where I can find him before then?'

'No, sorry. He'll be around, dossing in a doorway, God knows where. Your best bet is to come along in the morning. You'll spot him straight away because of his new coat, it's long and fawn and obviously expensive. He might not want to talk to you,' he added. 'I'd appreciate it if you kept quiet about my speaking to you. The rough sleepers feel safe with us. They talk to one another, and if just one of them gets wind of the fact that I talked to you, we'll lose their trust. I shouldn't really have spoken to you at all, only it being a murder investigation, I thought I should pass on what I heard.'

Early the next morning Geraldine went to the church and found a group of rough sleepers gathered around the breakfast table. She was not sure which of the volunteer helpers had called the police station, but it was easy to identify an elderly man wearing a smart new coat. His wizened face was leathery from living outdoors, his straggly hair was in need of a trim, and his long fingernails were black with grime. When she sat beside him and introduced herself he seemed to close in on himself, like a tortoise. Without turning his head away, he refused to meet her eye, and he could have been deaf for all the response her words elicited. It was hardly surprising that he was reluctant to talk to her. Somehow she had to persuade him that she needed him to help her catch the killer who was targeting rough sleepers.

'You could be his next victim,' she muttered earnestly. 'So, is there anything you can tell us that might help us track him down?'

The old man shrugged. 'This was given to me,' he said, whining in outrage. 'You got no right to take it off me. It's mine now.'

The other people at the table were turning to stare at them so Geraldine suggested they move away from the group and talk discreetly in a corner of the room. Grumbling under his breath, the old man heaved himself to his feet, wheezing, and followed her, stumbling as he walked.

'No one wants to take your coat away, but we need to know who gave it to you. Whoever it was might be able to help us find the person who's killing rough sleepers like you.' She lowered her voice and glanced around the room. 'You, or any one of your friends here, could be next. I know you don't want that to happen. So you have to help us find this killer.'

'They're not my friends,' he replied in a voice that was slightly slurred.

'Malcolm, you have to help us.'

As she leaned towards him, Geraldine was not surprised to detect a strong whiff of alcohol on his breath.

'I don't know who it was. And even if I know, I don't have to tell you.'

Sensing his advantage, he looked at her with a sly grin. 'What's in it for me?'

'The knowledge that you're not going to be strangled in your sleep tonight. Withholding information from the police is a serious offence, especially in a murder enquiry.'

He shrugged and turned away.

'All right,' she agreed, showing him a couple of notes. 'That's all you're getting. Now talk, unless you want to accompany me to the police station and be questioned there.'

He reached for the money but she slipped it in her pocket.

'First, you talk to me.'

Scowling, the old man began talking.

'She told me her husband was dead, and she wanted to give me his coat so it would go to someone who needed it. That's all I know. Now, where's my money?'

'She?'

He nodded.

'Are you telling me it was a woman who gave you this coat?'

He grunted in assent.

'Are you sure?' she asked.

The old man turned away from her. 'I may be old but I can still tell the difference between a man and a woman.'

'What was she like?'

'I don't know. Where's my money?'

'Was she young or old?'

'I don't know. I didn't ask her age.'

'Was she tall or short?'

He shook his head. 'She might have been taller than me, she might not. I'm not sure.'

'You must recall something about her,' Geraldine urged him. 'What about her hair? What colour was it?'

'She was wearing a scarf wrapped round her head. I couldn't see her hair.'

It was not clear whether the old man could not remember anything about the woman who had given him his new coat, or whether he simply did not want to tell Geraldine what he knew. However much she tried to persuade him, he remained adamant that he could remember nothing else. When she wanted to take the coat from him, he refused to give it up. Threats made no impression on him. In the end she had to offer him a new coat, and a further cash inducement, before he agreed to give her the coat which was sent straight off for forensic examination. With any luck, some helpful DNA evidence would be recovered from it. They might at least be able to trace whoever else had worn the coat recently.

'I read your account of the coat,' Eileen said to Geraldine at the next briefing.

'And the old rough sleeper was sure it was a woman who gave it to him?' Ian asked.

Geraldine shrugged. 'That's what he said.'

'Did you believe him?'

'I don't know why he would have lied about it, but who knows? He seemed more than a bit addled, although he was sufficiently on the ball to wheedle a new coat out of our chat, as well as a hefty tip for his information.'

'Well, man or woman, we could be dealing with a completely new killer,' Eileen said. 'The victim was strangled but not with the same noose, and so far there's no evidence of the DNA that was found on any of the other bodies. But equally it's possible David was acting as a one-man vigilante trying to find the killer. He tried to disguise himself as a tramp and was, ironically, caught by the killer and became his next victim.' She turned to Ian. 'What's your feeling about it all?'

'Given the absence of any matching evidence, this could be a different killer jumping on the bandwagon,' he suggested.

'Meaning we could have a copycat killer out there looking for rough sleepers?'

Geraldine nodded in agreement. 'For a psychopath wanting to kill, they might be an easy target.'

'But it's also possible this murder had nothing to do with rough sleepers and the earlier deaths at all,' Eileen said, 'except by association. Isn't this more or less the same as happened with Mark, who appeared to be homeless but wasn't?'

'But think about it,' Geraldine replied. 'If you wanted someone dead, and there were a number of murders in the local area, all targeting tramps, you might dress your intended victim in an old coat, strangle him, and hope everyone would think it was just one more rough sleeper being killed, or at least that the victim had been mistaken for a tramp. That way, the killer would escape suspicion.' She paused.

Eileen nodded. 'Yes, you're right. So are you suggesting we need to treat the murders of Mark and David as if they were completely new cases?' She frowned. 'And both their killers had the same idea about disguising their victims by dressing them as tramps?'

'If so, Mark's killer did a more thorough job of it,' Ian said.

'It seems unlikely,' Eileen said.

'But possible,' Geraldine replied.

'How do we explain the fact that three of them were killed with the same red fabric?' Eileen asked.

'We can't, not yet,' Geraldine admitted. 'But I think we should consider the possibility that there's another killer involved, perhaps an accomplice.'

'So what do you suggest we do now?' Eileen asked.

Hiding her gratification that the detective chief inspector was soliciting her opinion, Geraldine replied, 'We just have to do what we always do in a murder investigation.'

Eileen frowned. 'Very well, the first question to ask is: who benefits from David's death?'

'I'm guessing his wife? And Malcolm said a woman gave him his new coat,' Geraldine said. 'Shall I go and speak to Ann Rawson again?'

'That might be a good idea,' Eileen replied.

She gave Geraldine a taut smile. But it was a smile. Geraldine left Eileen's office feeling as though a dark cloud above her had finally drifted away.

49

RETURNING TO DAVID'S HOUSE, Geraldine tried not to be influenced by the wary expression on his widow's face. Once she was convinced that someone was guilty, it was difficult to remain completely impartial and continue to see only the facts. There was really nothing to implicate Ann in her husband's murder, other than the fact that she stood to inherit the house and a small pension. Those might conceivably provide a motive for murder, but she was only in the position in which many women might find themselves if their husbands predeceased them. With a twenty-year age gap between Ann and David that was quite likely to have happened at some point, even if he had died of old age. She was unlikely to have killed him in order to possess their house in her own right.

'Have you found out who did it?' Ann asked, without inviting Geraldine in.

'Not yet, but we're following several leads. How's your daughter?'

Ann flinched and her voice hardened. 'What do you expect? She's fifteen and her father was murdered. She's upstairs and I'd rather you didn't bother her. She had a bad night and she's asleep now. The other policewoman has gone for now, thank goodness, and we really don't want to be disturbed any more than is strictly necessary. We just want to be left alone. So when are you going to end your investigation and let us arrange a funeral? This waiting is unbearable. My daughter needs to say goodbye.'

'Like I said, we're following several leads,' Geraldine repeated phlegmatically. 'We've discovered where the coat your husband was wearing came from.'

For a second, Ann stood perfectly still. 'That's good, isn't it?' she asked, in a brittle voice. 'That must mean you know who killed him.' She hesitated, then frowned in disbelief. 'Are you telling me he was murdered for his coat? That's terrible!'

'That's a possibility,' Geraldine conceded. 'Nothing has yet been proved.'

'But you do have the person who stole David's coat in custody?'

There was an undeniable note of triumph in Ann's voice as she said that but it meant nothing. If she was innocent, she might be justifiably thrilled to know that her husband's killer had been apprehended. Geraldine left without mentioning that Malcolm was still at liberty, or that he had told the police a woman had given him David's coat. Her next visit was to David's work place, in a small office block on the outskirts of the city. It looked dingy from the outside but the interior of the building appeared to have been recently painted, and the furniture was smart and modern. A young receptionist looked up from her screen as Geraldine entered.

'Do you have an appointment?'

Geraldine held up her identity card and explained she was there to speak to David's partner.

'Oh yes, of course, we're expecting you,' the girl replied, with a hesitant smile, as though she wasn't sure whether her usual professional welcome was appropriate in these circumstances. 'We were all devastated by the news,' she added. 'Please, take a seat and I'll see if Geoffrey is free now.'

A moment later she returned and led Geraldine into an office. David's partner looked quite young. He had ginger hair and his face was covered in faint freckles.

'This is terrible,' he greeted her, rising to his feet behind his desk, 'just terrible. If there's anything I can do to assist your investigation, you will get on to me right away, won't you? I've spoken to Ann, his widow, and offered to do whatever I can to make sure she's all right. Do you have any idea who did it?'

'This is slightly delicate,' Geraldine said, as she sat down, 'and I need to know I can speak to you in complete confidence.'

The young man nodded solemnly as he sat down again. 'Of course.'

'Were you close to David?'

'We worked together.'

'I mean, in a personal sense.'

The lawyer frowned. 'We're – we were – we were both married –'

'I didn't mean anything personal in that sense,' Geraldine interrupted, 'I meant, were you friends?'

'Not exactly. David was a lot older than me, and I've got a young family, so I don't really have much spare time. We didn't socialise, but we got on well as partners, speaking professionally.'

'Did he ever confide in you about any problems he might have been having?'

'What kind of problems?'

'I don't know. Anything really.'

'No, I can't say that he did.'

'Do you think he had any enemies?'

'Oh, I see what you mean.' He shook his head. 'If he did, I didn't know about them. David was a quiet sort of bloke. We didn't talk much about anything really, apart from the practice. It's not as if he specialised in criminal law, where he might conceivably have upset a violent client. No one he worked with was likely to want him dead. He dealt with conveyancing. So unless someone had a grudge against him because they weren't able to buy a house, I can't see how this could have anything to do with his work. '

'Did you ever talk about anything outside of his work?'

'We talked mostly about work but we sometimes talked about politics – David was worried about what's happening in the world, well, aren't we all? And he talked about his garden, but we didn't talk about personal matters, and we didn't really talk much at all.'

'Was he unhappy about anything, do you think?'

'Not that I was aware of.'

'What about at home?'

'You mean his daughter?'

'What about his daughter?'

'Well, she's a teenager, you know. He used to worry about her, but that's par for the course, really, isn't it?' He gave a short laugh. 'Our oldest is seven, and David used to tell me I had it all to look forward to!'

'Did he ever mention his wife?'

'Ann? No, not as such. She used to get stressed about Aimee as well, but well, that's teenagers for you, isn't it? I can't say I'm looking forward to it. And it's not going to be easy for Ann now, is it? Poor Aimee. She's only fifteen. That's a hard age to be, and more so now she's lost her father. Seriously, if there's anything at all I can do to help, you must let me know.'

Geraldine tried to probe gently, but she had to conclude that if David had been experiencing any problems with his wife, his business partner knew nothing about them. She questioned the receptionist briefly but she hardly knew David and had only met Ann once. Clearly David had not confided in either of them.

Her next visit was to David's GP who was also not aware of any problems, marital or otherwise. An enquiry into David's financial affairs was similarly unhelpful. His whole life appeared to have been generally steady and uninteresting. There was no obvious reason why anyone might have wanted to kill him and disguise the murder as part of a campaign against the homeless. Back at the police station any suspicions of Ann were quashed by the discovery that David had no life insurance policy and his wife was actually worse off now than she had been while he had been alive and earning. If she was responsible for his death, she had not killed him for his money. Geraldine was relieved she had not told anyone else she had been convinced Ann was guilty of murdering her husband.

50

THE SERGEANT ALLOCATED TO work with Ann and her daughter came to the police station to report back. Ostensibly visiting the bereaved family to offer them support, her job was also to get to know them and gain an impression of how they really felt about David's sudden death. Linda Bennett was a plump woman in her early forties, and very experienced. Her wavy blond hair was obviously dyed and probably permed, framing a smiling face with round cheeks. Looking more like a nursery school teacher than a police officer, she was ideally suited to her role as a family liaison officer.

'The young girl is understandably all over the place,' she said.

'What about the widow?' Geraldine asked and stopped abruptly, afraid she had spoken out of turn.

'Ann's worried about her daughter,' Linda replied, not at all put out at being interrupted and slightly misunderstanding Geraldine's question. 'She's doing everything she can to calm the girl down, but it's not easy. Aimee's clearly volatile, even for a teenager, and according to her school she's been slightly wild recently.'

'Wild in what way?' Eileen asked.

'Oh, nothing untoward, and certainly nothing that suggests any particular disharmony at home. She's fallen in with a crowd of kids who are experimenting with alcohol and other substances. Nothing too hard core, just cannabis from what I can gather, but they are only fifteen and sixteen so the school's getting involved and the parents are concerned. And from the way she conducts herself, I'm pretty sure Aimee's experimenting with boys as well.' She shrugged. 'She's only fifteen, but she's physically very mature and could easily pass for eighteen or more. It's a confusing rebellious age to lose a parent like that. There is something else we need to follow up,' she added. 'According to Aimee, her father played squash every Tuesday evening, although she told me she didn't know who her father played with.'

This revelation was greeted with a suppressed buzz of excitement. According to Ann, both she and David spent every evening together.

'And that's not all,' Linda went on. 'Aimee told me both her parents went out on Tuesdays, but not together.'

Eileen nodded. 'How many squash courts are there in York?'

'I'm on it,' Geraldine replied.

Remembering her gut feeling about Ann, she was keen to investigate anything that might point to a schism within the family, however small, one chink in the wall that could bring the whole edifice tumbling down. But all she said was that she would follow up Aimee's statement, and try to track down anyone David might have spent time with.

'Presumably he's not been playing for a while, or Ann would have known about it,' Ariadne said.

Geraldine nodded. 'Let's just find out about these squash games before we dismiss what Aimee said,' she replied. 'Or before we start to draw conclusions,' she added under her breath.

'What's that?' Ariadne asked.

'Nothing. Just thinking aloud.'

The third sports club that Geraldine contacted confirmed David was a member who played a regular weekly squash game. She drove straight there to find out more.

'And you're sure he played here regularly?' she asked the manager. She was irritated that she had been kept waiting for half an hour by the manager who was in his early twenties, and cocky.

'Sure, I've got the attendance record right here,' he replied, nodding casually at his screen. 'I'll tell you whatever you want to know, as long as it doesn't break any confidentiality.'

'Can you let me have a printout of that?'

'No, I'm not prepared to share our records. You have heard of GDPR?'

'I don't think you understand,' Geraldine replied. 'I need a printout of all your records, showing dates and times of attendance, so we can see who was here at the same time as David Rawson.'

'No, I'm sorry, that won't be possible. It's against our rules.'

'I'm not interested in your rules,' Geraldine replied. 'Now please let me have the records I'm asking for.'

'I've already told you I can't allow –'

Finally Geraldine lost her patience. 'If you're not willing to hand over the information we need, then the police will contact your head office to advise them that your club is closed with immediate effect, while we take charge of your records.' She pulled out her phone. 'A team of uniformed officers will be here in a few minutes to evacuate the club.'

The manager gaped. 'You can't expect us to close. The weekend's our busiest –'

'We not only have the power to take any steps necessary when investigating a serious crime, but I must warn you that you're about to be charged, personally, with obstructing the police in the course of a murder enquiry, a charge that carries a custodial sentence. This is wasting police time as well as yours.'

Keeping her own expression impassive, it gave Geraldine some satisfaction to see the self-important young club manager's eyes widen in alarm.

'OK, OK,' he babbled, 'wait, wait here, wait here, just let me call head office and then tell me what to do. I don't want to obstruct you. I was just trying to protect our customers' privacy.' He grabbed his phone and began talking very fast. 'No, no, she's here, she's here right now, and she's threatening to shut us down if I don't co-operate. Yes, yes, of course this is genuine.'

With the manager's help, Geraldine established that David had been visiting the sports club every Tuesday for at least the past three years. Having obtained the contact details for his sports partner, she left. David's squash partner was a man called Norman Gregory, who worked in the same building as him, only for a different company on a different floor. Geraldine went straight back there and found Norman at his desk. The encounter was brief but interesting. Norman confirmed that he had played squash with David every Tuesday. He even checked his diary to confirm that. He also confirmed that David's wife had never accompanied him to the squash club. His assurances failed to explain why Ann had lied about being at home with her husband every evening when she must have known perfectly well that he had been out on Tuesday evenings for at least a few hours each week. It seemed that Geraldine had been right to mistrust Ann. They now needed to find out what she had been up to while her husband had been on the squash court.

51

LINDA REPORTED THAT SHE had questioned Ann who had persisted in denying that David had gone out on Tuesday evenings. It was a stupid lie because obviously the police would be able to establish the truth if they looked into the matter, but Ann had evidently not thought this through and had not expected them to check. If Aimee had not mentioned it, they might never have suspected David had gone out on Tuesday evenings. Now they were faced with a lie, either from Aimee or Ann. As a rebellious teenager, Aimee was perhaps not the most reliable of sources, so Geraldine began with her. Aimee was at home, probably happy to take the opportunity to avoid school, so Geraldine went straight there. Ann insisted on being present, along with Linda. The small living room felt crowded.

'Aimee,' Geraldine began gently, 'I'm so sorry about what happened to your father.'

Fidgeting with her fingers, Aimee grunted without looking up. Her hair looked greasy, and there were pouches beneath her eyes, either from crying or from lack of sleep, or perhaps both. Geraldine hated having to question her. She glanced at Ann who was leaning forward in her chair, an anxious expression on her delicate face. In these circumstances, any mother would be worried about her daughter's state of mind, but Geraldine wondered whether Ann was more worried about her own lies being exposed. Dismissing that thought, she focused on Aimee.

'Aimee, we're doing everything we can to find out who did

this terrible thing, and you may be able to help us. I'd like to ask you a question.'

'Can't you leave her alone?' Ann burst out. 'Can't you see she's upset enough already?'

'Just one question,' Geraldine said.

'What?' Aimee demanded gruffly. 'What's the question?'

'You told Linda your father had a regular squash game. We'd like to know who he played with.'

'I don't know.'

'Right, that's enough,' Ann interrupted as Geraldine was about to press on. 'Aimee, you can go to your room now.'

Aimee glared at her mother, but she did not move.

'He played on Tuesdays, didn't he?' Geraldine asked, although she already knew the answer. 'We've confirmed that with the sports club and spoken to his regular partner, but we wondered whether he might have played with anyone else.'

Out of the corner of her eye Geraldine was aware of Aimee shrugging, but she was more interested in watching Ann's response to what she had said. Ann sat motionless, and her face remained completely blank.

'Thank you, Aimee, you can go now,' Geraldine said.

Realising what was about to happen, Linda stood up. 'Come on, Aimee,' she said, 'let's go and put the kettle on and then we can watch some TV.'

Once Linda and Aimee had left the room, Geraldine closed the door.

'Ann, I'd like you to accompany me to the police station so you can answer a few more questions,' she said. 'This is just routine,' she added, although they both knew that was not true.

'You can ask me whatever it is you want to know here,' Ann replied. She spoke calmly, but her eyes betrayed her alarm.

'Why did you tell us your husband was at home with you every evening?'

'Oh that,' Ann raised her eyebrows dismissively. 'I was

confused. And I didn't think his squash game was important. It was just squash.'

'You told us he was here with you every evening,' Geraldine repeated.

'Yes, well, I forgot he went out sometimes.'

'You were here on your own every Tuesday, and you forgot he wasn't in?'

'Well, that's because I wasn't here without him. I went out as well.'

This was becoming even more interesting than Geraldine had expected.

'Every Tuesday?'

'Yes. We agreed we'd both go to our classes on the same night.'

So far the story made sense, and David was no longer able to confirm or refute anything Ann said.

'Did you go to the sports club as well?'

'No.'

'Where were you?'

'I was having guitar lessons.'

Geraldine glanced around. She did not recall seeing a guitar in the house, and said so.

'No,' Ann agreed. 'But I was going to get one. That is, David promised to get me one for my birthday.' She dropped her head in her hands and began to sob.

'Ann,' Geraldine said gently, 'is there something you're not telling me?'

Ann raised a tear stained face. 'No,' she replied, with a faint frown. 'What do you mean?'

'Very well, who was your guitar teacher?'

'His name was Mark.' Noting the past tense, Geraldine knew at once who Ann meant. Ann gazed at Geraldine in consternation before adding, 'He was murdered as well. I saw it in the paper.'

Geraldine nodded. She knew who Mark was.

'Where did you meet him?' she asked.

'I bumped into him by chance at a school concert, and we got chatting. He told me he was a music teacher and I asked if he ever taught adults and he said he did, so he agreed to try and teach me and, well, I wasn't very good, but I did enjoy learning. That's why I wanted to get a guitar, so I could practise at home. Mark said it was no good only being able to play once a week. David wanted to wait and see how I got on. He thought it might be a five-minute wonder, you know. But I wanted to carry on and so he was going to get me a guitar.'

Tears leaked from her eyes again at the memory. Geraldine kept quiet, but her suspicions were rekindled. Ann's story made sense, but Geraldine did not believe her. Thoughtfully she returned to Fulford Road.

'What's going on?' she asked Ariadne.

'We're trying to identify all the women who went to Mark's flat.'

'One of them might turn out to be Ann Rawson,' Geraldine replied.

Eileen had followed Geraldine into the room and asked her to repeat her remark.

'Ann just told me she was having guitar lessons with Mark Routledge.'

'Guitar lessons?'

Geraldine shrugged. 'That's what she said. There might have been more to it than that, considering Ann's age and looks, and how much older than her David was. Perhaps it was clever of her to have admitted she went to Mark's flat. She might have realised there was a risk we would find out she was going there. But Mark's dead, so if she's lying about their relationship, it's going to be difficult to prove, isn't it?'

'Why would she be lying?' Eileen asked.

'Well, it's odd that she knew both victims who were disguised in a clumsy attempt to make them look like victims of the Tramp Killer. You don't really think that could be a coincidence, do you?'

52

A SEARCH WARRANT WAS issued urgently and later that evening a team arrived at Ann's house. Geraldine was already there. She rang the bell and they waited. After a few moments, Geraldine rang again, and knocked loudly. At last Ann opened the door a fraction and peered out.

'Who is it?' she called out.

'We'd like to take a look around inside,' Geraldine said, pushing the door open.

'What for?' Ann stood still, blocking the doorway. 'I've already told Linda, we want to be left alone.'

'I'm afraid that's really not possible under the circumstances. We're looking for anything that might help us discover who killed your husband. Surely you want to help us in any way you can?'

'Yes, of course I want to help, but you're not going to find anything here.'

Ann still had not moved from the doorway.

'Please, stand aside,' Geraldine insisted quietly. 'You're not going to help us if you try to obstruct us in carrying out our work.'

She took a step forward and placed one foot over the threshold.

'I refuse to give you permission to enter this house,' Ann said, her voice rising in agitation. 'You have no right to force your way in here after we've asked to be left alone to grieve in peace.'

'I'm afraid you have no choice in the matter. We have a warrant to search the premises,' Geraldine replied. 'Now, we'd like you and Aimee to accompany us to the police station while we take a look around here. It will really be easier for everyone if you give us your full co-operation, and this needn't take long.'

'No! Get out of my house! Get out!'

Just then Linda came down the stairs followed by Aimee, who was crying.

'I don't want to go,' Aimee was sobbing. 'I want to stay here. I don't want to go.'

'It won't be for long,' Linda reassured her. 'You'll be home again soon.'

'Come along now,' Geraldine said as a group of officers joined her on the path. 'We'll drive you to the police station and you can wait there while the team do their job.'

Scowling, Ann fetched her bag and coat and followed Geraldine to a waiting police car while Aimee drove to the police station with Linda in a second car, leaving the search team to hunt for anything that might assist the investigation.

At the police station Ann and Aimee were invited to sit in a quiet room where they were offered tea and biscuits. Aimee continued to be sullen and unresponsive, while Ann grew increasingly agitated. After about an hour, Ann's neighbour arrived to take Aimee home with her and she left, willingly enough.

'What's going on?' Ann cried out. 'You can't take my daughter away like that.'

'Don't worry,' her neighbour replied. 'We're going to have supper and watch TV. Aimee'll be fine.'

'I don't understand. Why have you sent her away?'

'She'll be perfectly safe with your neighbour,' Geraldine said, 'and we didn't want to keep her here any longer than was necessary. This is no place for a teenager.'

'But what about me? Why am I still here?'

'I'm afraid we can't release you just yet,' Geraldine told her.

'Why not? You can't keep me here. This is outrageous! I'm

still in shock over my husband's death and now you're detaining me against my will. I want to go home.'

'We'd like to interview you now. You have the right to a lawyer.'

'What?'

Ann listened, her face a mask of horror, as Ian arrested her for the murder of Mark Routledge.

'Mark?' Ann repeated. 'Mark? You think I killed Mark? That's insane!'

Screeching in protest she was led to a cell to await the arrival of a duty solicitor. Fortunately someone was available to come to the police station almost straight away, so they could resume without too much delay. But this time Ian and Geraldine addressed Ann across the table in a formal interview room with a tape running.

'The search team found a phone at your house,' Ian said to Ann, ignoring her muttered protests.

'It's not mine,' Ann replied quickly. 'My phone's in my bag.' But her face betrayed her unease.

'The phone records show texts to Mark Routledge's number, almost on a daily basis,' Ian went on, glancing at a document he was holding. 'There were also calls, sometimes several in one day.'

'Mark Routledge? Are you talking about my guitar teacher?'

'Yes, Mark Routledge, your "guitar teacher",' Geraldine confirmed, stressing the last two words as though she was being sarcastic. 'There have been a lot of calls to him, and none to anyone else. Not even one.' She turned to the lawyer. 'Perhaps your client would like to clarify what that means?'

'It means,' Ann said, 'that I had to call my guitar teacher to confirm the times of my lessons.'

'So you bought this phone specifically to stay in contact with your guitar teacher?' Ian said. 'Can you tell us why you were so keen to keep your relationship with him a secret?'

'No, no, I wasn't. It wasn't a secret. That's not true. You're making this sound like something it wasn't. You can't put words in my mouth like that. Mark was my guitar teacher. I didn't phone him every day. Why would I?'

'That's exactly what we've been wondering,' Geraldine said. 'Why on earth would you want to text him every day? And so far we've only been able to come up with one conclusion. You were having an affair with Mark, weren't you?' It was not a question. 'We know it's your phone, because it was found concealed at the bottom of your wardrobe, and your fingerprints are all over it.'

For a few minutes Ann continued to deny knowing anything about the phone, but finally she broke down. 'Yes, yes, all right, it's my phone and I used it to call Mark. If you've got my phone, you know that anyway, so why are you asking me? We were having an affair! There! I've said it. Are you satisfied now? We loved each other. It's not a crime to fall in love. And yes, I kept the relationship a secret because I didn't want my husband to find out. I was afraid of upsetting him if he discovered I was seeing someone else.'

'You were in love with Mark, but then you became jealous and so you killed him,' Ian suggested.

'No, no, I wasn't jealous. Why would I be? You've got this all wrong. David was the one who was jealous. He was a monster.' She was crying now. 'I would never have hurt Mark. I loved him. It was David. It was David.'

'When you discovered Mark was seeing other women you became jealous and so you killed him,' Geraldine said.

'What do you mean? What are you talking about? Mark wasn't seeing other women. He loved me. Me!'

'Oh yes, there were other women. Several of them, in fact.'

'No! That's a lie!'

'It's true, Ann.'

'No, no. It's not true. It can't be.' Ann was trembling. 'I loved Mark. I loved him! And he loved me. There weren't any other women in his life, only me. He loved me. I know he did, and this is all lies. Lies! Mark loved me!'

'Did you kill Mark?' Ian asked.

'No, no. I keep telling you, I loved him. I loved him!'

Watching her, Geraldine could believe her capable of a crime of passion. But that did not mean she had murdered her lover. They still needed proof.

53

PEERING OUT FROM LITTLE pouches of flab, the lawyer's beady eyes seemed to bore through her skull. Ann was not sure she wanted him defending her, but there he was, solid and unmoving, and she did not know who else to call. She sat on her bunk facing him across the tiny cell, trembling, and struggling to believe what had just happened. Her daughter had been taken away from her, and now she was locked in a police cell, reliant on a tubby stranger to clear her name. She was not sure she had much confidence in the lawyer. He did not seem to believe a word she said, any more than the police had.

'You have to tell me the truth,' he said.

Strutting around her cramped cell, he pointed a plump finger at her.

She glared back at him. Fat, sweaty, and middle-aged, he was probably the most unhealthy-looking man she had ever met, and certainly the most unattractive.

'I've told you everything there is to tell,' she replied, 'and I told it all to the police as well. I admitted I was having an affair with Mark. We were in love.' Trying not to cry, she put one hand to her lips. 'I still love him,' she mumbled, stifling another sob.

The lawyer nodded. 'Good,' he muttered.'That's good.'

'What's good about the man I loved being dead?' she cried out.

'I meant that what you're saying is good. A jury may well believe you,' he explained, tilting his head on one side. 'What you're saying is very credible. That's important.'

'What are you talking about? Of course what I'm saying is credible, because I'm telling you the truth. Listen, you have to get me out of here. I can't stay here, and I can't go to court accused of killing Mark. It's – it's impossible. I told you, I loved him. Why would I want to kill him?'

'The police are convinced he was seeing other women and you were driven to attack him in a jealous rage.'

'That's poppycock and they can't possibly prove it, because, as I keep telling you, it's not true!'

'Oh, I think they'll be able to prove he was promiscuous, or they wouldn't be so confident in their claim. They have all sorts of ways of tracking down any other women he was seeing. I suspect there were a few, but they only need one of them to appear in court to build a case for saying you were jealous.'

'He wasn't promiscuous. That's a terrible thing to say. Stop saying that about him. You didn't know him. I'm telling you, there were no other women. Mark wasn't seeing anyone else. He loved me.' She paused, aware that she was beginning to sound hysterical. 'Listen,' she went on in a more reasonable tone, 'Mark wasn't seeing anyone else, and the point is, you have to get me out of here. That's why you're here, so do your job and stop repeating those filthy lies the police have told you about Mark because I'm your client and I'm telling you none of it is true.'

Back in the interview room, the police kept going on and on at her about the other women Mark had been sleeping with. At last they realised she was never going to believe their lies about him and they changed their tack, asking her about the coat she had exchanged with the old tramp. She was shocked to discover they knew about that, but she hid her surprise well, aware that she was fighting for her freedom.

'We know you gave David's expensive coat to a rough sleeper,' the dark-haired sergeant said.

Ann pretended to look puzzled. 'Why would I give a perfectly good coat away to a homeless person?'

The detective replied with a shrug, as though the answer was obvious.

'You swapped it for the rough sleeper's old one.'

'I did what?'

Outwardly sneering at the questions, Ann was secretly terrified, wondering how the police had found out about David's coat. What else did they know about her movements? The lawyer who was supposed to be defending her sat quietly beside her. He did not even appear to be listening. Trying to sound contemptuous, and not too vehement, Ann denied any knowledge of the coat they were talking about. As she spoke, she tried to interpret the detectives' expressions but they remained inscrutable. It was like a game of poker. She would have to keep to the truth as closely as possible. Somehow they had found David's coat and traced it back to him, probably through his DNA. She had to think carefully.

'David did lose his coat,' she ventured. 'A few weeks before he died. He left it in the park, and when he went back it had gone. Are you saying some tramp found it?' She shivered. 'I don't think I want it back now. Tell him he can keep it.'

The tramp must have told them what happened. There was no other way they could have found out. Recalling what the lawyer had said earlier, she resolved to stick to the story she had just told. If it turned out to be her word against that of a homeless person in court, she was confident a jury would believe her. As the lawyer said, she would be credible in court. Reassuring herself of that, she felt unassailable. As long as she held her nerve, she would survive this ordeal and walk away a free woman. It was just as well she had had the foresight to get rid of the rucksack which had been in contact with both David's coat and the one she had exchanged it for. She had even chucked her own coat away, in case the tramp had touched it. A horrible thought struck her. She could not remember what she had done with the scarf she had been wearing when she had met the tramp. But it was only a scarf. In any case, the police would never be able to prove she was guilty of murdering Mark, because that never happened. She would never have hurt Mark.

But when she was alone in her cell that night, she remembered how Mark had claimed a pair of knickers she had found in his bed had belonged to his sister. For the first time, she acknowledged the possibility that the police were right about Mark two-timing her. All at once, unwelcome thoughts began to crowd in on her. Mark had never wanted her to leave her husband, on the pretext that he had not wanted to wreck her marriage. Now she wondered whether she had been kidding herself that he was being thoughtful, when he had said he was concerned about the effect on Aimee if her parents were to divorce. Perhaps he had not encouraged her to leave David because he had never wanted anything more from her than sex once a week. She had no idea what he had got up to the rest of the week, or who else he had been seeing. She had wanted to end her marriage and move in with Mark as soon as Aimee left home. He had never once said anything to suggest he was looking forward to that happening.

'Let's wait and see,' was all he had been prepared to concede.

The lawyer seemed certain the police would not have said Mark was seeing other women without evidence to back up their claim. She had been an idiot to be taken in by him. And now the police thought she had killed him, because they could not believe she had been stupid enough to trust his lies. When she learned Mark had been killed, she had honestly thought her life could not get any worse. Now it had. She was locked up, accused of murder, and Mark had never loved her. All she could do was continue to insist she had loved Mark. Luckily, when the police had found her phone, she had not tried to stick to her original claim that he had merely been her guitar teacher. In admitting the truth about their relationship, she had avoided being caught out sticking to an obvious lie. Now she just had to sit this out.

She told herself the police would not be able to find any evidence of her committing a murder of which she was innocent, and eventually they would have to let her go. In the meantime, she just had to keep on protesting her innocence. She wondered whether she ought to try and find a better lawyer, even if she had to pay for it. But it hardly seemed necessary because the police would not be able to make their trumped-up accusation stick, and she could not face a prison sentence for having a love affair, however misguided it had turned out to be.

And all the time, the police had arrested her for the wrong murder. If her situation had not been so terrifying, it would have been laughable. It was reassuring to know she was not the only stupid kid on the block.

54

WITH ANN ARRESTED FOR killing Mark, one murder case was solved.

'That's one out of the four,' Eileen said. 'It's not good enough but it's better than nothing. At least it's got the Powers that Be off our backs for a while.'

Geraldine was not sure why Eileen got so worked up about her superior officers' opinions of her work.

'We're all doing our best, you included,' she said. 'I don't see what they can possibly have to gripe about.'

'What about her husband?' Ian asked. 'Who killed him?'

They had all agreed to focus their efforts on Mark and David's murders for the time being. Hopefully, whoever had killed the two seemingly random tramps would be revealed, once they had found the killer or killers who appeared to have selected particular individuals for reasons more personal than their lifestyles.

Eileen had assumed David had been mistaken for a rough sleeper by the Tramp Killer with the awkward gait, but Geraldine was not convinced. Malcolm might not be a particularly credible witness, but he had seemed certain a woman had given him David's coat. It proved nothing that the coat bore traces of DNA from both David and Ann, but nor did that evidence disprove anything. Just as Ann's apparently innocent reason for phoning Mark was not proof she had not killed him, so her contact with David's coat did not clear her name in connection with his death.

The next morning Geraldine went to the breakfast club and showed Malcolm a photo of Ann.

'Malcolm, look at this and think very carefully. Was this the woman who gave you a new coat?'

Malcolm screwed up his eyes and shook his head. 'It could have been. I told you, I didn't see her face clearly. She was wearing a scarf.'

'Yes, you said. Can you describe the scarf?'

He frowned. 'It was a scarf.'

'What colour was it?' Geraldine asked patiently.

Prising information out of Malcolm was like getting blood out of the proverbial stone.

He shrugged. 'It could have been black. It was dark.'

'And what else was she wearing?'

He shook his head. 'I don't know. I can't remember.'

'But it could have been the woman in this photo?'

'I suppose so. Her or another woman.'

It was frustrating and pointless. She returned to the police station where the technical team had traced the two other women whose numbers appeared most frequently on Mark's phone records. One was a thirty-year-old mother of a pupil at the school where he worked, the other a twenty-seven-year-old wife of an English teacher from his school. Both had called Mark's mobile regularly, and a little investigation revealed they were both attractive, blond, and married. The two women lived in York, so Geraldine went to question them, first going to see the mother of the pupil at Mark's school. The woman Geraldine wanted to see came to the door herself, and Geraldine recognised her from her profile picture on Facebook.

'Melanie Jones?'

'Yes.'

A man's voice called from inside the house. 'Who is it, Mel?'

Geraldine held up her identity card. 'I'm here to ask you about your relationship with Mark Routledge.'

Melanie's smile faded. 'I don't know what you're talking about.'

She spoke softly, and her anxious glance over her shoulder was enough to confirm that she knew exactly who Geraldine meant.

'You were having an affair with him?'

'What are you talking about? Look, can we have this conversation another time? Only my husband's here and –'

Reluctant to alienate Melanie, Geraldine reached a quick decision.

'Sure,' she said. 'If it's easier, you can come to the police station and we can talk there.'

'Who is it?' the man's voice repeated.

'Come back in half an hour. He'll be out then,' the woman mumbled hurriedly. 'No one,' she added, shouting over her shoulder.

She nodded fiercely at Geraldine and shut the door. Geraldine went back to her car and glanced at her watch. There was barely time to go and see the other woman on her list and come back within thirty minutes, so she decided to stay where she was and wait. Sitting in her car, she watched the house with one eye on the time and, after about twenty minutes, Melanie's front door opened and a man emerged, climbed into a car that was on the drive, and drove off. Geraldine hurried back and this time Melanie opened the door straight away. She had evidently been waiting for Geraldine's return.

'What's this about?'

'You were in a relationship with Mark Routledge?'

Melanie nodded. 'Yes. What of it?' Her defiant tone fizzled out. 'You won't tell my husband, will you? I heard what happened, so it's not as if I'm going to be seeing him again, is it?' She gazed at Geraldine with tears in her eyes. 'Mark was a good man. You have to find out who did this to him. I know we screwed around a bit but he was a decent man. It was just a bit of fun.'

'We're doing our best to find his killer. That's where we're hoping you might be able to help us.'

'Yes, yes, of course. I'll help you if I can, but what can I do?'

'Tell me about your relationship.'

'I was seeing Mark, on and off, for nearly a year. It started one Christmas. We used to meet in his flat so there was no risk that anyone would see us. I didn't want my husband to find out. But I've no idea what happened to him. I mean, I know he was murdered by someone who thought he was homeless, but I don't understand how that can have happened. He had a flat, and a job, and it wasn't as if he was desperately short of money.'

'Did he ever mention anyone who might have held a grudge against him? An ex-girlfriend, perhaps, or the husband of one of the women he was sleeping with?'

Melanie stared at her in surprise. 'One of the women he was sleeping with?' she repeated. 'You make it sound as though he was sleeping with more than one woman at a time.'

'He was,' Geraldine said.

Melanie frowned and shook her head.

'Didn't you know?' Geraldine asked lightly, hoping the information would persuade Melanie to speak more freely. 'Oh well, don't shoot the messenger.'

'What did you say you wanted?' Melanie asked coldly. 'Only my husband will be back soon and I'd like you gone when he gets here.'

'I just want to know whether Mark ever mentioned anything to you about having an enemy, or a stalker, or anything like that? Or perhaps he confided in you,' she went on quickly, realising her plan had misfired.

Melanie shook her head slowly and solemnly. 'No,' she said. 'He never did.' Her voice softened and she gazed at Geraldine earnestly. 'You will catch whoever did this, won't you? I know he was a bit of a player, but he wasn't a bad person.' She sighed. 'It was stupid, I know, but we were just having fun.'

'We'll find out who did it,' Geraldine promised, and Melanie gave her a genuine smile.

Geraldine was not sure how they were going to manage it, but she knew those had to be more than empty words.

55

THE OTHER WOMAN WHO had been in regular contact with Mark was called Kelly. Her husband worked at the school, and her eleven-year-old son had recently started taking guitar lessons. Subsequently, according to the phone messages, he had taken to having private lessons at Mark's flat, although knowing what they did about him, they quickly realised that some of these after-school 'guitar lessons' were a different kind of assignation altogether. It was not difficult to read between the lines of messages like, 'Enjoyed the lesson today', and 'Can't wait for the next lesson'. There was never any mention of times and dates, just expressions of appreciation for the 'lessons'.

Kelly lived with her son in a terraced house in The Crescent, near Holgate Road, along with her second husband, Charlie. Geraldine found the house and rang the bell. She was not sure whether the bell worked, so she was rapping on the door with her knuckles when the door opened. A young woman frowned at her, looking harassed.

'Are you Kelly Harris?'

'Yes. What do you want?' the woman replied, 'only my husband'll be home soon and wanting his tea.'

She brushed her hair back off her face and Geraldine saw a row of small dark red blotches on the inside of her wrist. Someone had grabbed her arm with enough force to bruise the skin. Without betraying that she had noticed the signs of aggression, Geraldine held up her identity card.

'What's he gone and done now?' Kelly asked.

She frowned, but her eyes did not look worried. If anything, they seemed to darken, while her shoulders straightened and her head lifted.

'Don't tell me the school called the police. He's only eleven! And he wasn't the one who started it. You should talk to the other kid's mother.'

'This has got nothing to do with your son,' Geraldine assured her.

Almost imperceptibly, Kelly's shoulders slumped again, and she assumed an interested expression that was obviously fake.

'What do you want then? Only I'm kind of busy. If it's not about my boy, what is it?'

'I'm here to question you about Mark Routledge.'

The telltale shoulders jerked and this time her eyebrows shot up as well.

'Who's that? Mark who?'

'You know very well who I'm talking about,' Geraldine replied quietly.

Kelly bit her lip and did not answer for a moment. Then she shook her head. 'I'm sorry. I don't know anyone by that name.'

'Your number came up on Mark Routledge's phone records. Do you really want us to question your son about his "guitar lessons"?'

'I lost my phone,' Kelly said, panicking.

'I just want you to answer a few questions and then I'll be on my way. There's really no need to involve anyone else if you don't want to.'

The shoulders visibly relaxed as Kelly nodded.

'OK,' she agreed. 'But make it quick, please. He'll be home any time now and – and he doesn't know about Mark.' She shook her head. 'Poor Mark. When I saw about it on the telly, I couldn't believe it. What a terrible thing to happen. Who would do that?'

'That's what we're trying to find out.'

Kelly nodded. 'What do you want from me?'

'Did Mark ever mention anything to you that might help us in our enquiries?'

'Like what?'

'Did he have any enemies that he talked about? Anyone who might have had a grudge against him?'

Kelly shook her head. 'He did say he thought he was being stalked,' she said. 'But he didn't know who it was. I thought he was imagining it. I'd told him about –' she broke off in confusion.

'About what? What did you tell him about, Kelly?'

'Nothing. It's just that – well, Charlie can be a bit of a lunatic.' She forced a laugh. 'You know how crazy men can be.'

Geraldine restrained herself from glancing at Kelly's wrist, but she thought she understood what Kelly meant.

'I just told Mark we had to be careful, that's all. I was afraid of what Charlie might do if he found out. And then, not long after that, Mark told me he thought he was being stalked.' She shook her head. 'I put the wind up him all right. But that's all it was. He just got the jitters for no real reason. I mean, nothing happened.'

Geraldine did not point out that murder was hardly 'nothing'.

'Charlie's not a bad guy, but he gets funny ideas.'

'What kind of ideas?'

'He's crazy possessive, you know. If I so much as look at another man he gets mad.'

Perhaps because he discovered you were screwing someone else, Geraldine thought, but she kept that thought to herself.

'Was he ever violent towards you?'

'Who? Mark? Don't be daft,' Kelly replied, deliberately misunderstanding the question.

But Geraldine thought her shoulders tensed.

'Not Mark, Charlie. Is he ever violent towards you or does he ever show signs of –'

Before Geraldine could finish her sentence, Kelly's eyes flicked past Geraldine's shoulder and her expression hardened.

'No,' she said, very loudly, 'I just told you we're not interested.'

Looking round, Geraldine saw a man striding down the path towards her. He was about thirty, heavy set, with dark hair, and as he walked his left arm swung to compensate for his slight limp. Geraldine took a step back from the door.

'Thank you,' she said, 'I'm sorry to have bothered you.'

'Who are you?' the man asked politely.

'She was trying to sell –'

He turned to Kelly with a scowl. 'Did I ask you? How can we help you?'

'I'm here doing a survey for the council,' Geraldine answered quickly. 'But I won't take up any more of your time. I can see you're busy.'

She passed the man and hurried away, concealing her excitement. She intended to take up a lot more of his time, far more than he could possibly imagine, and most of it would be behind bars. Standing by her car, she called the police station for immediate backup, aware that if she attempted to tackle Charlie alone, there was a risk Kelly might pitch in and help him to get away. But she had not reckoned on Kelly telling Charlie who she really was. Before she had finished speaking on her phone, she heard screaming from inside the house. Afraid that Kelly was injured, Geraldine summoned urgent medical backup as she ran towards the house. She glanced around but there was no sign of any vehicles approaching. Then, in the distance, she heard sirens and a moment later the first police car swept into view at the far end of the road, siren blaring and lights flashing.

Turning, Geraldine banged on the door.

'Open up!' she shouted. 'This is the police! Open this door! Kelly! Kelly!'

The door flew open and she saw Charlie, red-faced with fury.

'Step outside –' she began.

He raised his hand and she saw he was holding a gun.

56

'GET IN HERE, NOW!' Charlie said. 'Move!'

He was holding the gun close to his chest, the dark circle of the barrel pointing straight at her. The weapon jerked in his hand, ushering her inside. Behind him Geraldine could see Kelly lying on her front at the far end of the narrow hall. She was not moving, and Geraldine could not see whether she was badly hurt. There had been no sound of a shot being fired, but the thought that Kelly might be in need of urgent medical attention decided Geraldine. In any case, there was no arguing with a man holding a gun. She stepped over the threshold and called Kelly's name but there was no response. Behind her she heard the front door close.

The end of the gun pressed against her back, between her shoulder blades.

'Charlie, I think your wife's unconscious,' she said, doing her best to focus on Kelly and ignore the gun which jabbed her viciously in the back as she spoke. 'We need to check whether she's still breathing.'

'Never mind that,' Charlie replied. 'Get in there.'

He grabbed her arm and steered her towards the front room.

At that moment someone banged so loudly on the front door, the door frame shook.

The flap of the letter box was pushed open. 'Open up! Police!' a voice yelled through it. 'Open this door or we'll break it down!'

'Shut up,' Charlie growled. 'I can't think with that racket going on. It's doing my head in.' He poked her in the back with the gun. 'They need to stop that din.'

She wondered whether the gun was loaded. Charlie probably did not even know how to fire it. But she was not taking any chances.

'They don't know you've got a gun,' she said. 'So they're not going to take your threats seriously. Any minute now, they're going to smash all your doors and windows in, and if enough of them rush into the house at once, you'll be pinned to the floor because you won't be able to shoot them fast enough to stop them overpowering you. But by the time that happens, I'll have a bullet in my back, won't I?'

He grunted.

'I'll be dead and you'll be locked up for life for killing a police officer.'

'What are you saying?'

'Just that this is going to end badly for both of us, because there's a small army of policemen out there who don't know you're armed.'

'If you don't shut up, you'll be dead, anyway.'

Geraldine took a deep breath, aware that it could be her last. 'Once they know you're armed they'll have to negotiate with you, and I'll get out of this alive, and you'll get a car, and whatever else you need. Of course, if you shoot me first, you won't have anything left to bargain with.'

Her captor seemed to have forgotten about Kelly, so Geraldine did not mention her. Charlie was no fool and he must have realised a police officer was a more useful hostage than a woman who might already be dead. Presumably that was why he had invited her into the house in the first place. Behind her she could hear him breathing heavily as though he was struggling with a heavy load.

'This is your final warning!' a voice reached them through

the front door. 'The house is surrounded and we're coming in.'

At the same time they heard a loud banging coming from the back of the kitchen, and more voices calling to Charlie to open up.

'I told you to get in there,' he cried out, grabbing hold of her arm again and propelling her into the front room.

He gave her a final shove that almost caused her to lose her balance. She stumbled forwards into the room and grabbed on to the back of a chair to stop herself from falling. Gasping, she swivelled round to look at him. He was standing in the doorway, one arm hanging loose, the other pointing the gun at her head. Seeing the manic glare in his eyes, she nearly panicked; it took all her willpower to control a surge of terror that swept through her as she realised she was seconds away from almost certain death.

'Tell them they've got to stop that,' Charlie cried out in fury, as the thumping at the door resumed. 'They've got to give me time to think. I need time.'

'Shall I call them and tell them you're armed?'

'Go on then. And no tricks,' he added, his gun twitching in his grasp as she reached for her phone.

Geraldine spoke as calmly as she could. 'I'm getting my phone so I can call and say you have a gun pointed at my head so they have to do whatever you want.'

He nodded. 'Go on then, do it. Now! Now! Before they kick the bloody door in!'

'I'm in the house and he's got a gun,' she gabbled into her phone. 'One other hostage is injured.'

'That's enough,' Charlie shouted. 'Drop the phone. Drop the phone!'

Geraldine let her phone fall to the floor and kicked it towards him. For a few seconds they heard a voice calling from the phone, and then there was silence. Hours seemed to pass while they stood there, facing one another across the room, waiting for something to happen.

'What's going on?' Charlie blurted out at last. 'What are they doing out there?'

Geraldine pictured the silent activity taking place in the street outside. Nearby houses would be evacuated, and the area cleared and cordoned off. Paramedics might already be standing by, ready to step forward as soon as it was safe to do so. A trained negotiator would be on his way, with an armed response team moving into place, surrounding the house. A helicopter would arrive shortly in case Charlie tried to make a run for it. It was hard to believe that such a large team were arriving outside, when inside the house they could hear no sound from the street.

'What's happening? Why is it so quiet out there?' Charlie shouted suddenly.

Beneath his short black hair he looked very pale. Although it was chilly in the house, beads of sweat trickled down his high forehead, while his narrow, dark eyes glared anxiously at Geraldine, and his fingers holding the gun seemed to twitch nervously. Half expecting him to pull the trigger, she stood poised to duck, even though it would be futile. No one could react fast enough to avoid a bullet. Behind her, she heard a faint moan.

'I think Kelly's recovered consciousness,' she said. 'We ought to see if she's all right.'

'Don't move. I told you, I need to think.'

Out in the hall, they heard Kelly groan.

'She needs medical assistance,' Geraldine said. 'She could be dying.'

'You need to shut up. What are they doing out there?'

Geraldine struggled to maintain her composure, while Charlie grew as jittery as a fish caught on a line.

If Geraldine could just kick the gun out of her opponent's grasp, she was confident she would be able to subdue him, in a one-against-one struggle. But even with all her training, she was no match for an armed man. And should Kelly recover sufficiently to do anything at all, there was no way of knowing whether she would want to help Geraldine or Charlie. Against two opponents and a gun, Geraldine was helpless.

As she was considering her limited options, a voice hailed them from outside. The police had responded to the situation quickly.

'We have the house surrounded, Charlie,' a negotiator called out in a calm unhurried tone. 'Come out with your hands in the air.'

'Not bloody likely,' Charlie replied.

No one but Geraldine could hear him.

'I think Kelly might be dying,' she urged him. 'If she doesn't get help soon, you'll go down for murder. At the moment you haven't hurt anyone. Let them take her away to safety. You'll still have me as a bargaining chip. Then you can tell them everything you want in exchange for my safe return.'

'Not bloody likely,' he repeated. 'I'm not a complete idiot. They're not getting in here. Now shut up, will you, and let me think what to do. I can handle this, I just need to think.'

57

AT LAST CHARLIE SEEMED to make up his mind. 'Tell them I want a car,' he said, 'and no one's to follow me. If I see anyone on my tail...' he jerked the gun meaningfully. 'And to make sure there's no tricks, you're coming with me.'

Geraldine nodded to show she understood. 'I'll need my phone if I'm going to talk to them.'

She pointed at her phone, lying on the floor between them.

'Put your hands on your head and sit down,' he said. 'On the floor. Over there.'

He was waving the gun at her wildly now, so she did as she was told. Once she was on the floor, leaning against the far wall, he stepped forward to bend down and pick up the phone. Geraldine suppressed a crazy impulse to fling herself at him and knock him off his feet. If he had not been clutching a gun, she would have done it without any hesitation. As it was, she sat perfectly still, watching him, praying the gun would slip from his grasp and skitter across the floor in her direction. It did not.

'Here,' he said, sliding the phone across the floor before straightening up. 'Call them. Tell them I want a car. A fast car.' He paused. 'A police car. No, no, a Ferrari. Make it a Ferrari.'

'A Ferrari? Are you sure?'

'Call them! Tell them I'll shoot you in the head if they don't give me what I want.'

Although she felt strangely calm, Geraldine could see her fingers shaking as she made the call.

'This is DS Steel,' she said, and broke off, unable to speak.

'We're listening,' the voice called from out in the street. 'We can hear you. Are you all right in there?'

'Give me the phone!' Charlie shouted. 'Give it to me! Throw it over here.'

Geraldine held out the phone and he lunged forward to grab it, still pointing the gun at her. He was not quite close enough for her to feel confident that she could safely reach out and seize his arm, twisting it so the gun was no longer pointing directly at her. Regretfully, she decided to be patient instead of taking such an unnecessary risk. She might be angry and frightened, but she was not suicidal.

'I want a car! A Ferrari!' Charlie bellowed into the phone. 'Give me what I want or the sergeant gets a bullet in her brain!'

He turned to Geraldine whose eyes had not shifted from the barrel of the gun. It stared back at her like a malevolent eye.

'Now, get up, slowly. You're coming with me.'

She understood that she was to be used as a human shield, but at least she was still alive. Suddenly each moment felt precious. Her gaze wandered around the untidy little room where every object now assumed a significance she had not noticed earlier. She felt as though a grey filter had been lifted from her eyes. An irregular stain on the carpet seemed to take on a new significance. Someone had spilt their tea there, or their beer, and left it to soak into the carpet. Perhaps they had tried, without success, to dilute it with water and mop it up. It seemed inexpressibly sad that she would never learn the truth about its history. There was so much she would never discover if Charlie shot her dead. She avoided thinking about people she knew. She did not want to spend her last moments wracked with guilt over her flawed relationships with her sisters, or filled with regret over what might have happened with Ian Peterson, if only he had never fallen in love with his wife years before Geraldine had first met him.

She turned to gaze at the net curtain over the window. Out of sight, just a short distance away, her colleagues were playing a waiting game, hoping for a positive outcome from this tense situation. Through the curtain she could make out the faint outline of a tree. If she was going to die here in this stuffy room, she would like her last view of the world to be a tree, not the face of her killer. But the thought of the world outside gave her hope. Her colleagues were working to rescue her and restore her to her career, her friends and family. She had a life. Somewhere out in the street, not far away, Ian Peterson was waiting to see her walk out through the front door. She could almost hear the cheers of the watching team as she stepped out of the house, unharmed. She was not ready to die. Not yet.

Raising her eyes she saw Charlie, his top lip and forehead glistening with sweat, his eyes flickering nervously at her, his lips stretched in a triumphant grin. And over his shoulder she saw Kelly, clinging on to the door for support, blinking and swaying on quivering legs.

'Kelly?' Geraldine said.

'Forget about her,' Charlie replied, oblivious that Kelly had just clambered to her feet behind him. 'You and me, we're leaving here together.'

Before he finished speaking, Kelly hurled herself forward with a shriek of rage.

'You're not leaving me for that bitch!' she screeched, completely misunderstanding the situation.

Startled, Charlie looked round. As he turned his head, Geraldine dived at him, knocking the gun out of his hand. It went skating across the floor and landed by Kelly. At once, Geraldine had Charlie's arm twisted up behind his back.

'Stop it! You're breaking my arm! Kelly, give me the gun. Give it to me, you stupid cow!'

Kelly stood, trembling, clutching the gun which could go off at any moment. Light glinted off the metal shaking in her grasp.

'Drop the gun, Kelly!' Geraldine called out, trying to keep

her voice steady and conceal her panic. 'Drop the gun before you kill someone!'

As Kelly stared around wildly, Geraldine struggled to work out how she could control the situation.

She lowered her voice and tried to sound encouraging. 'Drop the gun, Kelly. You're going to hurt someone if you're not careful.'

The retort as the gun went off was deafening.

58

THROUGH THE PAINFUL RINGING in her ears, Geraldine was only hazily aware of another crashing sound. She barely had time to register that she had not been injured by the gunshot when two armed police officers in riot gear burst into the room.

'Drop your weapons!' the first one shouted. 'Hands above your heads!'

For a second no one moved. Then Kelly threw the gun down and fell to her knees, holding her arms up and whimpering in terror. Geraldine released her grip on Charlie, put her hands on his shoulders and pushed him to the floor where he lay, whingeing that she had broken his arm.

'You're going to regret this,' he cried out. 'This is police brutality. You'll be in trouble –'

'At least I'm not threatening to put a bullet through your brain if you don't shut up,' she interrupted him.

'Are you all right, Sergeant?' one of the armed police officers asked her.

Geraldine nodded uncertainly. 'I need to get out of here,' she replied, for the first time aware of the sour stench of sweat and gunpowder. 'And that woman needs to get to a hospital.'

Holding on to the wall for support, Geraldine made her way to the front door. She stood for a moment, enjoying a blast of cold fresh air. She had not realised how stifling it had been inside the house. A little revived, she stepped outside and a familiar figure ran forward.

'Ian,' she muttered, as his arms wrapped round her.

'Come on,' he said, 'let's get you to hospital.'

'I don't need a hospital,' she replied.

She stood perfectly still for a moment, trying to memorise the sensation of his embrace, and he seemed in no hurry to release her. There was a faint smell of perspiration that his aftershave failed to mask.

'Are you sure you're all right?' he asked in a curiously husky voice, holding her head tightly against his chest.

His hand felt warm on the side of her head, and against her other ear she could hear his heart thumping.

'I'm not hurt. What I need right now is a shower and a stiff drink,' she replied, as he loosened his hold on her.

He gazed at her for a moment. 'I was afraid I'd never see you again,' he said softly.

She smiled. 'I don't think you're going to get rid of me that easily.'

'I hope not.'

As soon as she had showered and changed, Geraldine returned to the police station and went straight to Eileen's office.

'I didn't expect to see you back here until next week,' Eileen said. She spoke severely, but she was smiling. 'Although knowing you, I'm surprised you didn't come straight here from the house where you were being held hostage at gunpoint.' She shook her head. 'Seriously, Geraldine, it's admirable the way you take everything in your stride, but don't you need to take a few days off, at least? Go and visit your sister in Kent, and have a break. You've been through quite an ordeal and you might not be as tough as you think you are.'

'OK, keep me behind a desk for a few days if it makes you feel better,' Geraldine replied. 'But I can assure you I'm fine.' She hoped her expression did not betray that she was still feeling shocked by her experience. 'The thing is, I had to come in to tell you what I've learned.'

Eileen nodded. 'Go on,' she said.

'Charlie killed the first two rough sleepers.'

'Did he tell you that?'

'No, not in so many words, but I know it was him.'

'Be careful, Geraldine. After Charlie held you up at gunpoint, it's understandable you're going to feel a little disorientated, not to mention keen to see him convicted – who wouldn't be after what he put you through? But without clear evidence or a credible confession, there's nothing further to be said.'

'No, no,' Geraldine said, trying to control her impatience. 'This isn't a petty attempt to be revenged on that cretin. Listen, you remember I questioned Molly after she witnessed the attack on Alf when he was strangled in Nether Hornpot Lane?'

Eileen nodded. 'Yes, of course I remember.'

'Well, Molly described the way the killer walked. She said his left leg swung out to the side, and he moved his left arm more than his right one.'

Eileen nodded again. 'Something like that, yes.'

'Not something like that,' Geraldine replied. 'Those were her words. I checked before I came here to speak to you. And remember we have CCTV film of a hooded man walking away from the scene of Bingo's murder, walking with a similar gait?'

'Yes.'

'All of that would probably be enough to establish that the same killer strangled both Bingo and Alf, even without the forensic evidence that the same noose was used to strangle both victims.'

Eileen nodded. 'Is this going somewhere?'

'Charlie walks with a slight limp, swinging his left arm to compensate for the way he drags his left leg ever so slightly to the side. I saw it myself. If we get the forensic podiatrist to compare Charlie's actual gait with the film we have of the unidentified hooded suspect near the first crime scene, we might find proof that Charlie killed Bingo.'

'And then we would have him for Alf as well!' Eileen cried out, catching the excitement that Geraldine was no longer bothering to try and conceal.

'The murders of two rough sleepers,' Geraldine said, 'assaulting his wife – if we can persuade her to talk – and taking a police officer hostage. He won't have much wriggle room after that.'

'Do you think he suspected her of having a relationship with a rough sleeper, and that's why he targeted them?'

Geraldine shook her head. 'I think killing the rough sleepers was a calculated smoke screen to enable him to get away with killing Mark because he found out Kelly was having an affair with him.'

'Do you think he killed David as well?'

'I don't know about David, but I'm almost sure he killed Mark,' Geraldine said. 'We know Charlie's possessive and has a history of violence, and his wife was sleeping with Mark which gives a vicious brute like that a motive, however crude.'

'Did he know about their affair?'

'We'll have to ask Kelly. To be honest, I'm not sure she's going to help us, despite the way he's treated her.'

Eileen raised her eyebrows. 'Blind love?'

'Not so much love on her part, seeing as she was sleeping with at least one other man, but plenty of fear. If we can convince her he's going down anyway, she might talk, but we won't really need her evidence, will we?'

'Let's see what she has to say anyway. I'd like you to speak to her, Geraldine. But I'm not sure you're the right person to question Charlie after what he put you through.'

'I'd say that would make me the ideal person to question him. He can hardly lie about what happened to me, can he?'

'Are you saying you want to interview him?'

Geraldine smiled. 'Oh yes. I think he'll realise the game's up as soon as I walk through the door.'

'Very well. Let's see what Kelly has to say for herself first, though, as she might give us some useful information that we can use to put pressure on him.'

'Yes, at the very least it'll unnerve him to know she's been talking to us. It's possible he confided in her and I don't think he'll trust her to keep her mouth shut now he's been arrested.'

Kelly had not yet been released from hospital where she was receiving treatment for several injuries, including a fairly serious blow to the head which she claimed she had sustained when she accidentally fell down the stairs at home.

'Don't let her talk for long,' the nurse on the desk told Geraldine, 'and try not to disturb her. She's in a delicate state, mentally. She's been crying a lot and we've put her on antidepressants, temporarily, as well as painkillers.'

'It sounds as though she's in a bad way,' Geraldine replied. 'Is she going to be all right?'

The nurse shrugged. 'We think so, but she needs quiet.'

'Where's her son?'

'He's been visiting her. He's staying with friends for now.'

Geraldine thanked the nurse and went into the ward. Kelly appeared to be sleeping, so Geraldine pulled the curtains closed around her bed and sat down to wait for her to wake up. After a while, she stirred and Geraldine called her name softly. Kelly opened her eyes and they widened as she recognised her visitor.

'You didn't get him,' she said, her voice slurred with sleep and drugs. 'He wouldn't leave without me. He wants me. Not you.'

Kelly was still under the impression that Geraldine had been trying to run away with Charlie.

'Kelly, I'm a police officer,' she said quietly. 'Charlie didn't want to run off with me, he had taken me hostage and wanted to use me as a human shield, to help him escape from the police.'

Kelly frowned. 'You just said you *are* the police.'

'Yes, but I'm only one police officer. Don't you remember? Your house was surrounded. Charlie was afraid he would never be able to escape. That's why he wanted me to go with him.' She paused. 'You can trust me. I wasn't trying to steal your husband, I was trying to arrest him.'

Kelly closed her eyes. 'Where's Charlie?'

'He's in a police cell charged with multiple murders.'

Kelly's eyes flew open. 'What?'

Geraldine frowned. Evidently Kelly had no idea what her husband had been up to.

'I'm sorry to tell you Charlie killed two men, possibly more.'

She was taken aback when Kelly began to giggle. 'No, he didn't,' she said. 'Charlie never did.'

'He violently assaulted you on more than one occasion,' Geraldine said.

Kelly's laughter stopped abruptly. She closed her eyes. 'No, no, that's not true. That's not what happened. I fell down. I'm clumsy,' she explained earnestly, 'Charlie says I'm clumsy.'

'Charlie's in prison, accused of murder. If we hadn't stopped him, he would probably have killed you too, and your son.'

Kelly closed her eyes. Eventually she opened them again and looked directly at Geraldine, her pupils dilated and her speech sluggish.

'Bye bye, policewoman,' she said. 'Charlie doesn't want to see you again.'

'Well, that's a pity,' Geraldine replied, more to herself than to Kelly who appeared to have gone back to sleep. 'He's going to see quite a lot of me for a while, until he's convicted and incarcerated in a secure prison. Still, it's highly unlikely I'll ever go and visit him there, and then he won't have to see me again. Ever. Or you either for that matter, unless you go and see him during visiting hours.'

Sound asleep and snoring gently, Kelly did not answer.

59

HAVING WASHED HIS FACE and hands, and combed his hair, Charlie looked quite presentable as he faced Geraldine and Ian across the table in an interview room. The duty solicitor seated at the side of the accused was young and sharp-featured, with piercing blue eyes that watched the two detectives closely, as though she suspected them of plotting to seize her folder from the table by some sleight of hand.

'My client denies the charge,' the solicitor said, her decisive tone seeming to imply the interview was over.

'Charges,' Geraldine corrected her. 'Charlie, you're accused of killing four people. You understand the charges, don't you?'

Charlie scowled and turned to his lawyer. 'Four people? What are they talking about?'

'Please, leave the talking to me,' she replied.

'You can get me off, can't you?' he asked her. 'It's all a pack of lies. They're trying to pin everything they have on me.' He turned to face Geraldine again. 'You won't get away with this, you know, harassing an innocent man. You'll be in serious trouble over this.'

'You're accused of the unlawful killing of four men, assaulting your wife, Kelly, and taking my colleague here hostage,' Ian said in an even tone.

Charlie shook his head. 'It's not true. None of it's true.'

'Are you denying all the charges?' Ian asked, raising his eyebrows.

Charlie glanced at his lawyer.

'My client denies all of the charges,' she confirmed.

Ian sat forward. 'Think very carefully before you speak, Charlie. You are accused of murdering two rough sleepers, along with Mark Routledge, who was in a sexual relationship with your wife, Kelly.'

He paused, and Geraldine knew he too was watching for a response when Charlie heard Kelly's name. She was not sure if the suspect's face reddened, but he did not speak and his expression remained fixed.

'Mark was your real target all along, wasn't he?' Geraldine said.

Charlie gave no response, but she thought his eyes glittered.

'We know what was going on,' she said at last, giving Charlie what she hoped was a sympathetic look. 'We've spoken to Kelly. We know all about her affair with Mark Routledge.'

Charlie's bottom jaw twitched as he shook his head. 'Who?'

'The man your wife was having sex with,' Ian said bluntly.

Again Mark's jaw twitched. Watching him, Geraldine sensed an air of vulnerability which gave her a feeling that they would be able to break him soon. And then, without any further warning, he cracked, slamming his fist down on the table in a burst of rage. To his credit, Ian barely blinked, while Geraldine gasped, and the lawyer jumped in her seat and let out a yelp of surprise.

Geraldine suppressed a smile. 'It must have been very hard for you,' she said softly, 'knowing your wife was sleeping with another man.'

Charlie shook his head, his temper once more under control. 'Kelly was a slag,' he muttered.

'That's why you hit her,' Ian said. 'It's –' he hesitated to complete his sentence.

Geraldine finished it for him. 'It's understandable.'

'You don't have to respond to this needling,' the lawyer cut in urgently. 'We want to request a break.'

'We've hardly begun,' Ian protested.

'Please switch off the tape. This interview is suspended. I need to speak to my client.'

Walking away along the corridor, Ian and Geraldine went over what had just happened.

'We nearly had him talking,' Geraldine fumed. 'Bloody lawyers. Now she'll get him under control again and we'll be right back where we started.'

'Not quite back where we started,' Ian said, with an anxious smile at her. 'We know he's guilty, and he knows we know. We're getting there. Come on, let's go and have a cup of tea.'

Ian smiled at her and, just like that, Geraldine's anger dissipated. While they were in the canteen, Ian's phone rang.

'It's Eileen,' he mouthed at Geraldine. Hanging up, he said, 'She wants to see us.'

'What about our tea?'

'She said right now. I think there's been a development.'

They hurried along to Eileen's room. Without stopping to ask how the interview with Charlie was going, she shared the news that had just reached her from the team searching Charlie's flat. Armed with new information, they returned to the interview room to resume questioning Charlie.

This time Ian went straight in. 'We know you killed Bingo and Alf, we just weren't sure why,' he began.

'That's nonsense,' Charlie blustered.

'The search team have found the red tie you used to strangle them with,' Geraldine said.

'It seems you didn't hide it well enough,' Ian added.

Charlie frowned. 'I have got a red tie, yes,' he said cautiously. 'But so what? You think I'm the only man in York to own a red tie?'

'You might be the only man in York to hide his red tie under his mattress,' Geraldine replied. 'Microscopic fibres caught in the skin of your victims are being tested and compared with the fabric of your tie. It's not looking good for you, Charlie.'

'In fact,' Ian added, with a broad grin, 'I'd say we've got you bang to rights. Unless you have a good reason for hiding a red tie under your mattress?'

'I need to consult with my client,' the lawyer began.

'No, we're only just back from a break,' Ian told her. 'You can wait a few minutes. There's no way you can claim he's in need of another break yet.'

'In the light of new information –' she began, but this time Geraldine interrupted her.

'Oh, but there's more,' she said. 'Surely you'd like to hear it all before you go off again? We can't keep stopping and starting every time we catch Charlie out in a lie.' She turned to Charlie. 'You see, what was puzzling us was why you would want to kill those two rough sleepers. It all seemed a bit random.'

'That's because I never did it,' he protested lamely.

'I'm afraid the forensic evidence tells us that you did,' Geraldine said. 'But we now think it was all part of a bigger plan. That's what happened, isn't it? You discovered Kelly was having an affair with Mark and that's when you decided to kill him. But you didn't want to be caught, so you came up with a plan to disguise his death as one of a series of murders of rough sleepers. Bingo and Alf were random victims, chosen by you just because they happened to be homeless. You could have picked on any of the rough sleepers in York. It didn't matter to you who they were, as long as they looked like tramps. And then you killed Mark and David, and dressed them up to look like homeless people as well, so no one would suspect –'

Charlie frowned. 'David? Who the hell is David?' He gazed at his lawyer who warned him to say nothing.

'We thought his wife had killed him, but now we believe it was you.'

'Listen,' Charlie scowled at Geraldine, 'maybe you think

there's some sort of evidence that might suggest I attacked a couple of tramps – I'm only saying it's possible – and as for Mark, he got what was coming to him. But I never touched anyone but Mark. Why would I?'

'Because it was all part of your plan. You thought you were being clever, didn't you?' Geraldine went on. 'Only we saw through it right from the start because it wasn't the brilliant idea you thought it was. No, it was actually a really really stupid idea. If you hadn't killed those two old men who had done nothing to injure you, it's possible you might have got away with murdering Mark, who was the only one you thought you had a reason to kill. What hadn't occurred to you was that with each murder you risked being seen, and left more evidence of your presence, and massively increased the chances of your being caught. You couldn't have been more stupid if you'd tried.'

'Oh, very well,' Charlie blurted out, with an angry frown. 'Yes, I killed them two old tramps and the man who was shagging Kelly. I killed them all, and I'd do it again. So now you know. And all the time no one suspected it was me. You were running around in circles like headless bloody chickens, and *you're* calling *me* stupid!'

'Now you can take a break,' Ian said.

As they left the room, Geraldine turned to Ian. 'Was that very bad of me, to revel in his humiliation?' she asked.

'Bad isn't a word I would ever use to describe you.'

'How would you describe the way I behaved just then?'

He thought for a second. 'Genius is the word I would use.' He leaned down and kissed her on the forehead. 'But you do need to take care of yourself.'

Before she could respond, he turned and walked quickly away. His shoulders were slightly bowed, but there was more of a spring to his step than she had seen since he had started divorce proceedings against his wife.

60

GERALDINE WAS WRITING UP her decision log when Eileen came over and, leaning forward over the side of Geraldine's desk, confided that she was more relieved than she could say at the outcome of the investigation.

'I really didn't think we would put this one to bed so quickly,' she admitted. 'To be honest,' she glanced around to check that no one else was listening, 'there were times when I wasn't sure we would track him down at all, the whole thing seemed so complicated. Anyway,' she added, straightening up, 'now we have him, we can let Ann go.'

'We don't have any physical proof that links Charlie to David's death,' Geraldine pointed out. 'It's still possible she killed her husband.'

'Anything's possible,' Eileen replied, 'but we can't prove anything without evidence. We know Charlie's a psychopath. I'm not sure we need to look any further for David's killer.'

'Charlie has confessed to killing Bingo and Alf before he killed Mark, but he's adamant he wasn't involved in any deaths after Mark's. If it was all about Mark, once he was dead why would Charlie have wanted to kill anyone else?' Geraldine asked.

'There could be any number of reasons,' Eileen replied. 'He might have wanted to make sure no one connected him to Mark specifically, or perhaps he discovered he enjoyed killing people. Anyway, I dare say the forensic boys will come up with something. It's over to them now. We can release Ann. We haven't got any evidence against her. There's a perfectly good explanation for her DNA being detected on David.'

'What about the witness who said he was given David's coat by a woman? Isn't it likely that was Ann? Who else would have had David's coat?' Geraldine persisted.

Eileen frowned. 'Are you suggesting we rely on his statement in court as our only evidence of Ann's guilt? A befuddled rough sleeper who thinks he may have been given a coat by a woman? Surely it's more likely that he stole it, or at least found it somewhere, and invented a story to persuade us he was entitled to keep it. He didn't seem very sure of himself, did he? He certainly didn't come across as a reliable witness. And Ann did tell us David had lost his coat. No, the CPS is never going to pursue such a flimsy case against her.'

Geraldine had to agree that Malcolm might not be a credible witness in court. All the same, she could not help wondering whether he had been telling the truth. There seemed to be no reason why he would have lied so specifically about the woman who had given him the coat. Thoughtfully, she went to speak to Ann, who had been locked in a police cell for nearly forty-eight hours.

Ann looked stunned when Geraldine told her she was being released.

'So, I'm free?' she repeated, shaking her head in disbelief. 'I don't understand. What's happened?'

It was hardly the reaction of a suspect who had been confident her innocence would become apparent.

'We've caught the real killer,' Geraldine told her. As she spoke, she watched Ann carefully. 'I can't say who he is just yet, but I can tell you that David wasn't his only victim. After killing two homeless men, this man killed Mark and then David. The whole killing spree was all about Mark, who was the only real target, as far as we can make out. The other three victims were only killed to disguise the personal nature of the attack on Mark.'

Ann frowned. 'I'm not sure I understand what you mean.'

'I'm afraid your husband was murdered to disguise the reason for Mark's death. This all happened because the killer wanted to murder Mark.'

'But why?' Ann demanded. 'Why would anyone want to kill Mark?'

'Mark was murdered because he was having sex with the killer's wife,' Geraldine replied.

Geraldine was startled when Ann laughed. 'Well, that's not true,' she said. 'I've already told you, haven't I? I'm the one who was having an affair with Mark. There was no one else.'

Seeing Geraldine's expression, Ann stopped laughing and glared coldly. Once again Geraldine felt convinced that more lay behind what Ann had said than the words themselves suggested.

'You're wrong. There was someone else in Mark's life,' Geraldine said softly. 'At least two more women, in fact. We know he was seeing at least two other women, both blond and very attractive, and both married. Mark seems to have had a hankering for married blonds. Both these women have confirmed they were having regular sexual relations with Mark. There's really no doubt about it. Like you, they both believed they were his only girlfriend. Of course, he could have been seeing other women as well, women we don't know about, probably a series of women.'

'I don't believe you,' Ann said. 'It's a pack of lies.'

'We've found evidence –'

'What evidence?'

'Hair from at least two other women in his bathroom.'

Ann shook her head. 'I don't believe you,' she whispered.

'Anyway,' Geraldine went on, 'you can go home, for now.'

'What do you mean, for now?'

'If there's more to all of this than meets the eye, we'll find out.'

Ann laughed nervously. 'That sounds like a threat.'

'Only if you have something to hide.'

'We all have something to hide,' Ann replied.

Thinking about her own struggle to conceal her feelings for Ian, Geraldine did not answer, but she returned to her desk feeling thoughtful. There was still one last lead she had not pursued. It was unlikely she would learn anything new, but she was determined to try. Before going home, she ran her idea past Eileen.

The detective chief inspector nodded. 'You don't give up easily, do you?'

'I'm not sure I ever want to give up at all.'

Eileen smiled. 'Go on,' she said. 'Do what you can. Whatever it takes.'

'It'll probably be a waste of time.'

'Look, you might not get anywhere, but it won't be a waste of time because there's a chance we'll end up with another killer behind bars, and that's what we're here for. I'd heard about your reputation before you came here.'

'My reputation?' Geraldine repeated, puzzled.

'For having an infallible instinct for the truth. I have to say I was sceptical about what I'd heard, and I'm still wary. I've seen officers with more potential than either of us –' she broke off, frowning. 'Well, more potential than me, at any rate – I've seen them ruined by getting carried away with their hunches without any evidence to back up their theories. But, well, you might as well pursue this. It might come to nothing, but then there's no harm done, and it's certainly an idea that's worth investigating.'

The next morning Geraldine went to the breakfast club in the church to look for Malcolm. This time he seemed sober. Seeing her enter the room, he jumped up from the table and scuttled away, but he moved too slowly to escape from her.

'Malcolm, you're looking very smart. How are you liking your new coat?'

The old man clutched the coat, pulling it tightly around him, and scowled.

'Malcolm, I need your help,' she said.

'Jesus, what now? Haven't I done enough for you?'

Ignoring his protestations, Geraldine outlined her plan and Malcolm nodded to show he understood.

'Come on then,' he said. 'Let's get this over with. But first, I'm going to finish my breakfast.'

Within an hour, Geraldine had Malcolm seated at the police station, with a cup of tea and a plate of biscuits. Even after his cooked breakfast, he tucked in with a will.

'All right, all right,' he spat out a few crumbs as he spoke, 'I'm thinking, I'm thinking. It was dark, black or navy with thin diagonal white lines, like fish bones. It could have been a square, folded in two.'

'What about the coat she was wearing?'

'That was a light colour.'

'Long? Short? Loose or tight?'

The old man shook his head. 'I can't remember. I'm not a machine.'

'Was the pattern on the scarf anything like this?'

The e-fit officer held up a screen with several similar patterns displayed. Malcolm frowned and then pointed at one.

'That's nearly right, that one.'

'Right.

Malcolm sipped his tea and they waited for the e-fit officer to finish his next screen.

'Was it like any of these?' Geraldine asked.

Malcolm studied the sketches on the screen. 'Could have been,' he said.

'Which one?'

Painstakingly, the e-fit officer produced an image which Malcolm confirmed more or less matched the outfit worn by the woman who had given him his new coat.

'And she was holding a bag,' he added. 'That's what she was carrying the coat in.'

'What sort of bag?'

'It was like a rucksack.'

'Like this?'

'No, she was carrying it over one shoulder. Yes, that's it. That looks something like the woman who gave me that coat.'

Now it was a question of setting up a team to scrutinise any CCTV footage they could source of the streets around the town, starting at Coney Street and spiralling outwards from there, looking for a woman in a dark scarf and light coloured coat with a rucksack over her shoulder. At the same time, the search team returned to Ann's house to look for a rucksack, coat and scarf matching the ones captured on film. They found only a scarf, but no light coloured coat or rucksack. Eileen had been right when she had said it would be a long shot.

61

It was only two weeks since Malcolm had acquired his new coat, and several of the cameras around the streets still had film stored in them. Malcolm was vague about days and times, but the volunteer at the church remembered contacting the police the day after he had first seen Malcolm wearing the new coat, and Malcolm confirmed that he had started wearing it straight away.

'I had to, didn't I? That woman had taken my coat, hadn't she?'

So they knew the day on which the coats had been swopped. Malcolm thought the woman had offered him the new coat 'some time after breakfast', giving the police an approximate time frame for the exchange. Working closely with the local intelligence team, Geraldine identified every route that Ann might possibly have followed between her home and Coney Street, had she indeed met Malcolm there. A team were sent to download footage from every CCTV camera she could have passed on her route, so that it could be scrutinised.

At the same time, another team were checking any images of David they could find online, looking for a picture of him wearing a camel-coloured coat like the one Malcolm had been given. Examination of David's credit card records showed a purchase from an expensive menswear shop in York for a single item priced at over £900. It was hard to imagine many items of clothing other than a coat costing so much. Even for a coat, it was dear. A visit to the shop confirmed that they stocked a coat identical to the one Malcolm had been given. That did not prove beyond any doubt that Ann had given away David's coat, but it certainly made it feasible.

It took a week for the video images identification and detections officers to find an image of a woman matching the e-fit sketch of the woman Malcolm had described. Geraldine was at her desk when the VIIDO team called her and she hurried along the corridor to see what they had found. The image on the screen showed a woman wearing a dark scarf and a light coloured coat, carrying a rucksack slung over one shoulder, exactly as Malcolm had described her; she matched the e-fit picture exactly. Geraldine watched the video clips which followed a route through the city centre, with long gaps where her route could be roughly tracked. Working backwards took the woman out towards Ann's neighbourhood, but reaching residential side streets the film record petered out.

Another day passed and, having watched the film extracts through several times, a VIIDO officer isolated a frame where the woman's face had been caught on camera and he had run a visual recognition search. Geraldine almost could not bear to go and view the enhanced image, for fear it would prove they had spent all that time following a false lead. But as soon as she saw the VIIDO officer's face, she knew they had found what they needed. Two images were displayed on the screen: a mug shot of Ann when she had arrived at the police station, and a slightly fuzzy image, with her hair mostly concealed beneath a navy scarf. Grinning, Geraldine hurried to speak to Eileen.

The detective chief inspector had already seen the evidence.

'We've got her,' Eileen said, as Geraldine entered the room.

Ian was standing beside Eileen's desk, smiling. 'Geraldine got her,' he said.

'This was a team effort,' Geraldine corrected him. 'The VIIDO team did an outstanding job, finding that image.'

'But it was your idea to look for it,' Eileen said. 'Well done,

Geraldine. And now, in the light of this new evidence, perhaps you and Ian would like to have another chat with Ann?'

As Geraldine followed Ian out of the room, she glanced over her shoulder and saw Eileen grinning.

'Good job,' Ian said to Geraldine as they made their way to the interview room to wait for Ann and her lawyer to join them.

'We'd like you to take a look at these images,' Geraldine said, when they were all seated, and the tape was running.

Ann stared at the picture of herself in a navy scarf and beige coat. In the photo her eyes stared straight ahead, and her shoulders were hunched forward, the one with a rucksack over it slightly raised.

'Do you deny that picture is you?'

'It looks like me, but so what? It could be anyone.'

Geraldine placed an evidence bag on the table between them. Through the clear plastic, a folded square of navy fabric was visible.

'And this is your scarf?' It was not really a question.

Ann's expression grew wary. 'I do have a scarf similar to that.'

'Is this your scarf?' Ian asked. 'Please answer the question.'

'It could be mine,' Ann said. 'I can't say for definite. It's just a scarf.'

But Geraldine could see fear in her eyes, and knew that Ann was losing the will to fight.

Even the stout lawyer was silent, aware that the scarf would carry incontrovertible traces of DNA from skin cells, sweat, dandruff, and hair that would prove its ownership.

Geraldine leaned forward. 'We know what happened, Ann,' she said gently. 'We know you killed David. We have enough evidence to convict you. But if you co-operate with us now, you could be given a reduced sentence.'

'If you refuse,' Ian added, 'you could be going away for a very long time. No lawyer can get you off a murder charge when we have evidence of such careful planning.'

'What we don't know is why you did it,' Geraldine said. 'What had David ever done to you? From what we can see, he was generous to a fault. It looks as though you didn't want for anything.'

'It had nothing to do with money,' Ann muttered.

'You don't have to say anything,' her lawyer barked.

'David had what was coming to him,' Ann went on, her voice growing hard.

'That's enough,' her lawyer said. 'I insist we take a break.'

But Geraldine held Ann's gaze. 'What do you mean: he had it coming to him?'

'I mean I did what anyone would have done. David deserved to die.'

'Did you kill him?'

'Yes, I killed him!'

The lawyer began to trot out his set phrases. 'My client is answering under duress, she doesn't know what she's saying –'

'Ann,' Geraldine interrupted him. 'You don't have to say anything, but you do understand you just confessed to killing your husband?'

Ann nodded.

'Did you just nod your head?'

'Yes, yes, I did it. I killed him.'

The lawyer changed tack. 'My client deeply regrets what she did in a moment of passion. She wasn't responsible for her actions –'

'I killed him and I'd do it again!' Ann cried out.

'Why? What had David done to you?'

'I strongly advise you not to answer that,' the lawyer answered quickly. 'I demand a break. I need to speak to my –'

'He killed Mark!' Ann shouted.

'You're wrong. Mark was killed by a man we have in custody,' Ian said. 'He's confessed.'

'Exactly,' the lawyer replied. 'Now I need to –'

'He's confessed,' Ian repeated, interrupting the lawyer. 'We have proof. The man who killed the rough sleepers also killed Mark. That was the whole point of all the murders. Mark was the target all along. The rough sleepers were killed and Mark was disguised as a rough sleeper to hide the truth.'

Ann stared at Ian, aghast. 'What? No!'

'It's true. David didn't kill anyone,' Geraldine confirmed.

'That's not true.'

All anger and triumph faded from Ann's face, leaving only a scared and horrified woman.

'Oh my God, what have I done? What have I done?' she whispered, turning to her lawyer.

'We'll plead diminished responsibility,' he replied stolidly. 'That will get you a reduced sentence.'

'Will I really go to prison?'

'You killed your husband,' Ian pointed out.

'But what about Aimee?' Ann asked.

'You should have thought of that before you strangled David,' Ian replied coldly. He turned to the lawyer. 'You can consult with your client now. Take as much time as you want. She's not going anywhere.'

62

THE TEAM WERE OFF to the pub for a celebratory drink.

'You're looking very solemn,' Ariadne said to Geraldine. 'Are you all right? You of all people should be feeling pleased with yourself.'

'I'm fine,' Geraldine lied.

The thought of Ann's daughter was bothering her. She wondered what would happen to a fifteen-year-old girl who learned that her mother had murdered her father.

Ian walked to the pub with her. 'I wanted to say well done,' he told her as they set off. 'Why so glum?'

When she explained to him how she was feeling, he smiled sadly.

'That's so typical of you. But it's not our responsibility. If you think about it, every villain we put behind bars probably has relatives, and quite possibly dependents as well, who could be left high and dry. And Aimee's neighbour is going to take her in while Ann's away. It's not as though she's been left on her own to be taken into care. She'll still be able to stay at the same school so her routine will be disrupted as little as possible.'

'But this isn't just about who's going to look after her, is it? Her mother murdered her father. She didn't have to know about that, did she? We already had Charlie in custody. Adding one more murder to his tally wouldn't have made much difference to him. He's going down for life anyway. But Ann's conviction is going to destroy an innocent young girl's life.'

'That's not our fault,' Ian insisted.

'No, it's my fault. If I hadn't been so determined to find the evidence to convict Ann, she might have got away with it.'

'And you're saying that would have been a good thing? You don't really believe that. How could it be good to let a murderer go unpunished?'

'I just can't help thinking about that poor girl.'

Ian shook his head. 'Our job is to serve justice by discovering the truth and getting killers locked up, nothing more nor less than that. And that's exactly what we've done, thanks to you. It's madness to think we can do anything else.'

Geraldine nodded. 'Yes, I know you're right.'

But she could not celebrate the outcome of the investigation with a light heart and she left the pub early. Ian said he would accompany her back to the police station car park and they left the pub together.

'Well, that's over,' he said brightly. 'You know, waiting for you while you were taken hostage was one of the worst experiences of my life.'

'It wasn't great for me,' she replied, with a little laugh. 'Thank you, anyway. I appreciate what you're doing, trying to take my mind off how I've screwed up Aimee's life, but –'

'No, let me speak.' There was a kind of urgency in his tone. 'If anything had happened to you in Charlie's house –' having secured her attention, he broke off and looked away.

'Well, it didn't,' she said lightly. 'Nothing happened to me, and it's over.'

'No,' he seemed to be struggling to speak. 'The point is, if you'll just shut up and let me speak – the point is, I couldn't bear it if anything happened to you before I'd had a chance to tell you how I feel.'

'I don't know what you mean.'

'Oh sod it,' he burst out.

He took her shoulders firmly in both hands to prevent her

315

from moving, and bent down. His lips brushed hers so gently at first, she thought she might have imagined his touch. But he did not pull away, and neither did she.

Acknowledgements

I would like to thank Dr Leonard Russell for his medical advice, and all my contacts in York for their help, especially the Changing Lives shelter.

My thanks also go to Ion Mills, Claire Watts, Clare Quinlivan, Clare Holloway, Katherine Sunderland, Jayne Lewis and all the wonderful team at No Exit Press for their unflagging support, and continuing belief in Geraldine Steel. I would love to spend every working day in the company of such inspiring and generous-spirited people.

Geraldine and I have been together for a long time, and another woman has been with us from the beginning, guiding and advising. So I would like to conclude by thanking my brilliant editor, Keshini Naidoo, without whom Geraldine and I would never have come this far. What an exciting journey it has been... and it's not over yet!

Subscribe to the No Exit Press eBook Club and save up to 30% on your choice of eBooks from our extensive catalogue
Visit noexit.co.uk/subscribe/da and get your first month for just £1

A LETTER FROM LEIGH

Dear Reader,

I hope you enjoyed reading this book in my Geraldine Steel series. Readers are the key to the writing process, so I'm thrilled that you've joined me on my writing journey.

You might not want to meet some of my characters on a dark night – I know I wouldn't! – but hopefully you want to read about Geraldine's other investigations. Her work is always her priority because she cares deeply about justice, but she also has her own life. Many readers care about what happens to her. I hope you join them, and become a fan of Geraldine Steel, and her colleague Ian Peterson.

If you follow me on Facebook or Twitter, you'll know that I love to hear from readers. I always respond to comments from fans, and hope you will follow me on **@LeighRussell** and **fb.me/leigh.russell.50** or drop me an email via my website **leighrussell.co.uk**.

That way you can be sure to get news of the latest offers on my books. You might also like to sign up for my newsletter on **leighrussell.co.uk/news** to make sure you're one of the first to know when a new book is coming out. We'll be running competitions, and I'll also notify you of any events where I'll be appearing.

Finally, if you enjoyed this story, I'd be really grateful if you would post a brief review on Amazon or Goodreads. A few sentences to say you enjoyed the book would be wonderful. And of course it would be brilliant if you would consider recommending my books to anyone who is a fan of crime fiction.

I hope to meet you at a literary festival or a book signing soon!

Thank you again for choosing to read my book.

With very best wishes,

Leigh Russell

NO EXIT PRESS
UNCOVERING THE BEST CRIME

'A very smart, independent publisher delivering
the finest literary crime fiction' – *Big Issue*

MEET NO EXIT PRESS, the independent publisher bringing you the best in crime and noir fiction. From classic detective novels, to page-turning spy thrillers and singular writing that just grabs the attention. Our books are carefully crafted by some of the world's finest writers and delivered to you by a small, but mighty, team.

In our 30 years of business, we have published award-winning fiction and non-fiction including the work of a Pulitzer Prize winner, the British Crime Book of the Year, numerous CWA Dagger Awards, a British million copy bestselling author, the winner of the Canadian Governor General's Award for Fiction and the Scotiabank Giller Prize, to name but a few. We are the home of many crime and noir legends from the USA whose work includes iconic film adaptations and TV sensations. We pride ourselves in uncovering the most exciting new or undiscovered talents. New and not so new – you know who you are!!

We are a proactive team committed to delivering the very best, both for our authors and our readers.

Want to join the conversation and find out more about what we do?

Catch us on social media or sign up to our newsletter for all the latest news from No Exit Press HQ.

f fb.me/noexitpress **🐦** @noexitpress
noexit.co.uk/newsletter